THE
DARK FOREST
TRILOGY

PART III

JOURNEY
OF THE SOUL

By Lisa J Comstock

2019

Softcover ISBN: 9781096693826
PUBLISHED BY ENCLAVE PRODUCTIONS, LLC

Printed in the United States of America

START YOUR COLLECTION OF BOOKS BY LISA J COMSTOCK:

FOR MORE INFORMATION CHECK OUT:
www.brimtierchronicles.com
and
www.authorlisajcomstock.yolasite.com

The Dark Forest Trilogy is dedicated to everyone that loves to read! Thank you for joining the companions on their quest to save Ernel.

I want to thank all of my friends and family for their words of encouragement along the way on my journey of becoming a published author.

I want to say a special thank you to my husband, Steve Comstock, for always being supportive and understanding of my spending so much time with the characters in my books.

I also want to say an extra thank you to my parents, Royce Witham, who is smiling down on me from heaven, and Jane Witham, for encouraging me to use my imagination and to never give up on my dreams.

As well as to Nina Liv Witham, my sister and fellow author. Thank you for being my sounding board, editor and assistant, at times – I am glad we got to go on this journey together!

VIII

X

1

JOURNEY
OF THE SOUL

The blue colored man walked over to the fallen elf. He stopped a few feet from the cleric's back and watched as the boy tried to save the elf's life. He knew it was for naught. He knew the cleric wouldn't let him take the elf if there was even a chance, so he waited.

Aramis jumped when he felt a hand on his shoulder. He thought it was Nortus. He turned quickly; ready to shout at him to get the hell away from him and that this was his fault. He knew it wasn't – on either account. He looked up and froze. The man standing over him was beautiful beyond words, more than any woman could ever hope to be. He had a grace to his movements no human could ever match. Aramis thought he should know this man but he couldn't explain how or why. He wondered for a moment if this was an angel coming to take his friend to heaven. He couldn't make his mouth move to ask.

"It is time," said the blue man in his musical voice.

Aramis fumbled for his own voice, which sounded hideous compared to this man's lyrical one, "Ti... time for wha... what? Who are you?"

"I am called Azure in your tongue. It is time to break the cycle," said the blue man.

Aramis looked at him as if he were speaking a foreign language.

Azure knelt down, reached out his slender arms and lifted the elf as if he were a toy.

Aramis was weak from the exertion of trying to heal Eonard so all he could do was watch the man carry his friend from the chamber.

Darlyn and Iligra, who was supporting the wizard, turned as the blue man, with the elf in his arms, walked past them. They followed. Aramis was right behind them. Nortus, half carrying Phineas, was behind him.

Azure set Eonard on the only bit of grass on the once lush bowl of the cavern and turned to face the five as they exited the cave. "I must ask you not to stop me from taking him."

Aramis again asked, "Who are you?"

"He is a blue dragon. I had heard dragons could take on human form but... I had never thought to see it," said Darlyn in awe.

Azure smiled and nodded to the wizard to tell him he was right.

"I go where he goes," said Aramis, pointing at the elf.

Azure shook his head, "You cannot follow us."

"I don't want to lose him…" pled the cleric.

"I am bringing him to the place his soul has gone, in an attempt to reunite it with his body."

The breath caught in Aramis' throat as he realized that meant his friend wasn't dead yet. He wanted to ask how, why and when he would see him again but he only nodded. Tears were running down his face without even trying to stop them.

Azure smiled at him and said, "Dry your tears. Whatever the outcome he is and will always be remembered as a hero."

Aramis managed to nod.

Azure moved to the wizard and Iligra then. She was supporting the wizard, whose leg had stopped bleeding now but was still all but destroyed. He waved his hand over the wounded limb.

Darlyn fell to the ground and began to convulse.

Iligra stood in horror, unsure what to do to help.

After only a few seconds, but felt like an eternity to the wizard, Darlyn stood up, on his own. His leg looked to be healed but it hurt as if it were still damaged. He looked at the dragon much as he had Aramis the first time he had healed him, with suspicion and jealousy.

"I cannot take away all of your pain, you still have a lesson to learn from it," said Azure then he placed his hand on Iligra's stomach and added, "And, many to teach."

Darlyn tuned as white as a ghost.

Iligra had a huge smile on her tear-streaked face, realizing then that the nausea she had been suffering from was not just nerves.

Azure stepped up to Phineas, who was still woozy from hitting his head, next. He waved his hand over his wound. The cracked bones mended and the split in his scalp disappeared. In his case he did heal him completely.

Phineas mumbled a quick thank you.

The blue dragon next looked at Nortus. "You will help us, Nortus Elgin?"

"Of course," said Nortus without a second thought.

"What of Mahki?" asked Darlyn. "I am guessing his soul still lives too?"

"The elf and the dark cleric's souls have gone to the same plain. It is my hope that we will find it there and destroy it," said the dragon. He turned to Phineas and said, "You have a spirit knight bound to you. It is to his plain we must go. Might I ask your permission, and his, to accompany us?"

Moments later the ethereal form of Junt appeared beside them. His armor looked to be a little charred but he looked the same. He nodded to the dragonman as if he had heard his request then turned to face Phineas, "I must ask your permission to break the bond. Will you allow it?"

"Yes, go. Save the elf."

Junt turned to Darlyn to be sure he too was releasing him.

Darlyn nodded as well.

The spirit knight bowed to them both then turned to face the dragonman and nodded to him. Darlyn had planned for him to go to the Plains of Vethe to be certain the dark cleric was gone all along. He was pleased he would not be doing it alone.

Azure picked Eonard up again and said, "We must go now if we are to have any chance. Time is already acting against us. Spirit Knight, can you open a portal to your plain for us?"

Junt nodded. He waved his right arm and an ancient looking stone archway appeared on the rise just beyond them. Swirls of colors filled the opening. He motioned for Nortus and the dragonman, carrying the elf, to go through. The veil split to allow them entry. With one last look at the others, the spirit knight stepped through. The opening turned black then the archway disappeared.

2

MASTER
OF HIS DOMAIN

Mahki watched as his son launched himself at him. He thought he would just swat him away like a bothersome fly then he saw what he was holding. It was a thick sword with a very sharp looking blade that was blacker than night. Something he had never felt before gripped his insides then – panic. He knew this was no ordinary sword because the blade didn't reflect the light of the many candles around them – it absorbed it.

He was surprised when he felt the blade go into his chest as if there was no effort needed to puncture the leather armor, skin, sinew, muscle and tissue that should have slowed it down, and that he felt no pain when it did. The body of his son, who had used his momentum to make this powerful thrust, hit him then and he was falling back into the coffin. He did feel pain then – excruciating pain – the pain of something burning in his chest.

He struggled to get out from under the unconscious body of his son. He finally managed to push him off and throw him over the side of the box but he couldn't stand up. He fell back wincing in agony. He looked down and saw only the hilt of the sword sticking out of a hole in his chest. He knew the blade was close to four paces long so it had to have gone right through him, the padding and into the stone beneath him, pinning him.

Being immortal a sword through him like this shouldn't harm him but he still wanted it removed because he wasn't enjoying the pain it was causing. It was like nothing he had ever felt before. That pain was moving out, consuming all of his body. He saw a light coming from around the wound then and began to try harder to free himself. He wrapped his hands around the hilt and tried to pull it out but it wouldn't budge. The light was getting brighter now and it was moving outward – up and out – away from the blade. He screamed out in horror, knowing suddenly, from experience, what it meant.

He wanted to cry out that they couldn't do this to him but he couldn't make his mouth move. The flesh of his face and body had begun to disintegrate, falling off in chunks. All of the muscles that held him together twisted and burst leaving only his bones and his consciousness. He opened his jaw for what would be the last time and tried to cry out; no sound came from his throat because he had no throat for it to come from. Those bones dried up and began to break down into dust, leaving just his consciousness.

He was still writhing as the air around him became thinner and the light less bright. It took him a moment to realize he was no longer feeling pain, in fact he wasn't feeling anything at all. He opened his eyes and saw why. He remembered this feeling. He wanted to groan in anger but he couldn't get the ethereal muscles of his throat to accept any commands yet.

Below him he could see the chamber he'd been left in for so long. He could see the coffin with the still burning body that had been his physical form and wanted to scream at the injustice. He knew Nortus wanted him destroyed for what he had done to his daughter, it seemed this time he had truly succeeded.

He shifted his vision to a man that looked on the verge of death, walking lopsided with the help of a twisted cane. He watched the battle of magic begin between the wizard divine that had awakened him and this stranger. He could feel the hatred that radiated off them both as if it was a physical force. He could feel the tension build as the stranger began the words to a spell that was very strong by the currents he could feel flowing around him. A beautiful woman came in then and shouted for the other one, whom she called Darlyn, to stop. He watched him take the full brunt of the spell back into himself then and saw a bit of the man's soul leave his body when his heart stopped for a moment. He tried to grasp the piece, knowing the power it would yield, even though it was only a fragment of the wizard but it disappeared too quickly.

He saw Paitell attempting to cast the same spell that had killed a piece of the other wizard and readied himself for the blast that would follow – it would not harm him, since he was now nothing but a spirit mind, but it would still be disturbing. The explosion he expected did not come but something else did. He saw the forces the wizard divine had unleashed disappear into thin air and suddenly a burst of snow was falling and coating the floor. A blue colored man stepped into the chamber then.

He was astonished. He had only seen a dragon in human form once before. That one was green. It had changed to its natural form before him when he and his son, Darius were harvesting the herb from the elfish fields. This one was powerful in magic – it twisted his ethereal innards.

He watched the dragon throw air at Paitell then the man fall back into the coffin on top of the ashes that had been his physical body only moments before. He was surprised again as another spirit appeared inside the coffin. This one was holding the wizard divine in the embers of his own death.

The soul of Paitell left his body moments later. Mahki did not try to stop it. A full spirit was too much for his still too weak form to handle. He would find him when he was ready and make use of him then.

He heard his grandson scream then and saw the elf's blood was slowly dripping into the cracks in the chamber floor. He could not believe anyone of his own blood could befriend an elf, but then Darius had, and it seemed Phineas had as well. This one would not be a friend to either of them anymore, which was a sick bit of justice he supposed.

The room slowly began to dissolve then and he felt himself being pulled into a darkness that was deeper than anything anyone, that had never died or had the soul taken out of them before, would have ever experienced. He was screaming in rage but no one could hear him.

Mahki MaComber opened his eyes and found he was back on one of the hated plains of existence known as the Plains of Vethe. He swore colorfully and looked for anything he could hit. He could find nothing to quench his anger on. For all he had learned how to mold and sculpt this plain to his whims and wishes over the decades he had existed on it, it wasn't living. He had only his imagination to entertain him and he had grown weary of it over the many years as he waited for someone to find his body and figure out how to bring him out of the stasis. He knew there was nothing he could do right now to remedy the situation he had again found himself in though. He allowed the rift that was opening to take him as it had so long ago.

He appeared in the same chamber that resembled a library as he had the last time here. He waited for the insolent clerk-of-sorts who received new arrivals to appear, as one had so many years before when he first came. This time no clerk appeared, the room remained empty. He had no way to know how long he had stayed, time didn't progress on this plain like it does in the living world, before he finally said to the empty place, "Fine, don't greet me."

If he was forced to be here again there was only one place he would want it to be – the reality he had created. He closed his eyes, let the images around him dissolve into nothingness and allowed his mind to drift freely through the plain. He could see hundreds of points of light before him, each a different, or a group of, souls' world. He could have entered any one of them he wanted to but he had no desire to.

The dark cleric stepped from the nothingness to a grassy knoll overlooking the closest rendition of his estate on Ernel as he had ever been able to create. He wondered what his hated son and his grandson were doing with the real one, in the living world, now that they knew they were its heirs.

He really didn't mind his grandson having it. He could see bits of himself in the boy even in the short time he had spent with him. He had little doubt he could have had him as an ally if he had time to work with and mold him. Once he had gotten him past all the lies Nortus would have fed him. The thought of his first son, Phineas, having any part of his estate, lands and wealth was enough to make him claw his way out of this plain.

He stood looking over the sadly far from accurate view he would have had in the real world from this knoll and sighed. If only he had been able to see it for real – just once more. He knew it wasn't quite right, though he couldn't say what wrong about it now. It had been too many years since he had seen the real one to get it perfect. Thanks to Nortus Elgin, he would never see it again.

He had no way to get back to the real world now. His physical body had been destroyed. He wished he could get his hands on the disdainful cleric right then. A flash of dark, almost black, red flashed around the dark cleric as the malevolent thoughts of what he would do if he could ran through his mind. It was these thoughts that were staining the fabric around him.

Nortus had likely told the council putting him in stasis was a fitting punishment for what they saw as his crimes but he knew the man had actually only wanted to get his own vengeance in his own way – by using his own blood to get to him. To do that he had had to wait until his grandson sought him out. That man was far more evil than he could ever think to be.

Mahki was about to walk down the fake grassy over-look to his fake estate house when he suddenly convulsed and fell to his knees. He clutched at his chest in panic; he had never felt pain in this place before. He wondered what had changed this time. He felt something odd wash over him then and smiled sickly.

He could feel the plain shifting and forming around him, he had been able to manipulate it since shortly after the first time arriving here. After having been here for close to one hundred years, in Ernel time, he could form it to his wishes. He had taught himself to detect when new souls arrived. He often greeted those new souls, once the library clerk had finished processing them, to see if they were ones he might find use for. Newly arrived souls were easy to mold, they hadn't had the chance to fully accept that they were dead and they rarely had the power to fight him until it was too late. Some of these he used as servants, some he used as food of sorts, drinking in their desires and fears like a fine wine.

This time something new had entered the plain. This was something different, something that did not belong – something the plain was trying hard to destroy. He smiled as he realized what it was. The elf's soul, which had been spilled during the battle in his tomb, had entered the plain with him. This plain was constructed to hold only human souls. He could feel the elements of the dimension trying to tear it to pieces.

He would find and protect it from the forces here. Not because he wanted to save it from harm. He would use it to sate some of his need for vengeance. He knew of ways to inflict pain on a spirit – pain that would make it wish it *was* being torn apart. He would keep it going indefinitely.

He stood and started again for his ethereal estate then collapsed again as he felt another shift in the plain. He shook briefly and felt as if he was going to be sick. An odd feeling of his skin crawling washed over him. He had felt this once before, when he had been around a dragon that was trying to defend its elf master – it was the beast's form of defense. There was a dragon on the plain as well, but it wasn't in soul form – it was still alive.

Another wave of oddness gripped the base of his spine as he felt another being, almost alive, enter the plain. It took a moment for him to figure out what this was. When he did his smile widened. It was the elf's empty shell of a body. He thought, *how could this be* and, *how interesting*. He smiled even wider then as he felt a final entity enter the plain, this one was also alive – it was Nortus Elgin.

"Ah, at least now I shall have some sport!" He smiled as he again started for the faux image of his ancestral home.

3

THE
PLAIN OF VETHE

An odd wave of sensations washed over Nortus as he stepped out of the swirling portal. He looked around and was surprised to find his vision was no longer blurry and the aches and pains he had come to know so well were gone. He sniggered at how simple a thing it was to open and close his fingers here as he did so several times. It had been a long time since he had felt this good. It was bittersweet though.

He looked back through the shrinking opening, at those he was leaving on the other side. He knew odds were it would be the last time he would see them. His eyes lingered on his grandson. He didn't want to leave Aramis when he had just lost his best friend and just learned of his true ancestry but he had no choice; he had to finish this. The path had been laid long before now. He had to hope the boy was strong enough.

The portal closed, cutting off the image and throwing him into darkness.

The smoke around the unlikely companions slowly cleared, showing them they were in a large room with a vaulted ceiling. Bookcases filled with thousands of the same size, shape and color book, going up three floors, lined all four of the walls. There were two rods, one a few feet down from the top of the cases and the other about twelve feet from the floor. Several ladders were hanging from each of these rods. Wheels on these ladders allowed them to roll along the rods and give access to any of the books along the shelves.

"What is this place?" asked Azure. He had never had contact with humans and he knew of no elfish equivalent of the room before him.

"It looks like a library," said Nortus. He had been in several in his life, though none were as large as this one was and they were not filled with what appeared to be myriad copies of only one book. There were no chairs to relax in and read the books and no door to come and go from. The only piece of furniture in the room was a large mahogany desk on a raised dais near the back of the room.

"A what?" asked the dragon.

"A depository of human's written knowledge," said the old cleric.

"It smells like wood," said the dragon, scrunching his nose up. Having been raised with elves he was against the use of wood for anything other than the beautiful trees the Gods had intended them to be.

"The pulp that is used to make some kinds of paper is made of wood," said the old cleric, frowning to himself.

Azure sniffed out a small puff of icy smoke but said no more.

"Master Elgin is correct. The room is a library, of sorts, but not so much a depository of knowledge as it is of history. These books are, in essence, Ernel's memoirs." Junt explained.

Azure was about to ask who had written them, not understanding this concept. He stopped and they all jumped when they heard a slight cough from behind them.

They found an ancient looking man now sitting at the desk that a moment ago had been empty. A huge book just like those on the shelves around them lay open before him. That book was tilted up slightly on a stand and was opened to about its center. Beside it was a bottle of dark red ink and a couple long white feather quills. The man was dipping another feather quill like them into this bottle and was writing in the volume with great speed.

The man's hair was very long, halfway down his back, was beyond white and was thin and wispy. A thick pair of spectacles sat on a bump sticking up on the center, halfway down the bridge, of his nose. He was dressed in a long sleeved deep purple robe with golden scrollwork spiraling around the sleeves and down both sides of the front of it. The hood was hanging down his back to near the floor and the long draping sleeves were hanging off the sides of the desk.

He didn't seem to know he had company until Nortus cleared his throat.

The man looked up from the book and found four people before him, two standing and one kneeling beside the fourth, lying motionless between them. He smirked briefly then held the long sleeve back as he dipped the quill into the ink and moved his hand back over the page. Again he began to write rapidly, speaking aloud this time as he moved the pen, "On this day of August 1075, four appeared in the fourth realm of Vethe: a spirit already from this realm, a human cleric, an elf and a dragon in human form... *What*?!" The man dropped the quill and stood up menacingly. "What are an elf and a dragon doing here?" he screamed. His eyes shifted from one face to the next then they focused on the spirit knight. He pointed a long, thin, bony finger at the spirit, "You know better than to bring them here, Knight, it is forbidden!"

Junt stepped forward and dropped to his right knee, "My Lord, I beg you and the realm's forgiveness. We are here to track a great evil and return the soul of this elf to him before he is dead."

The man nodded to Junt then shook his head as he sat back down, picked the quill back up, again held the sleeve back as he filled it with more ink and began to write in his breakneck speed again. "An elf's soul cannot come to this realm, Knight; it is for human souls and human souls only."

"Be that as it may, it has," said Junt, more directly.

"*Preposterous!*" the man shouted. He slammed the quill down again, with far more force than his frail body implied it should have. The strength of the hit had broken that quill in half. The old man was now looking at it, holding the two pieces together, as if not understanding how it could have happened.

Azure stepped up, angry that the man seemed to be mocking them, and said, through a deep growl, "It is here, Old Man."

Junt stepped before him and quickly added, "Please, My Lord, if you check the waves you will see we speak true."

The clerk held the feather end of the broken quill up and used it to point at the odd bluish man. "Either way, you have broken the rules of the realm by bringing the elf and dragon and... Huh?" The man drew in a deep and surprised breath; he rose from his seat again as his eyes locked on Nortus, "You are immortal!"

"My Lord, please listen to me, to us. An evil force has taken the elf's soul but before he could use it for his perverted wishes it was lost to this realm. The dragon, immortal and I have sworn our souls to finding the evil man's soul, destroying it and restoring the elf's soul to him. We ask, no, *we beg you*, to allow us entry," pleaded the spirit knight.

The old clerk looked them each over then slowly nodded. He said, "Wait here," then he disappeared.

Azure waited a moment to see if the man returned then he turned to the spirit knight. His eyes were blood red with anger, which looked especially hideous with the beauty of the face surrounding them. "Why did you stop me? He needs to be made to listen. Why don't we just go ourselves?"

"We cannot," said the knight, with far more patience than he would have had when he was alive, "We cannot just go in, Dragon. If the clerk does not give us permission to enter the realm we will be destroyed."

The dragonman wanted to laugh at that; how could this place destroy his, the elf and the cleric's living flesh? The look on the spirit knight's face and knowing, being of this realm, he would know, made him think twice. "So what do you suggest we do then?"

"We wait."

Wait they did. It seemed like they had been forgotten, though time here didn't pass as it did in the living world.

Azure refused to stop pacing the library like room; complaining that he didn't like to be confined like this, that he needed to have room to breathe. Junt sat off to the side by himself. He and Azure had finally reached a stalemate at least. This left the cleric to care for the dying elf.

Nortus didn't want to think about how they were going to find the elf's soul. In the living world he could do a divining to find it. In the living world he could manipulate the currents, just by changing one or two variables, so that often times he could make a situation come out in his favor. Here he couldn't get any readings. He didn't like the feeling of being helpless. He also didn't like how much Eonard was fading. Mahki hadn't drained all of his soul but he had taken enough to potentially kill him.

Luckily Eonard's will to live was strong.

The elder cleric had done several healings just to get the elf to the point he was at now, weak but alive. Eonard had only awakened once since their arrival on this plain, and hadn't stayed awake long. Nortus had tried to rouse him again but couldn't. Now he sat by the boy's side to be ready if there was any change.

And so they remained, in their solitary thoughts, until finally the old clerk reappeared.

Azure turned from his pacing and started toward the clerk with obvious determination. Junt, anticipating the dragon's anger, dissolved and rematerialized before him. He placed his semi-invisible hand on the beast's chest, stopping him. The dragon looked about to continue but instead nodded in ascension. He reminded himself this was Junt's world.

The spirit knight waited until he was sure Azure wouldn't fight before he turned back to the clerk.

The old man seemed very amused by the exchange and disappointed when it seemed to have ended without any punches or sour words being thrown. He shrugged then started to sit down. He took his time getting himself seated. He played with the long, dangling hood, trying to arrange it just right on his back, so it spread across the floor, and the equally long sleeves so they were just right on his desk. He waved the quill pen he was holding, that was once again whole, several times over the page, as if unsure where he had stopped writing. Once he seemed happy with all his fiddling he looked up at them. He had a look that seemed to say, 'why haven't you already gone?'

Junt, though barely visible, was obviously not amused, "What say you?"

The clerk waited a moment longer before answering. He had a strange looking smirk on his pale face, as if enjoying a private joke. "There is indeed an evil on this plain that threatens to corrupt the realm. It has existed here before without causing harm... It is effecting it differently now but we have yet to determine if this is a detriment. The realm must remain neutral. The consensus is that it must be removed though. Bringing an elf and a dragon to this world may destroy the balance even more... and don't even get me started on what an immortal could do..."

Again Azure started forward.

This time Nortus started to go to him.

The clerk quickly began again, "*But* we do feel the evil *is* the greater threat."

"Then we have permission to enter?" asked Nortus.

"You do," said the clerk then he added, "However you must have a guide."

"A what?" asked the dragon. "We have the knight."

"Though the *knight* is from this realm, it has been too long since he was here. He has been tainted by the living. The guide will make sure none of you get into any real trouble," said the clerk, looking down his long, bumpy nose, over the edge of the frame of the glasses.

Junt wanted to argue but he couldn't, he turned to the dragonman and said, "He is right, Dragon, I no longer have control of this realm."

"I've sent a request out for any soul with the desire but it will be difficult to find one. There is no saying how long it may take," said the clerk. "I hope none of you are in a hurry."

"We don't have time to spare, the elf's soul may be very fragile," said Junt.

"Can't we start ahead and have this guide soul catch up to us?" spat Azure.

The clerk continued as if he hadn't heard the spirit knight or the dragon's words, "Most souls here are either too consumed with whatever tragedy they feel befell them to bring them here or have been here so long that they no longer care who or what comes and goes." He had no sooner gotten the last words out when a cloudy form appeared between the clerk and the four companions.

"I volunteer," said a gravelly voice from the vicinity of this cloud.

The clerk seemed surprised and a bit suspicious. He looked at the cloud over the top of the rim of his glasses and asked pointedly, "You do understand you must do this with no hope of redemption."

"I do," said the disembodied voice.

The clerk looked dubiously at the cloud. He shook his head and looked as if he were going to refuse the offer for them. He mumbled something under his breath that none of them could figure out then took a deep breath and said, "Very well." He turned to the other four and said, again pointedly, using the feather quill to act as his finger, as if hoping to make them answer a specific way, "Do you accept this offer?"

"Do we have a choice?" spit Azure.

Junt shook his head then asked for a moment to discuss this.

The spirit knight motioned the dragonman and Nortus to approach him and said, in barely more than a whisper, "The clerk is right, we must have a guide."

"We know nothing about this guide soul though. How do we know it won't try to destroy us?" asked Azure.

Junt stared at the shadowy form for a moment then he said, "I cannot explain it but I feel this soul is offering its aid willingly."

"Then we are agreed?" asked Nortus, looking to each, wanting to be sure before answering.

They all nodded, though Azure still seemed reluctant.

Junt turned to the cloud and the clerk and said, "We accept the soul's offer as guide and we thank you for allowing us entry."

The clerk shook his head. He held his sleeve back and dipped the quill into the red ink several times, since it was new it needed to be primed, then, with a flourish of the fluffy end of the quill, he quickly jotted down this answer. He shook his head then he disappeared, leaving them alone.

4

SPIRITS
& SOULS

"So, now what?" asked Azure after a moment, unsure if the clerk was planning to return or not or how quickly he would be if he was.

Nortus and Azure both jumped, Junt, the cloudy form and Eonard, because he was still unconscious, did not, as the library room disappeared and a desert scene formed around them. There was no heat or sun as in a real desert but the sand shifting with their weight beneath their feet felt real enough.

"What is this place? Must we be screened again?" barked the dragonman. He had rarely taken on human form so he had not gotten used to the emotions he got when in it. Anger was always the quickest to surface and the hardest to control.

"This is an anti-chamber, a lobby of sorts. From here we must decide where we wish to go or create our own place," said Junt, "We can build on our memories... or to what we wished our lives had been." The spirit knight had a look as if he were having memory flashes in his all but transparent blue eyes. He was. He would have thought he had been dead long enough to have forgotten his life but since re-entering the plain he was having flashbacks.

Nortus turned to the cloud-like form that was to be their guide and said, "We are looking to find the soul of the elf, it was sent here by accident and must be returned to his body before he is dead."

"The clerk relayed this to the plain... it is part of why I volunteered."

"Do you know where it is?"

"No. I do feel a wrongness on the waves that I am hoping may be it. I think I can follow it. First though, before we begin, you must eat. Though it feels like you have only been here a few hours, in reality on your world it has been eight," said the guide soul.

Nortus looked to Junt for confirmation of this claim.

The spirit knight nodded, "The other spirit is likely correct. On this realm time moves much differently, some-times slower, sometimes faster, depending on the spirit's will. If a soul is strong-willed enough it can essentially stop time entirely."

"Can you do this?" Azure asked Junt.

"At one time I could but as the clerk said I've been away too long," said the spirit knight.

All eyes turned to the shadowy form.

Though it had no face it apparently knew they were looking at it. "I can alter time a little but I am not strong enough to do much. I have not wanted to learn so I have not."

"What do you mean?" asked Azure.

Junt answered for the other soul, "A spirit must have the desire and the will to alter this realm and must practice it to be able to hold any image for any length of time. The image of the library we first appeared in was a reality the clerk projected."

"Does he work for this plain?" asked Nortus.

"Not really. There is no true governing body here but his need for some normalcy likely made him choose to continue his life's works. I would guess he was a librarian or a historian, perhaps a lord's clerk or a scribe at a monastery when he was alive... He acts as a sort of clerk here and records all that transpires here and in the living realm... likely in an effort to stay sane."

"He records all that transpires here, you say?" asked Azure.

Junt didn't answer, assuming it was only rhetorical.

Sounding annoyed that he was the only one that seemed to have come to the conclusion he had, the dragon grumbled, "If he knows all that goes on here why didn't we ask him where the elf's soul and the dark cleric's soul are before we let him go?"

"Because he would not have answered," said Junt

"Why not? If we are a disruption to this realm wouldn't him telling us that have gotten us out of here quicker, restoring the balance?"

"He would not do that because he must remain neutral so that his recount is as well," answered Junt.

"Why?"

"To maintain the balance."

"For whom?"

Junt's all but transparent eyes relayed his confusion well enough for them all to see.

"Who is he recounting it for?" asked the dragon.

"His own piece of mind," said the knight.

"Who was it he went to discuss us gaining entrance to then?"

"No one."

"Then his threat to have us removed was hollow?"

"No, not entirely. The clerk has been here for as long as any other soul I know. He has grown powerful in that time. Most all of the spirits here respect him and give him authority to... screen, I suppose you would say, the souls as they arrive – *they* trust him to maintain the order and balance here."

"How do you mean, to screen them?" asked Azure.

"This realm is neither heaven nor hell, it is more of a place of limbo," started Junt, unsure how best to explain it, he tried to in the simplest of terms. "It is only a stopping point for most souls. Those that are not willing to accept their fate remain here. In the living world, some people are good and some are evil and some are somewhere between, it is the same here with the souls that reside on this plain... The clerk has been given the authority to make sure that not too many of any of these categories are here... so no side is over-balanced."

"Why is this a bad thing? Aren't they only essentially ghosts with no physical power?" asked the dragon, nervous and intrigued at the same time.

"Though they are weakened, a soul has all the memories and abilities he or she had when they were living flesh – sometimes this realm enhances those abilities, sometimes it diminishes them. The clerk weighs the risk of allowing too powerful a soul to enter this realm," said Junt rather matter-of-factly.

"What if, when he uses his authority to screen them, as you say, he deems it unworthy – too powerful, for example – what does he do?"

"He will bar it from entrance and open a... portal, I suppose it is... to one of the other realms," answered the guide soul.

"Other realms?" asked the dragon.

"There are seven known realms of the world between life and full death. Some are closer to heaven some are closer to hell."

"This one is closer to which?" asked Azure.

"It is... somewhere in the middle, I would guess... the souls that come here are more or less equally balanced in their aspects of good and evil parts."

"So then why did the dark cleric's soul come here? He is about as evil a person as I have ever known to have existed," said Nortus.

"I am only speculating here... from watching my... Watching Master Algier, studying the dark cleric's past, that his strong belief that what he was doing was just has made it difficult to determine if he was truly doing it for evil purposes... He has confused the waves..."

This concept was too mind-blowing for anyone to even think on so they let it drop.

"I do not understand this need for balance," said the dragon. His species were neither good nor evil so the concept of this was beyond him.

"There are souls here that will try to lead other souls. In some cases this can be a good thing. If the soul was a lord or a mayor or such, they can help other souls that are lost or need more structure. Together they pool their resources and create towns that have all the things you would expect in the living world. The souls essentially go on with their lives as if still living... Others, those that were outlaws, for instance, may choose to continue their life pursuits here, terrorizing the other souls... The towns offer the souls some protection.

"Others choose to make their own reality. As I said before, whatever was their last living memory, or where and how they died. In some cases they create a place they wish they could've had when they lived," said Junt.

"And what if whomever is running these other realms decides they don't want the soul the clerk on this level sent to them in theirs either?" asked Nortus, thinking he already knew the answer and a bit frightened by it.

"He detains them," was all Junt said to this.

"Detains them?" asked the dragon, not ready to let it drop so quickly.

"Until they can be dispelled."

"Who would have come to dispel us if it was decided we would not be allowed entry?" asked Azure.

"I am not sure I can explain how it works well enough for you to fully understand it, Dragon, but I will try. The forces of this realm are not physical forces, in the sense that they can be touched or felt, they just are. Enough souls can band together to do another soul harm but they rarely have enough like desire to. Some souls can do it alone... Having done it for so many years now, the clerk has acquired the power to dispel a soul by himself."

"The clerk does all of this, choosing and recording the choices he makes, alone? Who would choose such a lonely existence?" asked Azure. He never had much contact with humans, what little he had wasn't on good terms so he didn't trust many of them.

"Not many but it is what he apparently desired."

"If he has essentially fulfilled his desire what keeps him here?" asked the dragon.

"His inability to accept that he is dead."

"He seemed to know he was only a soul though."

Junt only nodded then shook his head, telling Azure he had no explanation. "As the other spirit said, though you will not feel hungry or tired you must eat and sleep as you would on Ernel or your bodies will die and your souls will be trapped here."

The dragon and Nortus both nodded and went to their packs to find food.

5

GUIDE
SOUL

The cleric and dragon sat quietly, resting and eating, for several minutes before Nortus looked toward the guide soul and asked, "Do you have a name?"

"Call me... Rius," said the soul somewhat quietly.

"I am Nortus, the spirit knight is Junt, the dragonman is Azure and this is..."

"Eonard," finished the elf weakly. He tried to sit up but he couldn't make his arms and back work.

Nortus quickly went to his side and helped him to a rock then sat down beside him to make sure he didn't fall over.

"Are you alright, Elf?" asked Junt.

"I have been a blazing hell of a lot better. I know Nortus but who are the rest of you?" asked the elf. He knew the blue colored man was a dragon in human form, having seen Skyfire this way. He didn't know what had happened to the red dragon but that there was a blue dragon before him made him hope the red one had managed to get some of the other dragons free after Paitell had taken him away from the volcano cave. His eyes shifted to the smoky thing before him that looked to be a man, large like Torrin, but was all but transparent, like a ghost. He had never known that a ghost could speak.

"I am called Junt. I am a spirit from this realm. The wizard, Darlyn Algier, brought me back to the living world to act as a servant. I bound myself to your friend, Phineas, for a time and have now pledged myself to assist in finding and returning your soul to you."

Eonard had just barely awakened and was still very weak, in body as well as in mind, so his mind was still a little slow. He listened to the words and accepted them as fact though at the moment he had nothing to play them against. "You were a knight when you lived?" he asked, thinking he saw the image of armor on the man's ghostly form.

The spirit paused as if unsure how to answer then he said, "I was a…. a knight… indeed, Elf," said the ghost, bowing.

Eonard usually got a strange, prickly sensation at the base of his neck when someone lied to him. He felt something itching that place but this sensation was different. This may have been because he was weak or because wherever they were was clouding his perception. He knew the spirit was not being entirely forthcoming but he felt certain it was not with evil intentions – for what that amounted to. He could tell he didn't want him to dispute this claim before the others so he only nodded and said, "Thank you for helping me, Junt."

Junt only bowed to this.

The dragonman stepped forward then and said, "I am called Azure, in your tongue. Skyfire freed me from the cave and entreated me with seeing you safe. A pledge I have come here to fulfill."

"Thank you, Azure. And, where exactly are we?" asked Eonard as he looked around. He saw nothing but tan sand around them. This barren landscape dissolved into a sky that was only a slightly lighter shade of the same bland color with no clouds and no sun but felt warm. His last memory was of being in the cave being drained by the dark cleric.

"We are on one of the Plains of Vethe," answered the guide soul.

"*Where?!*" asked Eonard, completely confused now.

"The dark cleric all but drained your soul from you before Darlyn and Phineas arrived. In the fight what he had taken was spilled. When the portal opened to reclaim the man's soul yours was taken with it. We are here to find it and return it to you," said the spirit knight.

"Isn't this plain only for human souls though?" asked the elf.

"Yes, normally, but in the confusion of magic being unleashed in the cave your soul was… misdirected," said Junt.

"Okay… So, where is my soul?" he still looked like he hadn't fully grasped the concept.

"We do not know, Elf, we are here to search for it. I have scanned the waves of the realm and it appears to be spread out. It is probably the realm's attempt to break it apart and disperse it to keep it from disrupting the balance," said Junt.

Eonard nodded to that, it seemed to make sense. "Oh. And you are?" he asked the cloudy image that had floated over from somewhere behind him. Unlike with Junt, this one did not have even a faint image of a living embodiment, it was only coalescing smoke.

"I am... Rius, I have agreed to be your guide soul while you are here on this plain."

Now that the subject had been raised, Nortus took the opportunity to ask a few questions of his own. "Why have you agreed to help us, Rius? What is the redemption the clerk spoke of?"

"I did something before I died that was... terrible. The clerk believes I offer you help to seek redemption for those actions but I can never have salvation, my sin was too great..." the soul didn't have a body but it seemed its shadow slouched.

"Why *did* you offer your services then?" asked Azure.

"I felt your appearance on the plain and felt the evil you spoke of arriving; I believe I can lead you to it."

"Were you an empath when you were alive?" asked Nortus, the hackles on the back of his neck rising.

"In a sense, yes. You must rest now, I will return soon and we can begin this expedition," said the soul. He wavered a moment then blinked out.

He had no sooner disappeared when the dragon turned to the group and asked pointedly, "Do we trust this Rius?"

"We have no choice," said Nortus.

"I do not like this. How do we know this spirit thing is not the dark cleric himself?" asked Azure.

"It isn't. I would feel it if it were," said Eonard quite surely, slumping a little.

Nortus dropped his jerky and quickly moved to his side.

Eonard shook his head to stop the old man and said, "I'm alright. I can feel my life force draining but I am not ready to meet my ancestors yet. I am drawing on them to survive."

"Impressive," said Azure with true admiration.

"How is it you survived this thing when no other elf has?" asked Junt.

"I think it is something to do with my having more abilities than most elves. I have what the seer of my... of the elf village I was born in called soul memories. I sort of relive experiences my ancestors have had. I relived..." he paused and closed his eyes tight, as if doing it again now, "I relived the draining of my mother... I think seeing that gave me strength to hold out some of mine." He shook his head then, as if it sounded just as ridiculous to him, but the fact remained that he had, so no one even questioned it.

Eonard felt a sharp stab in his heart as he remembered Mahki saying it was Nortus that had gotten his mother's life force. He wanted badly to hate the man for this but he knew he hadn't wanted it... still it did little to ease his pain.

Nortus didn't need to be empathic to know this was what the elf was thinking. He wanted to explain how it had happened but he knew it would do no good to bring it up and reopen the still festering and fresh wounds. He hoped the elf could see past this and would eventually come to terms with it.

Eonard looked at Azure then. "What happened to Skyfire?"

The dragon looked down briefly before answering, "The wizard took you before I was fully free. He thought he killed Skyfire when he left but he had not… not yet. He was all but though. He used his dying breath to free me and made me swear to see you safe."

Eonard got a faraway look in his eyes as he remembered the battle with Paitell. "I am sorry," said the elf. He had relived several of his ancestor's memories of dragons; he knew what a loyal and proud race they were. "I only knew Skyfire briefly but I had a great deal of respect for him and the situation he found himself in."

"All of dragonkind owe you a debt of gratitude for freeing him from the constraints and offering help to try to free us all," said the dragonman.

"What of the other dragons trapped in the mountain? Did any of the others get free?"

Azure again paused before answering. When he did the emotion was thick in his words making his voice huskier, "Skyfire rescued several dozen eggs before the wizard found us. The wizard brought the monster in the mountain to life before he left… the rest of the eggs and all of the adult dragons are gone… I am the only adult dragon that was saved. My race's future now lies in the eggs being allowed to hatch."

"Will they?"

"They have been secreted away. As long as they are not disturbed they will begin to hatch in the next few years. The dragonlings you helped save will resurrect our race in time."

Eonard nodded then fell silent and closed his eyes.

Nortus again started to reach for him.

The elf gently pushed him away– knowing the man was only trying to help. "I only need to rest, as should all of you," he added pointedly.

Junt took the elf's lead and said, "The elf is right. The spirits of this place are essentially harmless but they can do damage if they wish to. I will watch over you as you sleep."

"Damage? You mean send us to another realm?" asked Azure. Being a dragon he feared very little but some-thing in the way this spirit said this made even him uneasy.

"No..." Junt paused, trying to find the best way to explain it without freaking them out. "But, as long as you are on this plain your souls are vulnerable. If a powerful enough soul wished it they can enslave, torture or destroy your souls, which would leave your body as an empty shell."

"Torture? You feel pain?" asked Eonard.

"We are no longer living flesh but we have not given up our emotions fully – which is part of why we remain here or haunt your realm. We can feel pain, pleasure, fear and happiness."

"You said a soul can be destroyed?" said the elf, worried about his – that didn't belong here. "Do you mean it moves on without finishing its unfinished business?"

"No. It is utterly and completely destroyed – ripped to pieces so small there is no hope of it ever reforming and no hope of salvation... it just simply... ceases to be," said Junt.

Even in spirit form the others could see how shaken this concept made him.

Eonard wanted to know what unfinished business the spirit that had taken on the form of a knight had but he didn't know the spirit well enough to ask such a personal question.

They all fell silent then, thinking over this frightening bit of information, which didn't help any of them find the sleep the spirits insisted they needed.

6

MANIPULATIONS

Leonard didn't really sleep, partly because he wasn't sure he would wake again and partly because he knew he would have more of the soul memories if he did. He now remembered what had brought him here, the act that had separated his soul from his body. He didn't want to relive it but he had not learned how to fully control his abilities yet. The one allowing him to recall his own memories was running unchecked; images were flooding in with no way to slow or control them.

"You are aware of what I am about to do to you, yes?" he could still hear Mahki saying. He had felt a flash of fear like nothing he had ever experienced before or had any but one of his ancestors. He did not want this to be his ending. He rubbed at his arm where Mahki had used a leaf from his own beloved trees to cut him as another phrase that would haunt him for the

rest of his days replayed in his mind: *"You know, I believe that it was your mother's warm sweet blood that gave Nortus his immortality, do you not?"*

His eyes went to the still form of the old man, trying to get some sleep across from him. He remembered looking at Nortus after, praying it wasn't true. He had seen it was by the look on the old man's face. He was upset to hear this but he couldn't be angry with him. He knew it had been accidental in his case – he wouldn't have wanted anyone to have his mother's or any of his peoples' essence but at least this man had used it only for good.

He also remembered the look on Aramis' face as he learned this; he could not imagine how he had felt as all of his world came crashing down. Learning the he and Nortus had both known who Mahki was to him and had not told him must have been a slap in the face. He wished he could have spoken to his friend one last time. He wanted to explain why he had not told him and why he had ignored him before they went into Mahki's chamber. He wanted to explain to him that no matter who or what they were he was not and would never be sorry for his life before – growing up as his best friend and all but blood kin. He could still see Aramis fighting to get free of the bonds of air holding him in his mind, as if it were a soul memory – it was, his own. He had wanted to tell him not to fight this but he couldn't make his mouth move to do it.

"Please don't hurt my friend," Aramis had begged.

"You say that he was like blood to you, I can make him truly your blood," Mahki had responded.

Eonard had almost hoped his friend would say yes, if he was going to die he would rather his life force be given to him than to Paitell. Aramis had spat back, with such conviction, "*I would die before I would stand with you.*" Another statement that would haunt the elf the rest of his days was the last words he had heard before awakening on this plain. Nortus saying, "*It is done.*" Eonard shook himself all over. He hoped his friend was alright without him and Nortus. Now he was truly alone. No he wasn't, he had Phineas, Darlyn and Torrin; they all would watch over him.

The elf didn't want to let his mind drift again; uncertain if the next thing it stopped on might be worse still, though he couldn't imagine such a thing at that moment. He didn't want to have these thoughts any longer – knowing they were not constructive – so instead he thought about what the guide spirit and Junt had said about some spirits being able to manipulate the forces. They said some could mold this plain to their wishes. He wondered if he could... though he wasn't truly a spirit... yet...

Eonard let his mind drift and felt what could be best described as waves of energy. He tried to reach for them with his mind and felt them shift a little, away from him at first, then toward him. At first he felt a funny fuzzy feeling along the edges of his senses, like he was half asleep, then everything around him became so clear it took a moment to breathe. Everything around him had a strange aura around it now, some single colors, some more than one – based on their complexity, he guessed. He reached further; all around him dissolved and he saw they were actually floating in a grayish like mist. It was dizzying, awe inspiring, beautiful and frightening.

He could see dozens of points of light in that mist and somehow knew they were each a different point in this plain, much like when he had looked for soul memories with Corintisia so long ago now. He thought about trying to enter one but wasn't certain how to get back out if he did. He would try something a little less dangerous to begin with. Slowly the desert scene reappeared before him again.

Eonard reached down and put his hand into what was supposed to be sand. He could feel the different size grains sifting through his fingers. He watched the smaller bits turn to smoky mist as they passed through. It felt and reacted like real sand. He wondered who had created this reality or if it was kind of a generic scene newly departed souls went to. He guessed it was like a clean canvas for a soul to begin with. He could feel all the various elements that made it up; it was all so simple yet so complex that it was hard to fully fathom.

He chose a single element and concentrated all of his energy on it: the rock beside him. In his mind he examined it, every crack and dent, every bit of lichen sticking to it and the overall roughness of it. He imagined how heavy it would be, how craggy it would feel, how cold and lifeless it was. He was no longer imagining these sensations now, he was feeling them. He would have sworn it was truly in his hand. He opened his eyes to find the rock was now in his hand. It felt as real as any he had ever picked up, maybe slightly lighter than a true rock but real enough. He closed his fingers around it and felt its shape and texture. He squeezed it. It felt a bit spongy then it broke into sand and fell through his fingers. He smiled and reached out again.

He formed an image in his mind, of a small spiny cactus with a tiny pink flower coming from the top of it. Aramis' mother, Leanne, had grown one like it in a terracotta pot on the windowsill of the kitchen in the cottage in Windsor. He remembered how sharp the spines were; he had learned this firsthand when he had reached for it to get a closer look at it and got several of the tiny spines embedded in his fingertips when he was a much younger elf. He remembered how each spring it would get the small pink flower at the very top of it, how she had been so careful to only water it when the sandy medium was completely dry and then she did it in a pan of water, so it would soak it up from the bottom. He had always wanted to cut it open to find out just how it held water for so long but he knew she would kill him.

Eonard looked at a spot before him and watched the top of the sand shift as if something was trying to break from the surface. He smiled as a duplicate of that cactus did. It was only about three tines tall but it was there just the same. It was such a simple thing but it made him feel wonderful. He wished Aramis was there to show him but was equally glad he was not.

He closed his eyes again as a wave of dizziness washed over him.

He had intended only to rest his eyes and then try something a little more complex than a cactus but without realizing it, he fell asleep. He didn't have a soul memory as he had feared he would but what he did have wasn't enjoyable either.

He felt like his soul was drifting, he could feel it being pulled apart by the forces of the realm recognizing it as not human. He tried to get a feeling of where it might be but there were no landmarks to follow; as Junt said, this plain shifted too much. It helped to know it was still here though. He would try to reach out for it when he felt strong enough to. Feeling a bit more at peace he fell into a deeper sleep.

The elf opened his eyes and shook for several seconds. He wasn't sure just where he was for a moment. He wasn't sure who he was for a moment. He saw a hunched form of an old man, snoring softly, and a blue skinned man opposite him, that sounded like he was growling deep in his throat. Nortus and Azure, his mind told him. That would mean he was Eonard Leatherleaf, or more officially Eonard Lorraine. He was still having a hard time accepting the second name. It took a moment longer to remember where he was.

All around him was sand, in every direction; broken by what he thought might be the horizon. There were no clouds or sun but he did feel warm. He guessed he was still on one of the Plains of Vethe; he had hoped that had been only a dream.

He had not meant to fall asleep and had no idea how long he had slept. He remembered the spirit knight telling them that time ran different here. As if thinking of the spirit had called it forth, a cloudy image appeared across from him, drifting around the edge of the campsite. He had the distinct feeling it was watching him, though it had no eyes.

"Junt?" he asked.

"No, it is your guide… Rius," the shadow said. He paused then asked, "Are you well?"

"Yes and no," said Eonard weakly. He tried to sit up, it took three attempts but he did finally. The spirit moved toward him, as if he were going to assist, then stopped as if realizing without form it couldn't help. If possible, Eonard would have sworn the form slumped. "What were you in the living world, Rius?" asked the elf. He didn't want him to dissolve and leave him alone.

"A husband and a father, but not good at either," said the voice with a lot of emotion.

Something tickled the back of Eonard's mind but it didn't stay long enough to become a solid thought, "Why did you offer to guide us if you have no hope of redemption for doing so?"

"I had no choice," said the soul as it started to fade.

"Wait, what do you mean? Did someone force you?"

"No, no. I have said too much. I must go. I will return when you are all ready to begin," with that it did disappear.

Eonard didn't like the sinking feeling he had in the pit of his stomach. Should he tell the others this? They may not have accepted the soul's offer to act as their guide if they knew he had not truly volunteered. What would make a soul do this, and why? And, more importantly, could they trust it? No sooner had he gotten these thoughts out when Junt appeared.

"Do you fare well, Elf?" asked the spirit, apparently seeing he was in distress.

"Why do you appear in human form, Junt?"

"I feel it is easier on my hosts," said the spirit knight matter-of-factly. "And I suppose because I am not yet willing to fully accept my existence as a spirit."

"Is it strange the guide, Rius, doesn't appear as anything but a misshapen cloud?"

"Not especially. Some souls take on an image similar to that of their living flesh out of familiarity, some choose an image of... what they wish they had been... and some don't take on any image. It could be for many reasons that Rius is but a misshapen form. He may have not liked how he looked as living flesh; perhaps he was deformed or injured in some way."

"That makes sense, I guess," said the elf.

"Why are you so curious?"

Eonard almost said *because I am an elf* but he decided now wasn't the time for sarcasm. Instead he said, "He was here just before you. He said some things that concerned me. I am wondering if I should tell the others."

"Like?"

"He implied he did not accept our request to act as our guide willingly, and gave me the impression he isn't so happy to be doing it."

"I do not know of any reason why a soul would be forced to offer us its service," said Junt. If he'd had a physical head he might have been scratching it.

"He said he wasn't when I asked him to elaborate."

"Do you think him evil or threatening?"

"No, nothing like that."

"We need a guide but we will do what you think is best. It will cause us great delay to have to go back to the clerk and request another but we will if you feel it is necessary."

"No. I dare say I don't have the time to go back."

"You will keep the guide then?"

"Yes."

"If it helps any, the dragon, cleric and I will do all in our power to prevent this or any other soul in the realm from harming you."

"Thank you, Junt," said the elf. It did help to hear the spirit knight say this. For all he had not known him before, he knew Darlyn Algier would have never used him as his head servant and left him to watch his tower and all his precious things in it if he wasn't trustworthy. He knew Phineas would not have accepted being bonded to him and would never have allowed him to go to this realm with him and Nortus if he didn't feel the same. Still, he had hoped he would give him some help in this decision. He had hoped that maybe, being a spirit as well, he might have been able to feel if this soul calling itself Rius was being completely forthright.

Did he think this soul was a threat? Truly? No. Had the soul lied? Maybe he was hoping for redemption though he said he could get none? Eonard had always had an uncanny instinct about people and situations; he had thought it was just a normal elf trait but now he knew it was part of his elfish powers showing themselves. That instinct told him they could trust the soul with their lives. But, he also knew the soul was keeping something important to himself.

7

ARRANGEMENTS
FOR THE CASTLE

King Uther paced back and forth before his throne. He had been king again for eight months now and he had felt more like one than he had in the twenty years before his usurp. He still couldn't get used to how helpless he felt sometimes. He had longed for friends and allies for so long that now that he had them it tore him up when they were away from him.

He knew Eonard was being watched over by three very capable people, or beings, but he was still worried for the elf. Sangas still had a connection to him, the same connection that had drawn him and his brethren to the cave the followers had held them all in, but he said it was not as strong as it had been before they crossed over to Junt's realm. That it was still there implied Eonard still lived. With Sangas leaving him soon he would no longer get regular reports on the elf.

He never thought he would miss Darlyn Algier. He had become a true advisor since his return to the throne. Now he too would be leaving. Though, he, at least, would return from time to time. That was mostly because of Iligra though. She was due in a matter of weeks, about to give birth to his son. She at least was staying with him.

Darlyn had been living at the castle with Iligra since he retook his kingdom but, ever the private man, he tended to stay locked in his tower most of the day. It wasn't the twisted black monstrosity it had been, the wizard had that one torn down and had another built of the same stone as the rest of the castle. Unless needed for state or official functions or was responding by specific request, he never saw him.

Aramis stayed mostly in Komac, which was about a day's ride north of Hundertmark. He was getting his newly found family estate back to livable condition. It had been abandoned to nature, the elements and animals for the last five decades so it was in dire need of cleaning and repairs. The city around it had been all but abandoned and been left in disrepair as well, so he had the added task of rebuilding that and bringing the tenants that had been working the lands around it back under control of the new lord of the land. He returned to Hundertmark every few days to check on Iligra's condition but once the baby was born he would come less and less.

Phineas had forfeited the lordship of Komac, which was his by birthright, to his nephew Aramis; he had also refused a commission in the king's royal guard. He was no longer a marauder, and had no need to be; he was being given a steady income for acting as an advisor to Uther as well as one from Aramis as his. In these capacities he went back and forth between both castles, helping to build relations and bring aid to both the king and his nephew. He would be leaving both of these positions soon as well. A fact that bothered Aramis as much as it did Uther – both had come to rely on him a great deal.

Torrin had been kept busy with his duties as first knight, and preparing Nasir to fill in for him as his next in command, so he saw very little of him now, and would see even less of him soon. He couldn't have asked the man to stay though, as king or friend. It was a mission for the captain of the guard that he, Phineas, Sangas and Darlyn were about to embark on.

Jacobi, one of the men Torrin had helped save from the brotherhood when the elves had attacked the cave, had disappeared with his grandfather's sword. Apparently using it as his tsiaga, the item Cieri said he had once let slip he was looking for. It was learned by accident that Jacobi was one of the thought to be extinct Green elves. Sangas didn't know much of this secretive sect of his race except that they did not believe in interaction with other races. They did not want their culture to be compromised as that of the Brown and Silver elves, who had more regular contact with humans.

'Tsiaga is ancient elfish for prize.' Sangas had told them. 'It is said that when men of the Green elf tribes come of age they are sent away to prove their worth. They are not allowed to return until they have found their tsiaga.' It appeared Jacobi had chosen Torrin's grandfather's sword to be this symbol of his worth. Needless to say, Torrin couldn't let the theft go.

The king of Hundertmark had just sat down on the throne he had fought so hard to get back again when the doors to the chamber opened, making him jump up. He half expected it to be someone there to take it away again. He relaxed when he saw it was his new captain of the guard and his second knight that entered. The two men were speaking of military matters as if any other day, further frustrating the king.

They went down on their right knees and placed their right hands over their hearts in mid-step, not even stopping. Both uttered, "Your majesty," as was customary when they were before him, but both said it under their breaths, then they rose and walked to the other side of the chamber and continued their discussion. Neither was paying him any attention as he fidgeted on his throne.

Though few disputed Uther's right to the throne some still thought he was unworthy of it. Torrin wanted to be sure Nasir knew where to place the men to keep these factions at bay while he was away. It was hard to keep secret that both he and the wizard would be leaving, no matter how loyal the men and castle staff were; someone always let news of such happenings slip.

Uther was now getting very frustrated. He wanted to shout at the men to notice him but he fought it back.

"My captain, be calmed. I will be ever-vigilant while you are away. Moreover, you will have the wizard giving you regular reports and he can return you here at any time if the need should arise. Please do not worry," begged Nasir.

"Of course you are right, Master Rogette," said Torrin at least relaxing a little.

The older knight put his hand on Torrin's arm and said, "I will honor you and keep your command, Torrin."

"Of that I have no doubt," said Torrin, actually smiling for the first time in days.

Nasir knew part of Torrin's unrest was his being so young and newly put to the rank; he felt as if he were constantly having to prove himself. Most of the men would never even think of disobeying the first knight but a few had let the second knight know, in ambiguous ways, that they didn't approve of him being given the leadership role at his age. It didn't help Torrin's self-esteem that three of them were his own brothers.

Though he too was older, Nasir was not among the doubters. He had known and briefly served with Kentril Radric, Torrin's grandfather. He could see much of the same spirit and drive in the young captain. He had seen it when he was training him at the academy but he knew the younger man hadn't seen it in himself yet. He would make certain that no one had anything other than praise for the young knight.

He knew too that part of Torrin's problem was guilt. He had allowed Jacobi the power to take his grandfather's sword and that truly bothered him. He was innately a trusting man and to have that trust broken hurt worse than the loss of the item that had been taken in a lot of ways. Nasir hoped, for Torrin's sake, he found Jacobi, and for Jacobi's sake, that the sword was still intact.

Torrin knew he could trust Nasir but he still couldn't stop his worrying. He didn't want to leave King Uther while he was newly returned to his reign, which was just getting stabilized. If anything happened to his king while he was away he would be all but finished as a captain and a knight and would be lucky to keep his head. Though he knew Uther would never tell him he had to stay a part of him did almost wish he would so he wouldn't have to deal with the guilt also of leaving him.

He couldn't handle the guilt of letting his grandfather down either. The mere thought of the long-dead man standing before him and shaking his head in disappointment and disapproval was enough to know he had to do this.

He had intended to go alone, he could move faster that way. Sangas and Darlyn had been in the chamber when he asked the king's permission to go on this mission. When they learned what Jacobi was they had asked if they could join him. The Silver elf wanted to see if he could act as liaison to bring the lost elves back to the elfish fold and the wizard was going looking for the knowledge he could glean from them. He had tasked himself with recording all forms of magic – from woodland creatures to plant.

Phineas had been visiting the kingdom in his new station as advisor to the new lord of Komac a few days later and had heard Darlyn speaking of his plans to Iligra. He had then gone to the first knight and asked to go along as well.

Cieri he knew was coming because she wanted to be near him. She knew the most about Jacobi from traveling with him so long so her insights would be just as welcome as her company.

He would never refuse their coming with him. The problem was this meant he now had people other than himself he had to watch over and protect.

The first knight looked at the angle of the sun shining through the window then and begged the king's pardon. He left him and Nasir to go over plans as he saw to his equipment for the trip.

8

RELIVING
MEMORIES

The king's advisor and master wizard was trying to prepare himself for this mission as well, though in an entirely different way than the First Knight. His was more a mental than a physical preparation, though the headache he was fighting was manifesting itself very physically.

The throbbing in his brain was due, in part, to the passage he was trying to record in his journal at that moment. His mind was trying to fight back the unpleasant memories at the same time as trying to recall them. He didn't want to relive the pivotal battle in the cave but he wanted to chronicle every detail accurately.

He wrote about how he had tried to walk into the chamber with dignity, even limping and using a cane. His eyes connecting with Paitell's, the aversion he had felt for the man when he was a boy, when they were in the Guild together, had returned then and did again now. He had seen that it had for the other man as well, which had made him smile then and again now. He recalled a day when hatred and anger had been comforting to him. A part of his old self still remained it seemed.

He remembered having looked around the chamber and snorting as he waved his hand to remove the spell holding Aramis and Nortus and the chains that held the elf. The cleric had run over to his friend to catch him before he hit the stone floor, Nortus had crawled to Phineas, who was lying beside the coffin, blood gushing from a wound on his head, and the dark cleric's body was being consumed in magical flames. He knew then it was just him and Paitell, which was just how he had wanted it to be.

Darlyn had thought there was nothing Paitell could do to surprise or harm him but his heart still clenched as he remembered the man saying, "*It was so much fun turning your dismal and weak-minded brother against you and your parents, and so easy, he was just aching for it, wasn't he?*"

He had never considered that his brother might have been used, that his actions hadn't entirely been his own. He had honestly believed his brother was capable of such actions on his own. Why had he been so quick and sure of that? He felt a wave of guilt at never having thought his brother might have been innocent of the crime. Did some part of him want them out of his life so he wouldn't feel any obligation to them?

Anger burst inside of Darlyn again, at his family having been used in Paitell's sick and twisted desire to avenge whatever wrong he felt he had done him and that he had allowed himself and his family to fall victim to it. How different might his life have turned out if that had never happened? Darlyn Algier did not like to be toyed with or made a fool of. If Paitell wasn't already dead he would have hunted him down then and killed him for having done both.

A bit of his old self had burst forth from him with this realization. Darlyn hadn't liked how quickly he had been able to throw all his hatred at Paitell. He knew then no matter how much others had thought he had changed that he hadn't.

He had been so enraged that he hadn't noticed the chalice of Eonard's blood flying backward and smashing into the wall until it was too late. If the elf was not able to get his soul back it would be his fault. This pained the wizard. Though he had been the cause of more than one death in his life this one he felt would be the one that would damn him the most.

Darlyn's back spasmed as he began to write about the spell Paitell had thrown back at him; sending him smashing against the edge of one of the golden doors. The force of that hit had taken the wind out of his lungs in an instant and broke open the scar on his thigh that was only barely healed as it was. Again his sanity had shattered then – he wanted to write that what he did next was due to the pain in his leg but inside he knew better. He had decided if he was going to die he was going to take Paitell Tobac with him as he began the words to the one spell he had sworn he would never use.

The look on Iligra's face as she heard the words of the spell had torn his heart open. He was still surprised how quickly the anger and hatred had just stopped and how dirty and ashamed he had felt when he saw how frightened she was, *how frightened of him* she was.

He saw his fate if he performed this spell in the reflection of the stone he had given her. He saw that his soul would be damned to an eternity of torture beyond anything his immense and dark imagination could ever even think to conceive. This fate terrified him more than anything he had ever experienced to that date and that said a lot. He did not want to become what he saw.

Paitell had not missed the opportunity he had given him, and he had no one like Iligra to stop him from beginning the same spell and no way to stop it once the other wizard had released the spell. Or so Darlyn had thought as he started to throw himself in front of Iligra to keep her from getting the full brunt of the burning flames that were to come.

Seeing a blue skinned man step into the chamber had shocked him, watching that man throw a spell that stopped balefire was awesome. He couldn't explain how he knew but he knew this was a dragon. He had heard once that they could do this. Dragons had not been seen for nearly a hundred years, many had thought the species had gone extinct. He knew Paitell had a red dragon that he was using as a riding mount. This one, being blue skinned, would be a blue dragon.

It was said there were also once green and white, and some believed black dragons as well. He wondered if they were still alive, where, and why they had hidden themselves. He had known dragons could use magic but, as with elves, he had thought only rudimentary spells. Now, he wanted very much to learn all about dragon magic. He wanted desperately to know how the beast had learned how to stop the most powerful spell known to man – but then he wasn't a man was he.

He was still stumped by Paitell's response to seeing the dragonman, *"I saw the mountain destroyed."* It bothered him that he didn't know what this meant. He tapped his lip with the tip of the quill, transferring some of the left over ink onto it then set the feathered barb down.

He recalled Paitell saying: *'They,'* meaning the Guild, *'have been just waiting for an opportunity to bind your powers, you know... just waiting for you to step too far over their line of tolerated transgressions.'* for the umpteenth time. Darlyn didn't know why those words had affected him so much then and continued to. He supposed he had always suspected the Guild masters feared him. A part of him knew they had wanted to restrict his powers before he left the Guild. If they knew half of what he had done since leaving it he would be lucky to still be alive. They took misuse of magic very seriously, as well they should.

Hot tears – of pain – physical, emotional and mental, and a little bit of pleasure – began to coat his cheeks and burn his eyes and he began to shake. He suddenly felt as though he had been beaten severely. He closed his eyes and mumbled the words to a *self-healing* and felt most of the aches dissolving. His head continued to hurt though – that pain did not seem to want to go away. He angrily wiped the tears off his face with the edge of his left sleeve then jumped as something brushed his leg. He looked down and found the cat, Onyx, at his foot.

The animal had been pacing the front of Darlyn's desk for several minutes, waiting for a sign that his master had returned to the present. As soon as he had he moved in to let him know he was there. The cat mewed at him, making the wizard smile in spite of himself. He was now rubbing against his good leg and the desk leg, alternating between the two. He would never have believed how much the animal would have ingratiated itself into his life or how much he had allowed it to. He had sworn he would never let another animal into his heart after losing his dog, Bonny. This one had somehow managed to wrench an opening.

The wizard tried hard to ignore Onyx's obvious unrest as he went back to writing in his journal. He wanted to get every detail of the experience he had just relived onto the paper – so he wouldn't have to relive it again. The cat would not allow him to concentrate though. Sometimes he got images of what the cat was thinking, like now – he was worried that he was going to leave him behind. Finally he put down the quill and said indignantly, "What?"

"Mer... ow," cried the cat as it jumped into his lap and began to purr loudly.

Darlyn couldn't stop the smile from coming to his lips as he stroked the cat's soft back and it began to relax in his lap. He couldn't prove it but he was more and more sure Onyx had been a familiar to a wizard in his past; he was too empathic to be anything else.

If Onyx had been used as a vessel then he might have some residual memories of what the other wizard had done while in his body. Being a lover of all things knowledge, he was curious what the other wizard had used the cat for – interested in whether the information could further him. He had tried to get him to relay images of his life before joining their party willingly but all he got was visions of pain so he did not push.

Wizards and witches had been using animals as magical servants for centuries. Some kept them as spies or watchers of their lands, others used them as vessels for their own minds, so they could go places no human could. Few wizards used familiars as vessels due to risks involved. If something happened to the vessel while their mind was within it, or if something happened to their physical bodies while their minds were away, their minds could become trapped in the void forever.

The Guild taught its students many uses of, and the spells needed for, this type of magic but they weren't required courses. They didn't interest Darlyn so he had never taken any of them. The thought of being trapped, even for a few hours, in something that cleaned itself with its own tongue and ate what many of them did, had never appealed to him.

He ran his hand along the cat's back again and said, "Would you be happier with me?"

The cat looked up at the wizard and its mouth broke into a smile as it mewed through the purring.

Darlyn shook his head and said, "Very well, but know this, if you get yourself lost I will not go looking for you!"

The cat sniffed indignantly, as if to say it wouldn't.

"Well then, leave me be so I can finish this," said the wizard. Again he smiled as the cat mewed and jumped down. It then ran from the room quickly, leaving him alone. The wizard shook his head.

He caught his reflection in the side of the glass of red wine before him. He was surprised at how soft he looked when he smiled, like a different person. He lifted the glass and drank down its contents, letting the bitter drink coat his throat. He thought of how rarely he had smiled just a year ago, at least as anything other than wickedly. Now it seemed to be all he could do.

How different his life was now.

He still spent much of his days in the tower at the castle but not the black horror chamber of before. He'd had it dismantled and rebuilt in the same alabaster stones as the rest of the castle. He now slept in a room in the castle proper and he no longer lived with spirit servants, the castle staff was now allowed into the tower to clean up after him.

He was surprised how much he missed Junt, and how many times he had caught himself calling out for the ethereal servant. The spirit had never once questioned his sometimes odd requests, had a way of knowing what he was thinking and anticipated his needs before he even knew them himself and had never judged him – all things that made a good attendant. He had not realized how much he had taken that for granted, how much he had simply expected it.

He had thought the ghost was simply a ghost, with no feelings, wants or needs. The spirit knight had never asked him for anything for recompense for his service. He again found himself thinking, and being surprised at, how often Junt had gone above and beyond for the wizard. He couldn't remember ever once having thanked him for his service.

He remembered the day he had decided he needed servants and had decided it was going to be of the spirit kind. He remembered screening many before he had found one he felt would be benevolent to him – which was his most paramount requirement. The spirit he had come to know as Junt had first appeared to him in cloud form only. He had refused to take on any image until his new master had demanded he do so. Darlyn had done this partly to set his place in the spirit's mind and because he wanted the semblance of normalcy.

He had been surprised to see the form the image took – that of a stately knight. He would have never thought a knight could die without honor. He had asked Junt how he had died but the spirit had refused to tell him; saying only, "I will ask no questions of you if you ask none of me." This was a thing Darlyn could appreciate and had accepted. He truly hoped Junt found whatever he needed to release his soul and find the peace he deserved while he was completing his mission on the Plains of Vethe.

Instead of the ethereal servants, Darlyn now shared his space with the cat and Iligra, and soon a son. He had always been a lone creature, even before he lost his family, now he couldn't imagine not having people around him. He was still acting as the king's high counselor but now he truly counseled and advised instead of manipulated. Nortus had been right when he had said immortality was in other's memories of him. Now, he looked only to secure his son's future.

The journal the wizard was working on was a true telling of his past, beginning when he first became conscious that he was alive, at about the age of three months – he guessed. It went through his early days, before entering the Wizards Guild, through his time there and the years after – covering all the things he had done, had done to him and had seen. He didn't know if his son would show any abilities, and surprisingly didn't care. He wanted him to know everything either way.

Iligra knew almost everything now; there were some things he couldn't tell even her though, knowing it would drive her away. He was well aware some of what he had told her had sickened her greatly, making her stay clear of him for days sometimes. He knew she was also intrigued and excited by it as well, which was part of why he had likely kept her around.

It felt good to have someone with similar desires – she had some that were nearly as dark as his. She had proven to be quite the partner to him. Like him, she had a lust for knowledge. She had poured through and devoured the words of any of his magical volumes he would let her see. She had even been able to learn some minor spells, giving him hope for his son. She had made him promise, and he had agreed, that the boy would be allowed to decide on his own, with no force or pressure.

That was part of the reason he was writing down the things he had done in his thirty-nine years before now, so the boy would know what not to do, or at least not without having his eyes fully open when he did. Reliving some of the things he had forced himself to suffer in his pursuit of knowledge and power was painful, a *journey of the soul*, as Nortus would call it, but it was also liberating.

Darlyn never thought he would miss the old man so much. He knew Iligra missed him as well and tried to offer her comfort. The man had proven to be of much more value than he had ever thought he would. He had taught him many things without even knowing it, or without expecting acknowledgement for the lessons at least.

He was still translating the old man's journal. He was now long since passed the sealing of Mahki in his tomb. It told of his life after his daughter threw him out for not being able to save her husband, Aramis' father. How he had kept an eye on her, Aramis and Eonard through the years and had then begun to watch Torrin, Phineas, Haylea and he, himself, once the friends had joined him. He wasn't entirely surprised the man didn't have a high opinion of him in the beginning; some of his insights were surprisingly on target. He wished he could ask the man if his opinion had changed since the penning but guessed it was best he didn't know.

Eonard was another person the wizard would never have thought he would miss. He had never particularly liked or disliked the race of elves before meeting this one – he simply had had no use for them. The young elf had made him feel uneasy their first meeting, so long ago in the tournament field of Hundertmark Castle. He had known he was the one he wanted as soon as he saw him from the castle doors and had to force himself not to run to him directly. He knew in his heart then he would turn out to be more than just a piece of a prophecy he was trying so hard to make come to pass and was frightened and intrigued to learn what that was. Eonard had turned out to be a trusted ally and, as far as he was concerned, a friend. He hoped the elf was alright.

He had hoped to help Eonard learn to control his emotions, to better control his growing abilities, and had hoped to learn some of the elfish magics in exchange. He tried to tell himself he would still be able to, once his soul was returned to him, but he knew that was not going to be an easy task and seemed destined to fail. That was part of his reason for joining Torrin's group. If Sangas was correct, the Green elves could have very different magic than Silver and Brown elves. The chance to be a part of bringing their existence to light was one he could not refuse.

His other reason for joining this mission was that he simply needed to be away. Though he had fought against it, he cared deeply for Iligra – he supposed he even loved her, deep down – and he was finding a fast growing affection for his unborn child. He had never liked being cooped up for long. He knew once the child was born his life would change. He was still trying hard to fight it, some of his old stubborn streak.

He had changed in his physical appearance as well. He often worked out with Torrin and Nasir, and other soldiers that dared. They practiced fencing or threw a weighted ball between them, to increase hand eye coordination. His already ample muscles were getting larger. His leg, where Alistair Breman had sliced through to the bone during the final battle to retake the castle, had no scar, thanks to the dragon's healing, but the internal injury remained and refused to fully heal no matter how many times Aramis tried. He finally just told him to quit his efforts. Now he was forced to use a cane to walk long distances, sometimes even to stand, and he tired quicker than he used to. He supposed this was his punishment for being so vain.

His hair was finally beginning to grow some of its peppered black back. It was growing in from the roots making an odd stacked effect on his head. The white part was now only the last three inches of his hair. This added an even deeper air of oddity to him, and one he surprisingly wasn't looking forward to losing. Though most in Hundertmark knew him better now, some still looked sideways at him and strangers steered well clear of him. He'd had no idea just how much the last few months would affect and change him. He wondered sometimes, would he have undertaken this venture had he known?

The wizard finished the final word on the page facing him and slowly put the quill down. He was surprised and upset at how much his hand was shaking. He rubbed at his tired eyes and tried to get the images of what he had just finished writing to dissolve from his mind. If he didn't he would be seeing them again that night in his sleep.

He took the bag of sand from the corner of the desk, opened it, took a pinch of it out and sprinkled it onto the page then tipped up the book and let the excess fall to the floor. He closed his journal and placed his hand over the top of it. He shivered as he felt the power coming from the pages within. He had done nothing to enchant the book; his thoughts and actions were so magical in nature that he had empowered the pages with some of his essence without having to do any-thing. He didn't mind this side effect, nor did he do anything to counter it. He didn't want just anyone to be able to read these thoughts. He closed his eyes and sat back as a wave of dizziness washed over him; it was taking a lot out of him to put these thoughts on paper.

He had thought about bringing the journal with him so he could continue adding to it but decided he would make due with a small notebook to record his thoughts and transfer it later. He grabbed the cane that was leaning on the edge of the desk leg and used it to stand, grunting and clenching his teeth as he did. He had been sitting too long. Once he felt sure he could make it across the room, without falling flat on his face, he took the book and carried it to the shelf across from his desk. Behind it was a secret niche like he had in the original tower. He pulled the lever and waited for the shelf to slide aside then opened the alcove that hid the crystal scrying ball, dangerous scrolls and potions and the magical book he had salvaged from his old tower, and placed his journal inside. He avoided touching the red bound book in the bottom as he did this.

Though he had won the battle with that book, leaving him with the white hair that was now slowly growing out, he still felt uncomfortable using it. The old man had warned him he needed to know himself in order for the book to respond to him as it should; he was still learning who he was so he didn't wish to test it yet. He hoped by the end of this journey he would be able to.

He motioned to the cat, who was sitting and waiting, less than patiently, for him at the top of the stairs, to go on ahead then hobbled down the spiral staircase himself. He was using the cane as much to keep himself from tumbling over the edge as he was to keep him standing. His old tower had been a steep climb but this one seemed more so – even more so this day. He had been sitting at the desk for close to five hours without moving and none of his muscles seemed to want to stretch out. He knew Aramis and Iligra both would be quite angry if they knew this.

He locked the door as he left the tower, more to keep anyone from getting into things that could do them harm than to hide his secrets as he once had. He hooked the cane over his arm and started down the hall to his bedchambers to fetch his bags and say his farewell to Iligra.

9

PREPARING
FOR DEPARTURE

Darlyn found the cat waiting, still impatiently, for him at the door to his bedchamber when he arrived. He shook his head at the animal as he walked past him and stepped into the bedroom he shared with Iligra. He was a little surprised to find himself a touch nervous of the mood of the woman he expected to find waiting inside it.

He was surprised, and at the same time not so, to see that she had packed most of his things for him while he was busy working in his study and was now working on making the bed while she waited for him to arrive to say good-bye.

"You didn't need to do that, My Dear."

"I know but I wanted to stay busy," she said not looking up at him.

Though she was trying hard not to he could see she wanted to cry. She was having a hard time with the emotional swings of pregnancy but he knew this was more than that. She looked up at him when he stepped closer and then did burst into tears. "I will return through the portal as often as I can, My Darling. I hope we will be back long before your labor begins but I will be here either way. I promise."

"I know, I know... I don't know why I'm crying," she said as she wiped the tears away. "I wish I could be with you is all, I guess. I hate feeling useless."

"That is one thing you will never be, Iligra Almeas. You are to be the king's counselor while I am away, that should keep you busy enough, and Aramis will be arriving by week's end for your next check-up. You will barely even miss me."

"It will be you that will barely miss me. I know you are missing being by yourself to do as you please," said the woman, starting to cry again.

"Iligra," he said slowly. They had had this same conversation many times before. He knew she was only feeling self-conscious and insecure but he didn't know what he could do to make her see he wasn't sorry for asking her to live with him. Actually he did, three little words would do it quickly enough, but he wasn't ready to say them.

"I know I'm being foolish... I'll be alright," said the woman as she stepped into his open arms. "I love you and will miss you so much."

"I'll miss you as well," said Darlyn as he took her face in his left hand. He kissed each cheek then her full lips. "Especially on the cold nights," he added teasingly as his right hand traced down her back, came to rest on her bottom, squeezed it playfully and pulled her tight to him.

"Darlyn!" she squealed loudly. She pulled away from him and batted his hand away. "Don't be starting something you will not be here to finish."

He sniggered and said, "Seeing as you have done my packing..." He took the bag and set it on the floor by the door then turned back to her smiling. "I do have the time now." He took her into his arms, brought his eager lips to hers then to her neck as he began to pull the skirt of her dress up and gently direct her to the now empty bed.

The look in his eyes had told Iligra it wouldn't take much to get him into the bed at that moment and she was pleased he was still aroused by her even in her condition. She couldn't help but wonder if he wasn't doing it only to try to appease her, partly because he knew he wouldn't be able to have her this way for several weeks, she would be entering her final trimester in about a week. Sexual relations weren't recommended then.

They didn't spend as much time in their love making as usual, since time was limited, but both were satisfied when Darlyn stood to get himself dressed again.

Iligra got dressed as well and said, "I will walk you down."

"Very good," said the wizard. He kissed the side of her neck as he lifted the bag and looked down at the cat, "Lead the way, Onyx."

The cat mewed and ran ahead.

10

A
PLACE TO START

Torrin, Phineas and Cieri were already waiting by the stable doors when the wizard and woman arrived in the yard. Darlyn could see the warrior was growing impatient. Jacobi had a week's head start on them already and he didn't want him to have any more. The wizard had a plan to help with this, though he hadn't told the warrior yet.

Torrin was anxious, for many reasons. He tried to smile at Darlyn and Iligra as they came from the door of the tower but it was only halfhearted.

Cieri looked from him to Darlyn to Iligra and rolled her eyes, causing the other woman to giggle and the three men to harrumph. The women moved to the far side of the yard then, leaving the men to their planning.

"The last report I received had Jacobi in Sheffield two nights ago. The sentry there said he believes he took the west road towards Cutter," said Phineas.

"I have never been to Cutter but I have to Sheffield. I can teleport us there, saving us at least a week of travel time," said the wizard, shifting his weight on the cane.

"Are you sure you are…" Torrin didn't finish the question. He knew it would be an insult to imply the wizard wasn't strong enough.

Darlyn once would have barked at such a question, and might have struck out with magic as a reminder that he was still quite strong. He knew the man standing before him had only been concerned for his well-being. "I will likely need to rest when we get there."

"That would be appreciated then," said the warrior.

Darlyn was slowly regaining his strength from the sickness and fever the battle with the book had brought on and the fevers he had fought as his body fought the healing of the slice to his thigh he had taken trying to put Uther back on the throne. Aramis had wanted to do another healing on him before he left, sure that if he concentrated long enough he could heal it fully and rid him of the limp and slight nerve damage he was still suffering from. Darlyn had refused him, telling him he wanted it to heal on its own. It acted as a reminder of how foolish and complacent he had allowed himself to get.

They all turned as Sangas and the king stepped from the side door of the castle.

The king waved them all to stop before they made the customary salute, seeing them all moving to do so was enough for him. He was more than obviously upset, though he was doing a fair enough job of hiding it. "Are you sure you don't want to take a troop of knights with you?" the king asked his captain of the guard.

"I am sure, King Uther. The fewer we are the faster we move," answered the big warrior.

"What if the Green elves aren't friendly?" asked the king, the old whine was starting to creep back into his voice. A look from Darlyn stopped him from wringing his hands at least.

"We will all be well, Friend," said Sangas with the understanding and compassion he had given the king since their first meeting.

"I wish you all safe journey and that you are successful in your mission. I look forward to your reports, Master Algier," said Uther.

Darlyn bowed, as did the others.

They made their good-byes then the ones going moved to the center of the inner ward and waited as the wizard opened the portal.

The flashes, swirls and blasts of color and light of the portal opening broke the twilight sky around the field. Wisps of gray mist that had begun to form on the damp air blew away and around furiously, as if upset at being disturbed.

The five companions and their horses stepped out with the wizard in the rear, holding the cat in his arms. Onyx wasn't scared; the hairs on his back were prickly but only with excitement. He had witnessed more than one of the wizard's spells. The wizard stroked the animal a few times then allowed him to jump to the ground. He could easily keep up with them since they didn't intend to do more than a gentle trot into town.

Sheffield wasn't a large city but it was well enough accommodated. It had its prerequisite number of churches, schools, parks, a well-known library, factories, warehouses and storage silos; it boasted a fine selection of taverns and inns and a fairly large market square. Unlike most of the towns that began as a keep or stronghold and grew outward to form a city, Sheffield had been designed before it was built – which was for commerce rather than for protection. A tributary off the Eanon River ran through its center in a system of canals. Bridges spanned these waterways in several places and small boats traversed the watery lanes constantly. Some for enjoyment but most were delivering items from one side of the town to the other.

Since they were only passing through, hopefully leaving it in the morning, they had no need to go into that busy side of town. The five made their way to one of the inns, called the Rusty Nail. The name left much to be desired but Phineas, who had been there often, said it was actually one of the best in town and would keep prying eyes off them.

Not long after sitting at the table in the dining room, the wizard mysteriously announced, "There is someone I know in town I wish to visit with before we leave it." All but Sangas looked at him with a question on their lips, unsure if he would mind them asking for details or not. "The town steward, Antrim Galaer," he added without their having to.

There was no castle supporting the town but the lord that oversaw its running did have an estate near its center. He was away most of the time so his steward was the one looked to when a decision needed to be made. This kept the locals happy enough because in truth he was easier to deal with than the lord. Darlyn had known the steward since he was thirteen and considered him as much friend as he did most.

"Would any of you be interested in joining me?"

Phineas was curious what business the wizard had with the odd town steward, but he had no desire to go with him. The steward seemed to know things about people before they knew it about themselves, which unnerved him greatly. He'd had more than enough accidental run-ins with the lord and his steward both over the years and didn't particularly wish to see if either man remembered him. "I will decline the invite, Master Algier. I'm heading to the business district to visit some contacts, actually; hoping for news of our prey. Anyone care to join me?"

Sangas graciously said no to both offers. "I will stay in the room. Silver elves are an unusual enough occurrence that I will draw too much attention. Attention we don't need."

"I was thinking I would like to explore the markets," said Cieri.

Torrin wanted to go with Darlyn, concerned for the wizard, whose mood had seemed to get darker since leaving Hundertmark, and wanted to go with Phineas, anxious to hear what if anything he learned of where Jacobi had gone but he didn't want to upset Cieri. The look in her eyes told him if he didn't go with her she would be and he knew he would hear the details from Phineas later. "I will join you, if you like, Cieri."

Darlyn turned to the cat, who was sitting by the leg of his chair, "And you? Will you accompany me?"

The cat mewed happily and started for the door.

Darlyn shook his head and smiled briefly then said, "Meet back here for dinner?"

The others all nodded.

11

THE
STEWARD OF SHEFFIELD

Darlyn wasn't sorry none of the others wished to accompany him; part of his visit to the Steward of Sheffield, Antrim Galaer, was for something he would have preferred to do alone. He had felt obligated to ask. He was still getting used to this new, more diplomatic, role he had cast for himself.

He could tell by the look Phineas had gotten on mention of the steward's name that he knew of him and that he found him a little strange. The new underlord of Komac wasn't the only one who thought the man he was going to see was odd; Darlyn was one of the few people who knew the truth of why.

The man wasn't a wizard but he did have abilities – enough to be accepted into the Guild for a short time, which was where the two of them had become acquainted, and a kind of friends. Some people were born with lesser abilities – not being able to do much more than parlor tricks. They usually were no harm to anyone so they were left to their own devices. Others, like Antrim, would never reach full Mage status but they needed to be trained in how to control their slight powers to keep them from harming themselves or anyone else unintentionally.

Antrim's ability was reading people. The Guild had kept him enrolled for a year so they could help him learn to control it. It wasn't part of the usual curriculum of lessons but it was a dangerous enough skill they felt it necessary if they were to allow him to leave the facility unbound.

His knowledge and desires, like Darlyn's, tended to lean toward the darker side, which was why the two had become friends, and why the Guild continued to watch him.

Darlyn had been feeling a little lost the last time they had seen each other, which was nearly ten years after the steward had left the Guild. It was just after he had been on one of his attempts to delve into the darker side of his art. He had needed help getting some of the images to fade from his mind to allow him to sleep. He knew Antrim had been deeply bothered by what he had seen then, which was why he had stayed away from him for so long. The wizard hoped he still considered him a friend and he would be willing to use his skills to help stabilize his energy again.

According to the innkeeper, the lord of the manor was currently on a pilgrimage to Castle Lurkcross in Shadeport, seeking funds from his father who was its duke. This was just as well; Darlyn didn't care for him in any case so not having to kiss the man's ring and ass would make him happy. He made the old Uther look strong. Antrim was a far more trustworthy and just lord but he lacked the connections or blood to become more than just the second. Darlyn knew the man had no desire to be anything more.

The wizard looked down at Onyx and said, "Ready?" then he rang the bell.

It was only a moment before the door opened to a young woman dressed as a scullery maid. "Yes?" she asked, eyeing his odd hair color and looking even more oddly at the cat.

"I am wondering if the steward is available for a visitor?" said the wizard quite cordially.

"And, your name, Sir?"

"Darlyn Algier of Hundertmark."

The woman motioned him inside and asked him to wait as she disappeared down the hall.

The gong of the brass bells tolling, marking it noon, rang out from the top of the tower of the stone church opposite the sprawling home as Darlyn stepped through the door into the foyer. As always, when the wizard was in a place like this, his eyes wandered around the room, taking in all the details. This used to be looking for danger – marking escape routes and hiding places – now it was as much out of curiosity.

The estate was tastefully appointed but looked a little too manufactured for his taste – like its owner wanted to appear better off than he was. He found nothing that put him off his mark – of either his impression of the lord that lived in the house or of threat to his own person – so he allowed himself to relax a little.

He had been waiting close to twenty minutes and was beginning to get anxious, shifting his weight from his good leg to the cane every few seconds, when a smallish man stepped into the corridor with a smile on his face.

Antrim was a short, stout man of about forty with far more gray than brown hair, closely cropped on his head. He was wearing a white coverlet bearing his lord's coat of arms, a purple flour-de-lee over an off white tunic, and black britches. His face was clean-shaven, showing the cleft lip he had been born with. It had been partially fixed as a child but not well so the scar had never gone away. It gave him a slightly sinister look but Darlyn knew that was all it was.

Antrim tried to put a smile on his face as he stepped into the hall to greet his guest. He did want to see his friend but was also nervous at the same time. It had been close to ten years since they had last seen each other. He knew this was partly because Darlyn had known he had frightened him greatly by what he had seen inside him. The wizard had arrived on his doorstep unannounced then as well. Unless the man had changed, he was not the type to just happen to stop by because he was in the area, which meant... This sent a shiver up the steward's spine.

What he had seen and helped the wizard come to terms with and get beyond of then had given him nightmares for many months after. He would not refuse any of the man's requests, if that was what he was here for – Darlyn Algier was not a man to refuse anything of – he only hoped he wasn't now going to have new nightmares.

"My Lord, Master Algier!" Antrim said fondly. He brought his fisted hand to his chest and began to bow as was customary when before one of the wizard's rank in society.

"Please, just Darlyn is fine, Antrim," said the man, waving him to leave off the bow.

This took the steward up short. The man he knew had always prized his title, position and formality more than familiarity and used to get quite upset when anyone neglected to use them and forgo custom.

His attire was also out of place. Darlyn had worn magically charged robes and the odd light-sucking cloak since he was about eighteen. Today he was wearing a plain white tunic, nicely fitted deep magenta trousers and shiny black knee high boots. The top of the tunic was hanging open loosely, showing a far more muscled chest than he'd had as a young man, and giving him a very romantic air to his persona. The wizard's hair, which had been just beginning to get touches of gray when he last saw him, was now peppered black on top, from his scalp down the first three or so tines, the bottom three tines was beyond white. This combination contrasted strangely well with the peppered goatee on his chin. He wondered what had possessed the vain man to do this. He knew how much getting his first few gray hairs had irked him, barely in his twenties. He supposed it gave the wizard an air of oddness the robes and cloak missed. It looked even odder with the normal outfit he was wearing this day.

He was about to wave his friend to follow him back to his study when he saw that he was leaning on a cane. Again he was taken aback. The wizard he had known would never have willingly shown so obvious a sign of weakness unless it served some purpose for him to appear to be.

"What brings you to Sheffield, Darlyn?" Antrim asked.
"I'm... in need of some counsel."

The manner of this request took the steward up short yet again – it wasn't worded as a demand.

He was about to ask his friend of the changes to his behavior when he saw something that completely shocked him and actually made him take a step back.

A black cat came sauntering around the corner and sidled up to the wizard's leg. It began to rub itself on his shiny boots, first one way then spinning around and going the other. Antrim had no idea where it had come from. There were mousers living on the estate but most of them looked like wild animals, with dirty and matted fur. This one looked to be a pet to someone.

He was about to call it to him, thinking it must belong to one of the staff, not wanting to see it get harmed. His mouth stopped moving as he watched Darlyn lean over, pick the cat up, hold it close enough to his face for the animal to rub its nose and head against his chin and stroke it lovingly.

Now he knew something was seriously wrong.

Darlyn had not allowed himself to care for any animal since losing his dog all those years ago. The last he knew the wizard considered them nothing more than devices for his many dark experiments. When and why had that changed?

Trying to keep his voice steady, and not relay any fear, uncertain if it might be all it would take to send the wizard over the edge into whatever crazy dark reality he was apparently already skirting, Antrim said, "You are not the Darlyn Algier I remember."

"That is part of why I am here. The last year has been… illuminating and more than a bit confusing for me," said Darlyn.

"I am not certain if I should be pleased to hear you say this or if I should run for the hills now," said Antrim. He hoped the man before him could still take a joke as well as the old one had.

"There is times I would say to do the latter, Friend," said the wizard with a strange smirk, not unfriendly but not pleasant either. "This day I hope it is with pleasure. Pray-tell, what do you see?"

Antrim stepped back to get a better look at the man.

The town steward had a type of insight few in the wizard world had, or could understand. He had a way of *reading* a person's soul light that had worried and frightened many at the Guild. This was a form of magic but not one they trusted. He didn't learn the ones they did teach quick enough for them so he was released with only minimal training. He was taught enough to control his skills, nothing more. The rest he had learned on his own, through trial and error at times.

The wizard before him had allowed himself to be used for some of these trials, intrigued about the differences in their skills. Being a quick study, Darlyn had gleaned a few tricks himself, so it was a mutually beneficial experience. To this day, Darlyn was one of the few in the wizard world who were still willing to associate with him.

The master wizard was far from average himself though. The Guild had been confounded and excited at the thought that Darlyn, at only thirteen, had more self-awareness, control and strength of will than most three times his age and experience. Antrim knew the real reason the Guild had accepted the boy so quickly – going against all their own doctrines that it was unsafe for one under the age of fifteen to perform magic. He knew Darlyn knew this as well and that he had used the professors' desires to have associated themselves with one with his power for his own gain.

Darlyn's academic experience had been the exact opposite of Antrim's. He learned everything far faster than the instructors were comfortable with. In his case they didn't dare to release him – they wanted him to stay very, very close. Antrim had heard several rumors that there had been more than one Guild master who wanted him bound but they didn't dare to.

In truth, Darlyn frightened Antrim very much too. If the wizard knew just how much the steward knew of his true nature and the things he had done he would be frightened of the steward as well. This did little to ease the lesser magic user's mind.

The steward of Sheffield knew Darlyn Algier was very loyal and a sort of kind to those he liked or at least respected. He also knew he could be very cruel to them. He was especially cruel to those he disliked. Over their year together at the Guild he had *read* many of the wizard's dark thoughts, plans and aspirations, which had caused many a night's poor sleep. When he had come to him ten years ago he had been shown which of those thoughts, plans and aspirations had come true. He wasn't sure he wanted to see what new and terrible things the man had done since the last time but wasn't sure he dared to turn him away either.

He had learned to stave off his skills when he needed to. One could get themselves flayed alive if they read the wrong person, especially a wizard, against their will. Even though he had been given permission by this one, he stayed to only the surface of the man's mind.

He drew in his breathe as he opened his mind and allowed the currents of air to form around the man standing opposite him. His aura *had* changed, it had always glowed a strange purplish red before, now it was a purplish blue with a good deal of green.

The color of a person's soul light, their aura, told more than many would want known of their inner thoughts and desires to one that can read it. A person's current mood could change or cause a false reading for an untrained clairvoyant, to someone with experience it was easy to see a person's true self hidden underneath. Antrim was one of only a few considered adept at this.

A person's soul light can run from pure white to solid black, the first being one of a pure and good heart, in every way, the latter being pure evil, in every way. There were many stages between the two; most were a combination of several colors. The softer colors; yellows, oranges and greens were colors of peace and just thoughts; blues and purples were most often linked to mischievous or playful thoughts; reds to brown were the stages up to and before evil.

The steward had seen changes in Darlyn's aura before. When he first lost his parents and brother it had settled into a dull brown and had remained that color for several months after. Toward the end of his schooling it had changed to more purple and red. The last time Antrim had seen the wizard it was mostly reds and browns; due in part to having spent the previous few years deeply engulfed in the dark arts.

Now it didn't seem to know what color it wanted to be. It was changing so fast it was hard to name each individual color, it was flashing between every color except black and white – some for mere seconds others staying for several seconds before slowly changing – or more blending into the next. He wondered what had happened to the always so unwavering wizard to mess his aura up so badly this time.

The odd array of colors was making Antrim feel a little dizzy, he closed his eyes and forced his senses back to present with much effort.

The steward motioned for Darlyn to follow him into one of the side rooms so he could sit down. He did this also to give them some privacy. Few in his lord's employ knew of his ability and he wanted to keep it that way. He knew the very private wizard would want his reason for being there kept that way as well.

12

FLASHES
OF RED

The room Antrim led the wizard to was small but comfortable; it served as his office, where he conducted his business for Lord Grimmley, as well as his lounge. It had a small wooden desk set to one side with a stack of vellum, an ink well, a pot of feather quills, several seal stamps and wax for those seals spread across its surface. A land lease lay at its center just waiting for the lessees' name and the parcel of land to be entered; a quill lay across it as if he had been in the middle of filling it in when he was called away.

"Have I disturbed your work?" asked Darlyn. "I can return at a more convenient time."

Again Antrim looked sideways at the wizard. The Darlyn he knew wouldn't have cared because his needs were more important than anyone else's – as far as he was concerned. "I am always free for you, Friend," was what he said though. He motioned for the wizard to take one of the two chairs in the room. He watched his leg catch and him cringe and start to grab it as he sat down and asked, "Do you need anything for the pain?"

The wizard gave him a crooked smile then shook his head. "No thank you, I am learning to live with it. It's a reminder to me of how careless I have let myself become of late."

Antrim nodded at the statement. That was the first thing he had said since arriving that actually sounded like the old Darlyn. Still Antrim didn't allow himself to relax. "Your surface mind is cloudy. Let us sit and relax for a moment then I will try again."

He poured them each a bit a brandy and passed one to the wizard then moved to the chair at the desk, all the while watching his guest.

"Begin whenever you are ready," said the wizard as he sipped of the burgundy liquor.

Feeling a little more even minded, Antrim opened his senses again. This time the wizard's aura was a little more stable – now fluctuating between green and blue – and this time there were actually flashes of white, of all things. That was the one aspect he had never seen before. *How very odd*, he thought. The look on his face must have betrayed this because he watched the wizard get stiff then.

"Tell me what you find so odd. What do you see," spat Darlyn, getting some of his old impatience and arrogance back.

This changed the white quickly to red. "You're soul's light is all mixed up, Master Alg… Darlyn," Antrim said as he shifted in his seat. He moved it so he was directly across from the wizard. "I'm assuming you already suspected that, which is why you have come.

"I did."

"Do you want a full *discernment* or just a surface reading?"

"A full discernment, if you have the time."

"If I have your consent then I will make the time." said the steward, his curiosity piqued. He had made the mistake of *discerning* the wizard's aura once without asking permission, on a dare, and had felt only a tiny bit of the fury this man could wield for having done it. He'd had nasty nightmares, severe headaches and almost constant nosebleeds for nearly a month – a lesson he didn't need repeated.

"You do."

"Tell me when you are ready."

Darlyn remembered well all the times he had allowed the man to see inside him and had never enjoyed any of them. There really was no such thing as preparing to have your inner mind wrenched open forcefully, which felt a bit like thousands of tiny insects burrowing into your brain. He took several deep breaths, held the last, and tried to slow down his rapidly beating heart. He wanted to be in an almost trancelike state, not really fully unaware but numb at the same time. He decided it was now or never. He nodded his head to the man who was watching him intently.

Antrim took a deep breath and let it out slowly. "Steady your body and allow your mind to clear. Picture something that is calming and keep this image for as long as you are able." He leaned forward and stared deep into the wizard's blue-gray eyes, into what was left of his soul.

Antrim had been asked before what he saw when he did a *discerning* but he had never been able to adequately describe it enough for anyone to understand. It was a bit like seeing memories – not like living them himself more like watching a play being performed on a stage. The seer of sorts was now seeing Darlyn's memories like this.

Antrim saw the weeks before the wizard had left the castle on the expedition into the forest; all but torturing several men for information on the prophecy and him before a stack of books, pouring through dozens of dusty tomes in search of answers to his questions of how to achieve his single burning desire – to be immortal. He saw him find what he thought was the answer and him browbeating the king into funding the journey.

He watched him enter the forest with three people, one of them an elf. This struck him as odd; remembering what the wizard had once thought of that race. He truly cared for this one though. He saw how nervous, uncertain, jealous and intrigued he was made by a young cleric. Antrim was impressed that the man seemed to realize he was inferior to this young man in a lot of ways but was not especially upset by it. He knew the man had always disliked anyone knowing more than him about anything.

He saw the first days of him and these companions in the dark forest before they became separated and the strong emotions those images evoked. The wizard had truly been worried for them – as people not just pawns. These instances all seemed to have had a profound impact on the wizard but it wasn't enough to have caused the dramatic shift in his attitude and his aura.

Antrim flipped through the wizard's memories like turning the pages of a book.

He stopped on a battle the wizard was caught in the middle of with hideous misshapen creatures. Darlyn's mind said they were Torge. Antrim had learned of the beasts in history books telling of the Torge Wars that had been fought more than fifty years ago. He had never thought he would see one of them, let alone more than fifty of them, for real – even though only in a memory.

He was as shocked as Darlyn had been to see them able to incapacitate the powerful wizard. Darlyn's frustration at being overpowered was palpable. The fact that these things had known how to subdue the wizard was frightening. The darkness that descended as the band was tied over the wizard's eyes and the helplessness the wizard had felt at knowing he could not help his companions, who he could hear were still battling the same creatures, was disconcerting even to Antrim. The clairvoyant visibly cringed as he fought down the angst these memories brought out in his own innards.

Next he saw the wizard speaking with a man who he felt was far inferior to him, in mind and magic, yet this man had been able to render him magically impotent with only an herb. He had to take a deep breath to get beyond the anger and thoughts this act had brought up in Darlyn's mind. He would have more than a few nightmares after seeing the things Darlyn had wanted to do this man.

These memories had impacted the wizard profoundly but they did not explain his current state.

He flipped further and stopped again when he came upon his meeting of an old man, a recluse. A man he truly admired, envied and feared; one he looked upon as one of the few that might be an equal to him. That was the beginning of the change.

This man had become very important to the wizard. He saw him struggling to translate a journal the man had written many years before as if it were his bible and him discussing parts of it with the older man. The emotions these passages evoked were quite moving even now – pain and suffering, joy and tenderness, hatred and anger and a lot of loneliness.

Antrim saw that these entries had made the wizard see how being so closed off from the rest of the world had made the older man, how disconnected from it he had become, and realize how closed off he had allowed himself to become. He saw him realizing how much he thought he had missed out on in his all-consuming pursuit of knowledge and power. Meeting this man was what had made the wizard first question himself.

He saw a beautiful young woman that evoked feelings he doubted even Darlyn had fully admitted to himself. The name Iligra Almeas popped into his mind. He felt himself smiling as the wizard's heart skipped a beat when her face flashed through his mind. That was the second change.

He quickly flew past their sexual encounters, not wanting to anger the wizard for having invaded something so private. He was surprised, and gladdened, by how passionate the guarded man had allowed himself to be with this woman. He also saw how jealous he was of her past relationship with the young cleric. The man he had always thought of as pompous and so self-assured and used to always having things he wanted so easily truly didn't feel he could compete with the younger man if it became a contest to win her heart.

He saw him leaving the woman, uncertain whether he would ever be with her intimately again – fearing he would be driving her even faster into the cleric's arms, and the anxiety this evoked in his soul.

He saw him entering a very cold, dark, tower, one that the man had wanted that way but now didn't like, and him taking items he valued out of it, uncertain if he would ever step foot in it again, and the pain and anxiety this evoked in his soul.

He saw him magically battling a book he had warded himself to keep others from having access to the wonders and dangers inside. He saw what it had done to him and his soul and knew then what had brought about the change to his hair color. He saw just how close to dying the man had come and that he had no idea himself how close it had been. That had been the third change.

Antrim moved ahead in the memories then and stopped on the incident that caused the injury to his leg. He felt the pain of the sword cutting through the layers of skin, muscle, tissue, blood vessels and cutting into the bone as if it was happening to him now and had no idea how the man had been able to endure it and not go insane – or more insane. He felt all the shame and guilt the wizard had felt every day since for having allowed his guard down. The fourth change had come with this incident.

He saw a piece of the wizard's soul had been taken into one of the seven plains of hell. A spirit in knight form, that had strong ties to the wizard, had retrieved it but it had been in the realm long enough to have been altered already, which was why the wound wouldn't fully heal.

He flipped past all the attempts to heal the wound and all the months of frustrating and embarrassing rehabilitation he had endured just to be able to walk again. He was surprised by how much the vain and proud wizard had allowed the woman, Iligra, and another, Mari, to do for him, and how much it warmed the wizard's heart, and Antrim's, that the two had wanted to, no matter how much he berated them for it.

He stopped when he found the moment that had been the most intense change in the man before him. It was right after one of these embarrassing moments when the woman, Iligra, had finally convinced the man that there was nothing he could say or do that would make her leave him. He saw in that moment that the man had decided he could allow himself to completely and utterly surrender to this woman. Darlyn Algier had given a bit of himself to another, willingly, for the first time in that moment.

He saw him worrying and anxious about what was happening to one of the companions he had taken into the forest. It was the elf and he was truly worried for his life. He watched him entering a cave-like chamber. He felt the same anxiety and excitement the wizard had felt as he saw a man before him he had always wished he could face down, one he was now about to.

Antrim was surprised himself to see the very much alive Paitell Tobac standing before the wizard. The accident that was supposed to have killed the boy had happened just before he left the Guild. Like Darlyn, he had never cared for Paitell; he didn't trust him, partly because he had never been able to get a reading on him. It was as if his soul was... an empty void.

He heard Paitell telling Darlyn it was him that turned his brother into a killer and had provoked him into doing away with his parents and not to fight himself being hanged and felt the anguish in Darlyn's heart. He watched him hurl his anger at the man and saw him realizing he had just doomed the elf in the process. He felt the waves of guilt the man had at the thought that his actions and anger might be the cause of the elf's death. Antrim had always thought the wizard incapable of guilt.

He could feel the pain of the wizard hitting the door as if it was him hitting it and felt like his own leg was bursting open. He heard him begin the words to the forbidden spell, balefire, which equally did and didn't surprise him – to learn he knew the spell or that he would think to use it. He felt the shock, shame and pain as his eyes connected with the woman's and saw him see what he would become if he did this. He felt the pain he endured as he called the energy back and was awed that he was powerful enough to withstand it. A lesser wizard would have been destroyed by this act. He saw that a part of him *had* been destroyed. He wondered if Darlyn knew he had truly died for a few moments that day – not just come close to dying.

He felt the awe Darlyn had felt as he watched the blue dragon in human form stop the other wizard from throwing the same spell at him. He also felt the jealousy that this being was both beautiful and magical and that it was able to not only take on human form but that it could fly.

The steward saw him learning from this dragon that he was to be a father. The emotions this had caused ran the full gambit before settling on mostly pleasure.

The memories began to move faster then, mostly mundane moments, getting closer to present day.

He saw him helping the king of Hundertmark become the kind of ruler the people needed. Antrim found this surprising since an earlier memory had shown him that he had once thought the man was not worth half his effort. He saw him training with the soldiers of the king's guard, giving him the muscles he could see moving under the gauzy tunic. He saw him preparing for a journey, the one that had brought him here to Sheffield for a stop off.

He saw him writing in a journal, well into the evening hours, trying to record his life to date in hopes of giving his child some insight into his father. He wanted it to act as a lesson to him, hoping it would give his son the information to...

He saw what was truly distorting the wizard's aura.

Antrim drew in a deep and sudden breath as he pulled his mind back. He fell back as well from the force of it. He fought down the wave of nausea that always came after ending such deep readings. This time it was worse, it felt as if he might puke out all of his innards rather than just his stomach. He knew the wizard would want to know what he saw – all of it – he prayed he had the courage to tell him.

Darlyn shivered as Antrim moved around in his subconscious; he could feel him probing the surface memories and then felt an odd tingling as the man delved deeper. He had to fight the urge to close off his mind. There were things he didn't want this man to see but in order to get a thorough and useful reading he had to allow him to see everything.

He'd had Antrim *discern* him before but somehow this time was different – deeper and more intense. His stomach clenched tight and was getting tighter the deeper inside his mind he reached. He thought he might vomit if it didn't stop soon then it did.

He heard the man draw in a deep, sudden and shaky breath, loudly. He felt like his brain was being pulled out of his head through his eyes, telling him the man had just left his mind. He felt empty and hallow and battered and bruised. He closed his eyes tight, as if trying to prevent the last bits of his mind from escaping. He fell back in the chair hard, as if someone had pushed him, wiped sweat from his forehead and face with his sleeve and fought the dizziness that was washing over him. Once it cleared he opened his eyes and looked at the steward.

"What did you see?" Darlyn asked weakly.

Antrim was as white as a ghost. He stood up, poured himself more brandy, drank it, then poured another and drank it before he sat back down once more across from the wizard. "Where to begin? Where to begin? I... I saw a man. A cleric. Nortus Elgin. He made a deep impression on you. He has made you question yourself and your convictions. And..."

"And? And what?" asked the wizard. He wondered why the man, who was usually so quick and blunt, was drawing out his answer.

"I saw a woman."

"Iligra," said Darlyn, nodding. An image of her appeared in his mind and he felt himself smiling at the mention of her name.

Antrim saw a flash of green cross the wizard's aura as he said the woman's name but it disappeared quickly. He said the next part slowly, unsure whether the man knew yet what his feelings were on the subject, "And... you are to be a father as well."

The wizard nodded and the smile became almost a grimace.

Antrim watched a flash of green swept through again, this time it stayed a little bit longer. A flash of brilliant red immediately followed it, though it stayed only for a few seconds. This was part of why he was being so guarded with his answers. The steward still wasn't sure he had the courage to confront his thoughts. In his psychologically-mussed-up state the wizard might be even more unpredictable than usual. He did not want to find himself mentally or physically flayed.

Darlyn sensed Antrim's anxiety and wondered what could be so upsetting. The man had read all the horrific thoughts and feelings he had when he had thought his younger brother killed his parents in cold blood, and read more than a few of the questionable acts he had done between then and now. Surely this couldn't be any worse than that. The wizard spoke the thought aloud.

Antrim took a deep breath and quickly said, "You fear your son."

Darlyn broke into a deep and forced laugh. "Excuse me?" He couldn't believe he had heard right. How could he be afraid of a person that had not even come into the world yet? As those words sunk in he realized it was true. It wasn't because he was afraid to be a father, or not all that; this went far deeper. The wizard swallowed hard and said sedately, "Go on."

"You are afraid the woman will take your son from you if she learns all of your dark past and you fear your son will want to destroy you if he does... No, not fear, you... you almost... you hope he will..."

Darlyn wanted to laugh at the preposterousness of that statement but he could not. He felt like the man had just plunged a serrated dagger into his heart and was now wrenching it around inside of it, trying to carve it out without slicing him open to do it. He had to fight the urge to pull the non-existent blade from his chest. He wanted to deny it, he wanted to slap this man for even suggesting it, but he knew it was true. He suddenly felt like every nerve was fully exposed – raw and red and inflamed. He closed his eyes and held his breath for a few seconds before exhaling until there was no air left in his lungs. "Go on."

"Perhaps we should…"

"FINISH IT."

Antrim did. "The man, Nortus, made you question yourself so deeply that you have been severely emotionally traumatized. You are no longer sure who you are and what you truly want. You do not dare to let yourself learn either of these things for fear that they have not changed. All your beliefs and your core self are lain raw."

Darlyn only nodded to this.

Antrim didn't dare leave it just at this; he wanted to be sure the wizard fully understood how important – how dangerous – this situation was. "As long as you remain in this condition you are unsafe, not only to yourself but to everyone around you."

Darlyn brought the first two fingers and thumb of his right hand to the bridge of his nose and rubbed there, still nodding.

Antrim continued, knowing how much risk he was putting himself in. "I know I don't need to remind you it is your emotions that you rely on when casting spells."

"I know, I know," said the wizard shakily. He was having a hard time keeping them in check now.

"I suggest we do a complete mental purgative. It will be rough and painful. You will be reliving things you may not enjoy, but I feel it's needed if you are to remain or wish to continue to be Darlyn Algier."

Darlyn felt his body begin to shake and knew he couldn't go on this way. He hated what he was becoming but he didn't have time this day. "I fear you are more correct than you know, in more ways than you know, my friend. I have a prior obligation I must complete first though, so I have to decline... or rather postpone for now."

"As long as you continue as you are you will continue to be unbalanced..."

Darlyn stood up then and said, "I am aware of this. I will likely wish I had done different when this is done but I cannot back out of my obligation."

"If you feel you must..." said Antrim. He was equally pleased the wizard did not want to do this today; the procedure would not have been fun for him either – he too would be living what the wizard had – he would likely then need a cleansing of his own.

He wasn't sure that letting a wizard as powerful as this one was, given how unstable he was emotionally just then, to just leave was such a good idea. He wasn't sure if he wanted to do anything to stop him either though. He had no means, short of drugging him.

He could contact the Guild and inform them of the wizard's current condition. They would immediately send out handlers to bind the man's powers – or attempt to. This would anger Darlyn and would certainly make him lose control. Antrim was one of the few people who knew just *how* powerful Darlyn Algier really was. He doubted even the man himself knew. He knew this wizard could control his emotions more than most so he would honor his friendship and allow him to complete his goal and hope, and pray, he saw him again.

Darlyn started to take his scrip from his side, which was heavy with coins, intending to pay the steward for his services.

"Don't be ridiculous," said Antrim, waving him down. Darlyn had never once offered to pay before. This again surprised, perplexed and worried him. He didn't know if he had the power to be able to cleanse the man as deeply as he now believed he needed to be.

"Please accept my humble thank you for your time then, Sir."

"As always."

"I will return when my task is completed, if you are willing to continue this another day?" said the master wizard.

"I am willing and will be available to you whenever you are ready," said the man. He had decided when that day came he would be certain the Guild knew – to give them time to prepare.

He watched the wizard lift the waiting cat into his arms and stroke its head and back then set it back on the floor. He motioned it on as he took the cane and used it to steady his still shaking legs as he walked down the hall and out the door.

The steward shook his head at the wizard's back. He no longer had the walk of a man who knew he was powerful or dangerous. He had always considered Darlyn Algier one of the strongest people he knew. If this man could fall to pieces what did it mean for the rest of them? He suddenly found himself questioning his own beliefs.

13

MAKING REPORTS

Phineas completed his business in town before the others. He let the elf know this and the two went down to the dining room to await their companions' returns. They had tried to keep a conversation going, more out of politeness than true desire, while they waited but they both had too much on their mind so the silences between talking points became more and more extended. Sangas was worried about Uther and Phineas couldn't get Junt off his mind; neither could stop thinking of Eonard and Nortus.

Just before the others arrived, and after a few minutes of awkward silence, Phineas asked, "Have you gotten any recent feelings about Eonard?"

"His mind seems to be running over thoughts that are a bit jumbled and unclear. They apparently had to have a guide for the realm and he has concerns of the guide's intentions, though he doesn't feel like they are major," answered the elf.

Phineas started to ask about the spirit knight, Junt, when Torrin and Cieri walked in.

They made a quick line for their table.

Just seconds later the wizard, the cat perched on his shoulder, appeared in the arched doorway, looking more than a little bit preoccupied.

When the three reached the table Phineas made his report.

"A peddler coming in from Tanith saw a man fitting Jacobi's description in Venwar two days ago, which is a good day's traverse from Cutter. He is apparently still on foot at least."

"This is good news," said Torrin. "We can reach there in a day if we don't make any other stops." He turned to the wizard then and asked, "Were you able to conclude your business with the steward?"

"Not entirely but enough for now," said a pensive sounding wizard.

Torrin wasn't sure he liked the look of the man. He had not looked himself really since the injury to his leg but he was looking even worse than when he had been in the throes of the fever from that injury. He knew the wizard would not talk about whatever was ailing him unless he wanted to so he left it alone and instead said, "We will leave at first light."

14

A
BIT OF HIMSELF

Leonard was still weak but at least he was able to stay awake without needing help. Nortus preformed a healing on him each morning, or what passed for morning in this place, even the ones the elf said he didn't need. It did seem to help but he was still far from well.

There was no way to tell just how much time had passed in the upper world but it felt to them like they had been in the lower realm for four days – they had stopped to sleep that many times at least.

Their guide hadn't appeared the morning of their *fifth* day yet, which was making them all uneasy. The spirit knight was just about to see if he could find the absent soul on the currents that flowed through the realm when it appeared with a sudden and pointed pop beside Azure, making the dragon jump and growl deep in his throat.

Rius didn't say anything about his tardiness but he seemed anxious. His smoky form was usually white and wispy; this day he was turning grayish at his center then back to the white over and over like a tiny storm was raging inside him. This was disconcerting to the others and made them feel uncomfortable.

He floated over and stopped before Eonard. "I sense your soul is breaking apart further, Elf."

"I do as well," said Eonard. He hadn't told the others he had been trying to reach out for it ever since finding he could manipulate the plain a little.

Nortus picked up on the underlying meaning of this. His empathic abilities hadn't worked since arriving here, which he had been pleased with at first – glad to finally have only his own thoughts in his head – now he wished he had them. "You are too weak to be attempting such..." He stopped speaking when Rius suddenly vanished.

A slight pop sounded for a second time and the cloudy form was back. Again Azure jumped and growled, because he had appeared right beside him this time as well.

Eonard had sat up suddenly, at the same moment as the cloud reappeared.

"A piece of your soul is close," said Rius.

"I feel it too and I think I can lead us to it!" said Eonard.

"How do we move on this plain?" asked Azure.

"If we were all spirits looking to traverse the area we could each conjure a horse..." said Junt. "I am not strong enough to conjure one for each of us."

"Neither am I," said Rius.

Eonard thought he might be able to but he didn't tell the others. He might need the energy to get his soul from wherever it was when they reached it and that was more important.

"We can try jumping," offered the cloudy guide.

Junt's formed seemed to be considering this. He nodded his transparent head and said, "It is our only option. We will do it in turns so neither of us expends too much energy."

The guide had no head to nod but he wavered a little and said, "Agreed."

Traveling on this plain was difficult; since there was essentially no real end to it, a person could literally keep going forever. Junt and Rius took turns *jumping* them from one place to another. Sometimes they were in a desert, like the one they first arrived in, sometimes a forest, sometimes by a vast ocean. They stayed at each location just long enough to know it wasn't the right one then moved on. Their last jump was to a mineshaft, which bothered the two souls – neither knew how they had found themselves there. This was because it had been Eonard that had directed them to this location.

They were accosted by a strong wind and heat. The putrid smell of sulfur was heavy in the air. They could hear banging and voices shouting orders but couldn't see any people around to be making the noises. The dragon, Nortus and Junt looked around for signs of the soul or souls that had created this scene but couldn't find any.

Eonard stood frozen in the center of the cave like area.

Rius floated over to the elf and asked, with more concern than he probably should have, considering he hadn't known any of these people before they arrived on the plain, "Are you alright?"

"I've been better," said Eonard with more than a little sarcasm in the answer and in his stance. "I have been here before," said the elf suddenly – the attitude having been replaced by confusion.

This looked like the mine Paitell had held the other party from Hundertmark in; the place Raspal had been held and tortured. Just as he thought this a large, rusty gear wheel appeared before them. It was just like the one he had seen with his newly found ability to read peoples' thoughts as if his own as Torrin described the scene to him.

At first it was only the wheel, tinted orange with the years of oxidation. The teeth around its edge were clanking hollowly and a high-pitched squeal was ringing through the dead air as it turned. A body of a boy began to form on it as they looked at it. His bright red hair was matted with dried blood and dirt and his clothes were torn. Fresh blood, still red and tacky, coated his wrists and ankles where they were chained to the side of the wheel. More blood was dripping from his lips and the moans of pain were heartfelt.

"Good Gods!" shouted Nortus.

He and Azure drew in quick breaths and started forward to help the boy. Junt and Rius both disappeared and materialized before them to stop them.

"It is not real," said Rius.

"He is already dead," Junt, added after, as if he needed to make a point.

The boy looked so real and sounded in so much pain that they couldn't accept this. A sound, similar to the one Rius had made when he appeared to them earlier, made them turn around. They saw a new ghost-like image floating beside the elf.

Eonard turned toward it. He had no idea if it could do him harm so he wasn't sure if he should be frightened and should try to get away from it or not.

At first it was only mist, like Rius, then it became a mirror image of the boy on the wheel, then it changed to a much thinner, stark, white skinned image, then to what he had looked like when alive and full of life. His vibrant red hair was bouncing around his head with the blasts of heated wind coming from around the cave. He was staring at himself on the wheel, fighting back tears. He opened and closed him ethereal mouth a few times then asked a pain filled, "Why?"

Eonard looked from the boy to the others then back and asked, "What?"

Raspal jumped as if only just noticing them. At first he started to dissolve then he looked closely at the elf he had been standing beside and a spark of recognition lit in his eyes, "You are the elf the warrior, Torrin, was looking for, aren't you? Eonard, is that your name?"

"Yes, and you are Bergon's brother, Raspal, right?"

"Bergon..." the boy said with longing. He started to say something more then he drew in a breath quickly and said, "Why are you here? You aren't dead, are you?"

It took Eonard a minute to respond since it wasn't a simple answer, "No, at least not fully. The man the cleric, Helon, was helping resurrect took part of my soul. I am trying to get it back."

"And, my brother? Is Bergon here as well?" He sounded like he hoped he was but was about to cry because he didn't want him to be.

"No. He is alive and well," said Eonard. He hoped he had not lied.

"Good... good... He is good... That is good," said the boy as a tender smile broke his face. It faded quickly and was replaced with a strange look. "Did Torrin find you? I am sorry I slowed him down..."

"He did find me... though we had to separate again shortly after."

"He is well though?"

"As he can be... Jacobi took a sword from him, he is tracking him down to get it back."

"Jacobi had a lot of secrets," said the boy that most had thought was simpleminded.

Eonard could only nod to this.

"Helon is here, you know..." growled Raspal.

This response took Eonard aback for two reasons. First, because it was said with far more anger than the elf thought the innocent boy would have ever been able to muster when he was alive. Second, because he was a little surprised at the anger that welled up inside himself. He had known the man was dead; having watched Paitell rip his heart from his chest right in front of him, so he supposed he shouldn't be surprised to hear that he was here. He didn't get what he wanted before he died so he was wandering this place now... It was a sick sort of recompense. Elves were not typically vindictive but he wished he knew some of the ways to inflict pain on a soul, there were a few lessons he would very much enjoy teaching that man.

"You say you are looking for your soul?"

Eonard tried to shake off the less than normal thoughts he had just been having, not liking the taste they left in his mouth. "Yes, it has been sent here and is being slowly destroyed by the forces of this realm."

"I think I have a piece of it," the boy said quickly then disappeared in a pop.

Nortus, Azure and Eonard all said in unison, "How?" but the boy was already gone.

Seconds later he reappeared, in another loud pop, with a leaf from a leatherleaf tree held in his hand. He looked it over briefly then slowly held it out to the elf.

"It appeared at my feet out of nowhere. I have come to this place every day for I do not know how long and it never was here before... Tell me of Bergon."

Eonard held the leaf before him and slowly turned it by its stem. He didn't think he had seen anything so beautiful in all his life. It was green and supple, as if it had just recently been picked from one of his beloved trees. He held it up to the group for a moment then opened his shirt and placed it over his heart. It stuck to the skin of his chest for a moment then began to sparkle.

It slowly became only light as it was absorbed into him. At first nothing happened, the others stared, stiff, in wait, unsure what was supposed to or what was going to happen. The elf started to say that was easy when he began to convulse. His legs gave out and he fell to the ground hard, moaning horrifically. He was flopping around violently, bending up like a pretzel, first this way then that, and a blindingly bright light had formed all around him, which was pulsing and shrinking repeatedly.

Nortus went to his side but the aura was like a hard shell around him, it wouldn't let the old man touch him. He looked to the other two, hoping one of them could offer help but neither seemed able to. He was thrust backwards suddenly when the aura exploded outward, the blast blowing the thin hair away from his head. The elf appeared to have been unharmed by the blast but he now lay unconscious.

Without a second thought, Nortus went back to the elf's side and reached out to him. He breathed out a sigh of relief to find he was now able to touch him. He felt very hot to the touch, hotter than any fever Nortus had ever dealt with. He quickly said the words to a healing and was pleased at how much the elf's body responded to it this time. He did not awaken as the old cleric had expected him to though. "He is breathing," he said to the others. "I have to assume he is only in a form of stasis…"

It was several minutes before Eonard awakened again. He looked around, unsure where he was a first. They were no longer in the mine in the cave. He saw the bones of what was once a building. The roof over his head had gaping openings between the timbers. What was supposed to be the sky in this realm showed through these in a colorful mix of purples, blues and pinks. It didn't look very sturdy. He hoped it remained its roof; the idea of being buried alive while stuck in the realm did not sit well with him.

He was surprised to find he was lying on a lumpy cot. He looked to his rights and saw a row of what might have been other cots every few paces along the wall. Suddenly the elf recognized the building; it was just as Torrin had described in. This was the fort Raspal, Bergon, Torrin, Cieri and Jacobi had taken shelter in after their escape from the cave. More specifically, it was the barracks that was the last place the boy had been alive.

He slowly rose up on his elbows and found all but Rius and the boy standing across from him. They were all looking at him in anticipation. He tried to smile at them but he wasn't sure if his face responded. He swung his legs around and sat up. He waved Nortus away when he saw him start toward him. "I'm alright, Master Elgin."

He looked around for the spirit of Raspal. He found him floating near the only other still whole cot. He guessed it was the one he had laid on in life. He stood slowly and walked toward the boy. "Thank you, Raspal," he said weakly.

The boy smiled, a little sadly, then shrugged and said, "It was yours; I only returned it to you." He got a glint of life in his eyes again and he repeated his earlier request, "Tell me of Bergon?"

Eonard motioned the spirit boy back with the others. For all Raspal no longer needed to rest, the elf did. He was beginning to feel dizzy and he thought he might faint if he didn't sit down. He started to tell him how his brother had been when he had last seen him, which was just as he left with Torrin to find the black sword. He knew the boy wanted to know that his brother was good now. It was with great pain that he said, "I have not seen him in several weeks, Raspal. So, I really cannot say how he is."

The image of the boy looked ready to cry.

Eonard felt anger well up inside himself at the unjustness of this boy having to die so young and through no actions of his own – just being used as a pawn to cause pain.

Junt floated forward than and offered, "I was with your brother only a few days ago. He took a commission aboard Master Radric's father's ship; one called Ole' Bessie. To the best of my knowledge, that is where he remains."

"He *is* good then. He always loved water… This is good." Raspal opened his mouth a few times like he wanted to say more but he didn't know what more to say. He nodded his head slowly and whispered "Thank you," then he began to fade away.

"Wait!" Eonard said quickly.

Raspal's image became clear again. He looked at the elf and said, in a voice thick with emotion, "It is alright… Thank you for what you have been able to tell me…"

"Don't go yet. I can show you your brother," said Eonard.

This surprised everyone in the fake infirmary.

15

BOLD

DETERMINATION

"There is no way to do this," said Nortus, surprised the always-plainspoken elf would make an offer he couldn't follow through with. Barely over a whisper, hoping only Eonard would hear it, he added, "You do not even know if the boy's brother is alive. Accidents can happen on a ship, Eonard."

"I would be willing to bet their souls would have been drawn to each other if he were dead as well."

"Not all souls that die come to these places. If he had nothing to hold him back he would simply have ascended."

Eonard didn't say anything to this he only looked meaningfully at the floating image of the ever-eager looking red haired boy, nonverbally reminding the older man the boy's brother was filled with guilt at the loss of his younger brother and more than likely would have come here.

"Be that as it may..." said Nortus.

"There must be a way," said Eonard. He could almost see how to do it but it kept slipping away. "Can it be done?" Eonard looked from Junt to the smoky shape that was Rius and back.

Junt's ghostly image was shaking his head slowly, but not as if to say no, more as if to say not recommended. "It can be done but it would be extremely dangerous without some-one to call from your own realm, Elf, and you must have a strong connection to the living person."

"Can you reach Phineas or Darlyn?"

"I cannot reach Darlyn," said Junt very fast, more as if to say he *would not* rather than he *could not*. "And Phineas does not have the power to then connect to the boy's brother."

Eonard wondered why the spirit knight wished to avoid his former master.

Junt seemed to pick up on the elf's concern. He added, "The connection I once had with Darlyn and Phineas was severed when I came through the portal to assist in finding your soul and vanquishing the last bit of the dark cleric's. To contact them would put my own soul at risk of becoming fractured."

"If *I* could reach Darlyn, could it be done then?"

Again Junt shook his head. "It would require a connection to his mind."

"I was... briefly."

All but Rius and Raspal turned toward him then. Neither of them knew Darlyn so neither of them was disturbed by this.

"How? When?" asked Nortus. The sound of worry in his voice was very strong.

"When he first retrieved me from the elf village. I was still... am still very new to my abilities. He was telling me what had happened to him, you and Aramis and... I did not mean to but I sort of read his mind... I think some part of me is still connected to it. I get snippets of images that are not mine and are... too dark to be another elves' soul memories." Eonard would not meet Nortus' eyes after this admission. He looked back at the spirit knight and said, "Is it enough?"

Junt didn't want the elf to risk the little energy he had regained by getting the small piece of his soul back in a vain attempt to relieve the guilt he felt for Raspal's dying so young, but he knew if there was any way it could be done the elf would try. He reminded him of a much younger and riskier Darlyn – he had seen the same determined look in his former master's eyes when he was being told he couldn't do something. He wanted to be certain, if the elf did attempt this thing, that he fully understood all the possible consequences.

"When Master Algier opened a doorway to this realm to call souls to act as servants to him he risked creating a rift, one that could have been permanent. He also risked souls, such as Mahki, escaping. Though they would have been mere spirit forms, like myself, they still would have had the power to evoke great threat to the living."

"If you monitor this side none will get through," said Eonard, as if not really listening.

"I may not be strong enough to stop them, Elf. They can be held back from the living realm but there would be nothing stopping them from this side if several were to rush at it at once."

"Rius can assist then."

The smoky image of their guide kind of fluctuated but none of them knew whether it was in disagreement.

Seeing they were all against this made Eonard all the more determined, "I know none of you understand why but I must do this!"

"Young Elf," said Rius' disembodied voice, "I understand and commend your desire to help the boy but he must come to terms with his death on his own. Taking him to his brother most likely will only make it worse. A lost soul rarely leaves here. If he loses or forgets what his goal is he may never find the redemption he requires..." he let the last words kind of float a bit, with longing behind them.

Still the elf persisted, "Do any of you have brothers?"

Being a dragon, Azure considered all of his kin like brothers. He nodded.

Nortus shook his head. He was an only child.

Rius' smoking form didn't seem to react at all.

Junt's image took on an even paler color for a moment; implying he had.

"Then you know why I must do this."

"You must have control of the forces of this realm in order to do this," said Rius.

"I *can* control them," said Eonard, he hadn't wanted them to know this yet; hoping to be able to do more before he told them.

"What?" barked Nortus. "Do you have any idea how dangerous that was? You are weak … and elves do not belong on this plain. There is no way to know how this realm might interpret your desires."

"It did exactly what I asked it to do," said the elf in defense of himself and his actions.

"You always were so very impetuous."

"I am an elf," said Eonard smiling.

"Either way, you are too weak to attempt such again, Eonard," said Nortus.

"I am not too weak," insisted Eonard.

They all wanted to argue with the elf but none could. Elfish magic was different from human magic. Perhaps he could do it. The dragon, old man and Junt looked at each other and, almost in unison, shrugged.

"Very well, what can we do to help?" asked Nortus.

16

A
VISITOR'S REQUEST

The nights had stayed clear and warm so Torrin's group traveled through the dark, only stopping when absolutely necessary, and then only long enough to refill their waterskins, rest the horses, eat their meals and get some sleep. It was for the fourth they were stopped for when Sangas and Darlyn both suddenly cried out.

Cieri and Torrin had gone down to the nearby brook to clean up their dishes so Phineas was alone with the elf and wizard. Darlyn had just sat down and begun his evening meditation and the former marauder had been about to ask Sangas if he wanted to play a game of cards or stones when they made these sounds. He watched them both begin to convulse and fall over. He wasn't sure what to do, or which to go to first. The elf appeared to be trying to say something so Phineas went to him first.

Both men stopped spasming almost as fast as they started and shouted, "Eonard!" at the same time loudly.

This made Phineas jump anew, a flock of birds in the shrubs around the campsite take flight and brought the warriors running back from the river.

"Is he alright?" asked Phineas and Torrin at the same time.

Neither answered them, and Darlyn held up his hand to keep them from asking any more. The wizard had his head cocked to the side as if listening to something none of them could hear.

An image began to form in the smoke of the fire at the center of their campsite. It began to take on a humanoid shape then the features they had all come to know as Eonard appeared. He was much paler then when they had last seen him – although this could have been because he was semi-transparent.

"Blazin' hell… Eonard. Have your joined us?" said Torrin. He started forward to hug his friend. He realized he was only a ghost as he got closer and could see Phineas through him.

"Hello, Torrin, I wish my answer could be different but I am not able to yet."

"You aren't… Oh, Gods, Eonard… you aren't dead, are you?" asked the warrior.

"I am neither dead nor alive just now, Friend, but I am well enough."

They all looked confused by this answer.

"My soul is in pieces down here... I have only found one piece of it so far and have no idea how many others there are yet."

"Is there anythin' we can do to help?" asked Torrin.

"Not me. I have come in hopes of asking Darlyn a favor for another." Eonard's ethereal form turned in the direction of the wizard. Even in spirit form it was obvious the elf was surprised by the look of the wizard. "Sir Algier. You... you have changed."

Darlyn knew instantly that he had seen all and more than Antrim had seen in that brief moment. He was jealous, angry, frightened and awed even more by the elf.

Eonard *had* seen it all but he knew, more than probably anyone else, that there was more to a person than their actions – especially when they were the misguided and rash choices of a younger man only curious about his world and feeling like he needed to prove his worth in it. He could feel how anxious Darlyn was for him not to treat him any differently as well so he didn't.

"What is it you wish to ask of me?" asked Darlyn.

"I have met up with the spirit of a boy that was in one of the groups that entered the forest. He was murdered, unjustly and untimely. I know there is no way to give him the peace he needs to move on... but I'm hoping to ease some of his suffering by... reuniting him with his brother briefly."

"I wish very much I could help you, but having you, a dragon, and a living immortal there is already putting enough of a strain on the fabric between the realms," said Darlyn.

Torrin knew instantly the soul Eonard was speaking of. He still harbored a little guilt for the boy's death himself. If he could help the boy's spirit find some peace he wanted to do it. "Can it be done though? Is there a way to ensure no others, other than Raspal, will come through?"

"I have opened a rift to the realm before… though I had several protection runes in place when I did it…" said Darlyn. "It will be dangerous without them but, I am willing to attempt it. Is Junt still with you?"

"He is."

"Is he willing to stay close to prevent any others from his realm from coming through it?"

"Yes," the way the elf said this told them he was doing so reluctantly.

"Is the soul of the boy with you?"

"He is."

"Do you know anything of where the boy's brother might be?"

Torrin spoke for the elf then, "He took commission aboard the ship my father is now captain of. They will be somewhere on the Eonon River."

"I know most of the river… Assuming the ship is not moving at the moment, I might be able to reach him. Stay where you are on the plain, Eonard. It will take me a moment to prepare," said the wizard. "I need to try to discern the exact location of the vessel he is on."

17

A
DOORWAY TO PEACE

Darlyn opened the portal about an hour later. Sangas acted as a guard to keep any souls from escaping into the world of the living while Rius and Junt did the same on their side in Vethe. Eonard didn't come through this time, only an image of a red haired boy who should have still been playing at home.

The ghost of Raspal looked sadly at Cieri and Torrin then turned to the wizard and said, "I am ready."

Darlyn nodded, then turned to Phineas and said, "Hold the cat. Tight."

Phineas nodded.

Darlyn opened another portal then – this one to a location on the Eonon River.

Phineas squealed several times as the squirming animal fought to get free, wanting to follow the wizard. Somehow he did manage to keep hold of the cat until after the doorway had closed, getting more than a few scratches in the process.

Bergon was in the middle of wrapping the line for the anchor on Ole' Bessie, which was about to be dropped as they came to the dock in Hewlett. This was a task that required a lot of concentration to be certain you were not in those lines when the heavy bit of iron was released. Men had lost arms, legs and lives in that manner.

He jumped and nearly fell over the edge of the railing when a portal burst open beside him in a whoosh.

What he guessed was a man stepped through it. His image was distorted at first, as if coming from a great distance. He shouted out to the captain or first mate, thinking this was forest magic at work.

Taquel and Gregg both immediately started toward the form, thinking, as Bergon, that this was an evil-doing spirit come to wreck the ship.

"Don't move, Bergon," said Taquel. He stepped in front of him and pulled a dispelling charm from under the collar of his tunic. "Be gone, evil spirit!" he said boldly, through clenched teeth. He had the charm up to what would be the thing's forehead.

The form didn't even flinch but it did begin to clear.

Bergon recognized the wizard who had chosen him and his brother for the group to go into the forest, even though he was not wearing the long black robe and cloak that sucked all the light from around it, he now had half white and half black hair, which looked very odd, though somehow fitting for a wizard, and he was now using a cane. "It is alright, he is a wizard from Hundertmark."

"How do we know for certain? The forest may be able to read our minds and form beings from our memories," said the captain, still holding up the charm.

"Master Taquel?" Darlyn asked the captain.

"Aye?"

"I *am* Darlyn Algier, Master Wizard and High Counsel to King Uther Hundertmark." The wizard brought his hand forward and gently took hold of the captain's wrist to show he was real. "Your son, Torrin, sends his regards. I apologize for the odd manner of my appearance but I have been asked a rather odd request." A ghostly image appeared behind him.

"Junt?" asked Taquel, remembering the spirit knight that had been traveling with Phineas.

"Not exactly," said the wizard as he turned to face Bergon once more. "I have someone here that wishes to visit with your deckhand."

Bergon was shocked. "Why would a spirit want to speak with me?"

Darlyn didn't answer him; instead he turned to the ghostly cloud and said, "Well, Boy? I cannot keep you here much longer."

The image coalesced for several seconds, as if trying to form features but was unable to. Finally it began to take on human shape. The image of a boy of about sixteen with bright red hair appeared on the deck of the schooner.

"Ra... Ras... Raspal?" Bergon managed to spit out. He was not certain if he could believe his eyes. The image nodded. He looked to the others, wanting to know if they were seeing him as well. He could tell by the shock on their faces that they were. He stepped forward and threw his arms around his brother.

The smoky image broke apart, coalesced a moment then reformed, again as the young boy. He was smiling with tears in his eyes. "I'm sorry, Bergon..."

Bergon shook his head. He was also in tears now, "It is me that should be sorry. How?" he asked.

"I haven't... I am sorry I made you drag me along."

"Oh, Raspal... I know I acted otherwise but I didn't want to go alone."

"Really?... I wasn't just a... you didn't take me just 'cause Ma..."

"No, Raspal," said Bergon, it was actually a lie but he knew it would make his brother feel better.

"I... I thought..." the image said, looking at his feet. When he looked up again he had a huge smile on his face, "I helped the elf, Eonard, you know? I found a piece of his soul," said Raspal, pushing out his ghostly chest in pride.

"That's great, Brother." Bergon had no idea what he was talking about, not knowing what had happened to the elf. Seeing him so happy about it pleased him just the same. "See, I told ya' you were destined for great things."

"Thank you, Bergon. And, you? Do you like it here?" asked the boy, looking at the boat they were on.

"I do, Raspal. I think I have never been happier in all my life."

Darlyn stepped forward then and said, "I am sorry, I feel the currents shifting. We must go back now."

Bergon put his hand out and Raspal's ghostly one met it; for a brief moment it became solid enough for them to touch.

That momentary contact touched all the hearts looking upon the scene, including the wizard's.

Darlyn turned and reopened the portal. He waved for the soul of Raspal to go through. He turned then to the men on the ship and wished them safe voyage.

"Tell my son I am proud of him and will see him at Beltane," said Taquel.

Darlyn nodded and bowed then stepped through the shrinking portal.

The wizard had no more than exited the void when he was knocked back by Onyx jumping into his arms. He stroked the black cat's back then looked around. He'd hoped Eonard might come through before the boy's spirit was returned. He had hoped for a chance to speak to him. He was about to ask where he was when the other elf spoke.

Anticipating this was what the wizard was looking for, Sangas said, "He was feeling very weak so he did not dare to stay."

"You must return then, before he is forced to close the rift, Boy," the wizard said to the cloud that was Raspal.

"Thank you so much… I wish I could offer something in return," said the boy. He looked at each of them, his eyes stopped on the warrior. "Um, Torrin?"

"Yes, Boy?"

"Eonard said Jacobi stole a sword from you?"

"Yes," said Torrin.

"I know I acted a little unaware sometimes when I was… One night, when he and I had watch together, he seemed to want to talk and I needed something to keep me awake so I let him. He said his people live in the shadows of the Ashgroth Mountains. Does that help you any?"

"The Ashgroth Mountains?" asked Torrin. He looked at the others.

"I have been to them once, while escaping capture. I think, with a map, I can retrace my steps," said the former marauder.

Torrin smiled then turned to the spirit boy and said, "If you were solid I would give you a blazin' medal, Boy."

The most delighted look and smile split the boy's face as he dissolved before them.

18

A
SOUL AT PEACE

Eonard waited anxiously for the boy's soul to return. Nortus and Azure were still against his having done this. They were both pacing, not from worry over whether it had worked but because of what Junt had said just before Eonard made his attempt to reach Darlyn. The spirit knight was worried the forces that controlled this realm might feel he needed to be punished for having done this. Rius, if anything, seemed more envious.

Eonard was trying to reach out for the rest of his soul as he waited, before he lost what little power the first piece had given him. He couldn't fully explain the feeling of being half alive but it was uncomfortable. There were times he had to physically remind himself to breathe and times that his thoughts came so slowly he wasn't sure if he was awake or asleep. The piece of soul Raspal had returned to him was like a drug coursing through his body but the effects of it were fading away quickly. It had been an odd mix of pain and pleasure as the piece was absorbed into him, he could only describe it as a fire burning throughout his veins and feeling like he was frozen inside at the same time. He didn't want to go back to the odd nothingness feeling he had on first awakening on this plain.

He saw what he thought were faces flash before his eyes, he tried to concentrate to bring one of them into focus. Suddenly, in a flash, that made him jump and draw in a breath, he saw several faces clearly – one he was surprised was still here and three he had feared he might have to face.

Nortus and Azure quickly walked over to the elf's side; both had a look of uncertainty and anticipation on their face. When the spirit of Raspal appeared between them they calmed down, thinking the elf had only been sensing his return.

The boy could barely contain his excitement. He was dancing around them as if still alive. His pleasure was contagious, making the others smile. "Bergon is still on the ship with Torrin's father. They are teaching him to be a seadog. He says he has never been happier in all his life," said the boy. He stopped spinning and faced the elf, "How can I ever thank you?"

"There is no need," said Eonard as he slowly slumped back.

The boy was still smiling as his body began to blink and become all but transparent. His image faded away and the coalescing smoke that was in essence his soul turned into a hundred points of light then they flew upwards, through the open rafters of the dilapidated roof of the infirmary and disappeared. Shortly after the ruined building around them dissolved, telling them the boy had ascended.

Junt had an odd expression on his ethereal face on seeing this. He couldn't even fathom finding redemption and no longer being a spirit – he truly had no desire to ascend.

The cloudy form of Rius didn't show any expression but he seemed to be kind of jittery, as if he too were feeling unusual emotions at the moment. He was – a cross between joy, fear, envy and longing.

Nortus was also feeling a mix of longing and envy, though none of this showed on his face. He felt better in this realm than he had for a lot of years on Ernel but he still was tired of living.

Azure was unaffected – not being human he couldn't comprehend human emotions.

Eonard, who should have been happy with what he had done, seemed a million miles away.

"What is the matter, Eonard?" asked Nortus, seeing how gray he looked. He went to his side to see if he needed another healing.

Eonard gently pushed the old man's hand away and said, "I know where the rest of my soul is."

19

MATTERS
OF THE HEARTH

A red hawk was soaring low, along the still surface of the lake. Its movements were so precise that it did not even break the water's surface when it slowly shifted its wings on the wind currents. Suddenly it thrust its powerful legs, talons extended, into the water. When they came out it was holding a large trout in them. It turned its wings then to catch the updraft and began to climb. It came to rest on an outcropping of rock beside a gentle waterfall that feed the waterhole and began to tear at the still struggling fish with its powerful beak.

Aramis felt like he was that fish at the moment. He turned from the view and closed his eyes. There was a day he would have enjoyed watching that majestic bird and beautiful scenery around him but this one he couldn't even muster up a smile.

There were rolling hills, the breathtaking waterfall, a gentle lake, a babbling brook that emptied from it, acres and acres of fields of wildflowers and a friendly forest that surrounded the estate – all he could have ever dreamed of having as his own to explore – but he couldn't enjoy any of it. Instead of the feeling of warmth and happiness he should have, he felt only empty and alone.

Phineas, whom he now knew was his uncle, had left the estate three days ago to join up with Torrin and Darlyn. Torrin was trying to recover his grandfather's sword. They now believed Jacobi was a fabled Green elf, a thought to be lost sect of the elfish race. He had stolen the sword to take back to his tribe as some sort of proof of his manhood. Darlyn was hoping to learn all there was to know about the Green elves. He wasn't sure what Phineas was going for… He knew his uncle was uncomfortable in his father's home. He wasn't exactly at home here yet himself.

Thinking of the Green elves made him think of the other thing that was keeping him from being able to enjoy his knew found life – worry for the elf he considered to be his brother, though not by blood, and was his best friend, Eonard. Sangas' last report said Eonard was still holding on but there was no way to know if this was true without going to the realm the dragon took him to and asking him himself. Aramis would have done this in a heartbeat if he could figure out how and how to make it back safely.

He prayed nearly every hour of every day that Eonard would get his soul back and would return to him. A part of him was afraid of this as well. His friend would be different when he did – he had been through too much – they both had. He now knew Eonard was from another time. If he returned he would most likely have to return to that time – meaning he would be much older. He wished now they had never left Windsor.

Aramis turned from the window he had been staring out and walked from the rooms he had chosen as his – the only ones in the huge castle he felt even remotely comfortable in. He walked along the cold, dark hallway, down the cold, dark stairway and entered the cold, dark great hall of the cold, dark estate that was all now his.

He wasn't technically alone, he had a small staff now, but they were not familiar enough to him to have formed any kinship to them. He didn't want to get to know them since they were temporary. They were on loan from King Uther; meant to stay only until he'd had a chance to hire his own. He hadn't gotten up the stomach to do that yet. He passed two of them trying very hard to get the carpet off the floor in one of the many guest suites. Mold and mildew had sealed it to the wood planking of the floor. Their grunts and grumbles told him they weren't enjoying the work they had been assigned. Both quickly begged his pardon, which he gave with a nod. He would not call them out for the language, as he once would have.

They were trying to bring some life back into the stark fortress of a home. A task made more difficult by everything having been left unattended for more than fifty years. There were rooms they hadn't entered yet – ones they knew animals had moved into or in which trees and shrubs had sprouted from the cracks and crevices of and taken over. These rooms would need more than a thorough cleaning to make them livable to humans again.

The great hall looked much different than it had when he and Phineas first arrived, two months before. The dozens of owl nests had been removed from the rafters and ceiling beams and all their droppings and vomits had been cleaned up. The trestle table that had set across the back, where the head of the house and his particular guests would sit during audiences and dinners, had been burned – since no one would want to eat off it. A new one was now in its place. A hand-woven tapestry of a large blue dragon soaring over a snow covered mountaintop now graced the wall behind it. It was a gift from King Uther. This had added a small bit of color and life to the room, but again only reminded him of his missing friend. He never lingered on it long.

Several other tables were along the sides of the room, for when he had banquets; though, again, he hadn't gotten the stomach to hold one yet. The large brick fireplace had been cleaned and now had a fire burning in it, driving out some of the physical cold of the room. The stark black velvet curtains that had hung over the windows of the large room had all been taken down, they were dry-rotted and moth eaten anyway. As yet nothing had been put up in their place. Aramis wasn't sure he wanted anything put back in their place. It made the room feel more open and less ominous with the daylight flowing through the windows. Finding no comfort here, he turned and started to leave this room.

His eyes were drawn to a large portrait of the man that had last lived in the castle that was still hanging by the entrance. The man he now knew was his grandfather. He wondered why he hadn't had it removed and destroyed yet – as he had every other time he had started to leave this room. He stepped up to it and looked at it more closely – as he had every other time he had started to leave this room. He supposed he was hoping he might get a sense of how the man could be so evil, and how he could be related to a man that could be so evil. The man in the painting didn't look evil. He had an arrogant look about him and a glint in his eyes as if he knew something no one else did but he didn't look evil.

His grandfather looked to be about his current age in the portrait. His hair was cut in a style similar to his own and he looked to be built similar to him, broad in the shoulders. He was wearing a forest green velvet jerkin over an off white tunic and had a fine looking sword hanging from his left hip. He knew Torrin would have wanted to know what had happened to that sword, as yet it hadn't been found. He guessed it had been lost in battle – perhaps while slaughtering Eonard's people.

He had learned from a few of the locals that had relatives alive during the time of his grandfather's rule that he had not always been so evil – in fact some had said he was a sort of kind. He had never overly abused his serfs; he had expected a full day's work from them and would punish any he didn't feel had done so but he was also very generous with the bounty of their hard work. No one had ever gone hungry while he oversaw them.

The lands they had worked for the lord of the manor were now overgrown with weeds and small shrubs. He hoped by the fall they could get them cleared and planted with rye to make them fertile the following spring but as yet he hadn't seen about the labor to get this going – again his heart and stomach wasn't in it.

His eyes went to the depiction of the ring that graced the finger of the left hand that was resting on the hilt of the sword then he brought his own hand up to look at the ring now gracing his own hand. It was the same ring. One of the staff had found it when they were cleaning out the room that had been Mahki's bedchamber. It had a large green stone – jade, Darlyn had declared it – and had an image of a mortar and pestle engraved inside it. It was the same symbol as the one on the cleric's medallion he wore around his neck. That had been his family's symbol for he now knew to have been five generations.

He had thought about asking the cleric council for a different symbol, not wanting the reminder, but he didn't want to dishonor his father, or the rest of his ancestors. No matter what he grandfather had done and become, he now knew for certain his father had been a hero. He hadn't wanted the ring at first but he had taken it. He might not like the man that had made all this his but there was no reason why he shouldn't allow himself to have it.

He thought about the horrid event in the cave again then. He was still shocked at how it had all come down. He had learned that day that none of the people he had come to rely so much on were who he had thought they were, they had all lied to him – though not all knowingly. He was angriest at Nortus.

He now knew the old cleric was his maternal grand-father. There was a day he would have liked to know he had the familial connection to him, not now. Now he considered him as bad as his other grandfather. Nortus had known the dark cleric, Mahki, was his paternal grandfather and he had said nothing. He knew Phineas was his uncle and he had said nothing. He knew Eonard was from another time and he had said nothing. How could someone be so secretive and dishonest with their own kin?

Darlyn and Iligra had both tried to explain the man's reasons; they said telling him before the right moment would have caused the prophecy to fail. How would him knowing it all before that moment have made the outcome different? Did they think he would choose to help Paitell bring the dark cleric back by killing his best friend if he had known he was his grandfather? Did they know something about him that he didn't?

His eyes connected with his grandfather's painted eyes then and a strange feeling came over him. He felt as if the man was looking back at him through the portrait. He thought he saw him nod his head as if to say that all his fears and his friends' fears were justified. He knew, or more hoped, it was just his imagination or a play of light. He knew of stranger things in this world now – so anything was possible.

He remembered all the times growing up that he had thought and done things even he had thought were out of character for himself. He now wondered if they were because he truly had an evil nature – like this grandfather. His father had apparently been attracted to that life for a time as well. His father, Darius, had joined his grandfather willingly to begin with, as far as he knew. He was a little calmed by the fact that in the end he had refused to help Mahki and had taken Eonard to safety.

He remembered the day Nortus had given him his father's cleric arts book. The old man had said he wanted him to have it because he knew one day he would need it to know who he was. He wondered if that had been a sort of fore-shadowing – a warning that he would be tempted too and had to be sure he knew what was important to him.

Aramis thought then of just what it meant for Nortus to cross over to the Plains of Vethe as a living being and an immortal. Not wanting to frighten him – or so he told himself – one never knew with Darlyn Algier – the wizard said the balance of the plains would be disrupted having an elfish soul in it – that the forces would try to tear it apart. A dragon and a living man, especially one that was immortal, entering one of them would disrupt it further still. The wizard said they would have to fight very hard not to let the forces overwhelm them, trying to make them its own. He hadn't explained what this meant but Aramis thought he could figure it out on his own.

He remembered how kind Nortus had been to him, which at the time he had thought was just his way. He had been so down on himself thinking he was alone after Haylea had left him and because he had no blood family left. Now he knew he had two still living and felt horrible for having treated them both so poorly. He suddenly felt guilty for not saying good-bye to Nortus, for not wishing him good luck and telling him he would miss him.

The new lord of the manor jumped when a hand touched his shoulder. He looked over it and saw the man that was acting as his attendant and carriage driver.

"The carriage is ready, My Lord," said the man, bowing slightly at the waist.

Aramis was about to tell him he wasn't a lord then remembered he was. He hadn't wanted them to address him as their lord and master, he still didn't really want them to, but Darlyn had explained to him that if he didn't use his title the people would not be willing to do his bidding. He had agreed to continue the formality because he figured it would be easier on him than listening to the wizard lecture him on the importance of a person knowing their rightful place in society in order for it to function as it should. "Thank you, Charles, I will be right out."

The man bowed again and quickly walked through the doors.

Aramis had been looking forward to this trip all week. He was on his way to Hundertmark to give Iligra her check-up, and to see King Uther. Now he was dreading it. He knew they would both be feeling alone with Darlyn and Torrin gone. He wasn't in the mood to listen to either of them complaining, nor was he in the mood to complain to them about his feeling that way.

He sighed miserably, walked through the doors, out the main door and into the courtyard where the carriage, being pulled by four horses, was waiting for him. Charles had the door open already, waiting for him; he allowed the man to help him inside. The driver climbed onto the seat at the front of the carriage and shook the reins to get the animals moving.

20

BAD
DREAMS

It was a seven hour ride without stops from Aramis' estate to Hundertmark. They had to make two stops though, once to give the horses a rest and drink and once to allow him to stretch his muscles, which made it more like eight hours this trip. Riding all alone, the new lord found himself dozing through most of it. He was plagued by dreams most of it as well.

First he was in what he guessed was supposed to be the Plains of Vethe. It looked to be a barren place with the ground and sky all the same color: a faded out purple. Formless shapes that he guessed was the unresolved souls were floating around him aimlessly. It wasn't a place he would ever want to go; even one of the seven hells must be better than this place.

He next dreamt of being set into a stone coffin like the one Mahki had been sealed in, though he didn't know what his crime had been. He was bound and gagged and every time he tried to move he was hit with a thick club. He was more than happy to awaken from that one. He would rather have gone back to it than the one he had next.

It started slowly, with him walking up the street that Haylea lived on in Lancarst. All the houses looked as they had the day he had brought her home except for hers. It looked like it had been left to rot. He remembered her telling him how diligent her father was about keeping it up, how he insisted it be as well-kept as the homes on the rich side of town and how he'd had her and her sister both help him mend the roof on many occasions. What would have happened to make him stop that?

He walked up to the door and knocked – the sound of it echoed eerily as if coming from a vast distance. It opened to Haylea's mother, who was hunched over. Her once golden and reddish locks were all gray and her face was wrinkly, as if it had been twenty years since he had last been there instead of only about eight months.

"May I help you?" she had managed to say through a toothless mouth.

"I was wondering if Haylea is in?"

"Who?" the woman asked him, holding a hand to her ear and bending forward a little as if she was hard of hearing now as well.

"Your daughter, Haylea?"

"Oh... yeah... she is..." the woman gave him a look as if she wasn't certain where she was then her face lit up as she

remembered, "She is in the cemetery, cleaning up her father's grave."

"Her father died?"

"Yes, just end of the month... never got over her being ruined, I think. Did you want me to give her a message for you?"

"No... no thanks."

The scene changed then to him at the gate to the town's cemetery. It was immense, far bigger than the small town should have needed for a burial ground. He wondered how he was going to find Haylea's father's grave. He blinked his eyes and was suddenly on the other side of the great field. He was now standing opposite a small stone marker with a girl lying prostrate on top of it, crying her heart out.

"Haylea?" he called out.

The girl didn't move.

"Haylea?" he said more strongly.

The girl lifted her head then and looked around. "Who is there?"

She looked past him several times but didn't seem to see him. He stepped closer and waved but she still didn't stop her eyes on him. As he stepped up beside her he saw why. Where her eyes had been were now only burned out holes. "Blazing hell, Haylea."

"Aramis?" she said then. "Is that you?" She brought her hand out and touched his face; her skin was all clammy and cold.

"What happened?"

"My father... He said if I didn't want to see things his way then I wasn't going to see them in any way."

"Cripes, Haylea, I am so sorry."

He shook himself awake from that dream and refused to let himself go back to sleep again no matter how much he might want to.

The outer gate of Hundertmark came into view not long after in any case. He stretched and opened the windows to allow in some of the cooler fall air and let it awaken him the rest of the way.

21

MATTER
OF TRUTH

Uther was pacing the great room of his castle. It was back to how it had been, before he was tricked into going into the forest and then captured and tortured by the evil wizard divine, Paitell, and before his cousin, Alistair Breman, had taken over as regent when the nation had thought Uther was missing and or dead. Luckily the servants had refused to outright destroy their king's possessions, though they had told Breman they had. He had given them all a bonus to show how much he appreciated this.

He kept looking at the time keeping device on the back wall, trying to determine how much longer before Aramis would arrive. He jumped as it rang out five chimes and again turned to look at the doors. He waited for them to open and the herald to step in to announce the boy's carriage had been spotted for several moments before beginning to pace yet again.

The first sun had already set and the second wasn't far from it. If he didn't arrive soon it meant one of two things – either he had gotten a late start and had stopped for the night in one of the towns between Komac and Hundertmark or he had to stop en route for some reason. This second thought prompted another wave of uncertainties. If he had to stop it could be due to an injured horse or damage to the carriage, which meant he might need help, and if he had been forced to stop – by bandits – then he might even now be fighting for his life. He was just about to call out for the herald to fetch Nasir, intending to order him to take a squad of knights and go along the route to make sure nothing ill had befallen the cleric when the doors opened and the court announcer stepped in.

He was huffing as if he had run. "My Lord, King," said the man dropping to his right knee.

The look on the man's face made Uther fear the worst. "Speak, Herald."

"Lord MaComber's carriage…"

"What of it? *Speak*, Man," spat the king.

"It just entered the main gate, My Lord."

"Is it whole? Is it intact, with Lord Aramis inside it unharmed?"

"It looked to be, My Lord."

"Excellent. Alert the staff and send word to Miss Almeas." Uther could feel all of his worries of the last few hours leaving his muscles. He smiled and stepped down from the throne. He went to the doors, intending to be waiting for his friend on the stairs.

"Lord Aramis," said the king happily when the man finally appeared.

"Please, King Uther, I want to only be Aramis while I am here."

"Not liking your new role?"

"I am a little lonely all the way up there..." Aramis hadn't intended to let the man know how miserable he was but he found himself unable to lie to him once he was before him.

"I can understand, Aramis... even though I know many people in this castle and the town surrounding it I still feel very alone at times."

Aramis nodded, knowing it was self-absorbed of him to feel he was the only one that felt isolated.

"How long are you planning to stay with us?" asked Uther.

"I will be starting back first thing in the morning. I have a group of possible staff expected that I must meet with... so that I can return the ones you graciously loaned me."

"I will have a room prepared for you and see to a hearty meal for you for this evening then," said the man, clapping his much thinner hands together and smiling.

Aramis could see the man was very happy to be making such plans so he said nothing about the tight feeling in his stomach from the last dream he'd had on his way to the castle. It was refusing to diminish, making him doubt he would feel much like eating anything. "I will look forward to it. How has Iligra been?"

"She is complaining that her ankles are swollen lately," said the king.

"Yes, that is typical for one at her stage."

"She will be happy to hear that; she is sure it is because she has done something wrong."

"Is she in her room?" asked Aramis, looking to the doors.

"I believe she is in the gardens. She typically is out there to watch the suns setting. Ask her if she would care to join us if you like."

"I will do that. Do I have your permission to seek her out now?"

"By all means, I have plans to see to," said the king.

Aramis walked to the door that opened to the private gardens in the inner courtyard of the castle; it was positioned so the twin towers at the back of the castle framed the suns setting perfectly. The sky was just starting to darken as the last sun began her slow descent. The long thin clouds reflecting off her golden rays were making lines of pink and blue reflect across the sky. Even he had to stop for a moment and enjoy their beauty. He drew in a deep breath of the warm air and smiled then started toward the middle of the patch of flowers and trees.

He found the woman he was looking for sitting on a large flat rock set beside the path, her legs crossed before her, leaning back on her elbows. "Iligra?" he called out quietly, not wanting to startle her.

The woman looked over her shoulder and said, "Hello, Ari."

Aramis smiled and some of the tension in his shoulders melted away hearing her use her old nickname for him. It reminded him of days much less worrisome. "King Uther said you are suffering from swollen ankles?"

The woman held one of her legs up to show this was true.

Aramis stepped up before her and gently took hold of her right ankle. "This is normal for someone as far along as you are, Iligra."

"You are only saying that."

"I would never lie to you. I can give you a diuretic that will help with some of the water retention." said Aramis. He was surprised to see her tearing up "What is the matter?"

"I know you have never lied to me, Ari… that is part of why I feel so horrible."

"Excuse me?"

Iligra had been feeling terribly guilty every time she saw Aramis for the last six months, which was partly why she was glad he was away from the castle more than he was there now. She had been keeping Nortus' secret because he had said it wasn't the right time for the boy to know the truth but she couldn't imagine how that could still be true now. She could see how miserable he was when he looked at her, wondering how he and Haylea might be if they had stayed together. She had no idea how long Nortus had planned the secret be kept and had no way to know when or if she would ever see him again to ask him.

"What's the matter, Iligra?" Aramis repeated. He watched her begin to shake with tears, "Is something else bothering you?"

"Yes, but it has nothing to do with my pregnancy… except that my emotions are so hard to hide now."

"You are missing Darlyn."

"No... well, yes, but it's not that... You do consider me your friend, don't you?"

"Of course I do."

"Would you be willing to say that if you knew I had kept something from you? That I had helped keep something from you?"

"I suppose... Why? What are you keeping from me?"

"It wasn't her parents that told her she couldn't go with us..."

"Her parents? Whose parents?" asked Aramis.

"Nortus needed you to be focused... He... he didn't want you to be distracted... He knew... if there was a chance for you to be with her... you would take it and stay in Lancarst..." said the woman through wrenching sobs.

"Stay in Lancarst? You mean Haylea?"

"Yes."

"What do you mean?"

"He placed a spell over her, to make her forget you... She has no idea that she ever even met you... "

"Nortus did this?"

"Don't be angry with him, Aramis, he was doing what he had to do to save all of Ernel."

"So he made us miserable because he didn't trust that I would do what was right?" said Aramis. The pain of that statement made the dream he'd been so frightened of reliving disappear and replaced it with something that hurt his heart and soul even more. He remembered all the anger and resentment he had been holding against the man and wondered again how it was his other grandfather was the one said to be so evil.

"Haylea hasn't been miserable."

"What?" asked the cleric. Had she told Iligra that she really wasn't in love with him? That made his pain even more pronounced. "Is knowing she is perfectly happy without me supposed to make me feel better?"

"She isn't perfectly happy... she is oblivious. She will remember who you are and all you meant to her as soon as she sees you again."

"Lot of good that does me, I will never see her again," said Aramis bitterly.

"All you have to do is go to her, Aramis."

"She has been married to the local lord her father was pushing on her long since by now. What good would it do to remind her of me now? I don't want only to be her lover... and I am not evil enough to wish her to be miserable just because I am."

"She is not married."

"Then it is still being arranged, it is still not fair to see her now."

"There is no wedding planned for her. The lord wed another."

"Another lord will ask for her hand soon, no doubt, so it is still unfair."

"Aramis," said Iligra. She was surprised the usually so astute man was being so ignorant. "*You* are a lord now."

"No I'm nuh..." Aramis was surprised he had forgotten that, seeing as he had been fighting being one so hard for the last few weeks. He was suddenly pleased he was one. His heart was now beating strong in his chest and millions of plans and scenarios of seeing the girl he couldn't get out of his mind were running through his mind at breakneck speed. He was feeling a rush of adrenaline that was making him shaky. He took a slow, long and deep breath and said, "I cannot do anything before morning in any case and I need to see about these huge ankles," he teased.

Aramis didn't return to his estate as he had originally intended, instead he went right from Hundertmark to Lancarst. He wasn't willing to risk that another lord would come forward and ask for Haylea's hand before he was able to. He sent a messenger to his estate to let the attendant know that the planned interviews for staff was being put on hold; replacing the loaned staff could likewise wait for another day.

He was excited and nervous about getting to see Haylea again and how her father would react to him this time. What if it turned out it wasn't the spell that had changed her feelings for him? He had to know to be able to go forward with his life.

22

A PROPOSAL

Haylea was walking along Market Street barely paying attention to where she was going. She couldn't seem to break out of her melancholy mood. She had heard her parents talking about her and her sullen mood three nights before, saying if she didn't get better soon they feared she might need to be sent to an institution. There was a lot of talk of these types of places – places where people who had lost their grip on reality were sent. Had she lost her grip on reality?

She still couldn't remember where she had been for what she guessed had been about a four month period, during which time her sister had met, fallen in love with and split up with three different boys. The man she was supposed to have been betrothed to had married another; with no explanation to her – or at least none her parents had given her. And, it didn't appear that her father was trying to find a replacement for him – which completely confused her since she had always been told it was her place to bring the family name up in society by making a good bride. She wasn't sure if she had lost her grip on reality or not but it seemed everyone around her had.

She stopped to look at a display of hand carved wooden figurines. She had a sudden image of having watched someone making something like these but she couldn't see who it was or figure out where or when she would have. She kept having these sorts of strange flashes – scenes she guessed were from the forgotten time period.

She stood watching the man making a small dragon with large wings outstretched from its slender body. She strained her mind and saw the hands of another man making a similar one – they were slender, young, strong and friendly looking hands with long thin fingers. She moved her eyes up the forearms to the shoulders and across the chest of the man in her memory. She could see long, slightly curly blondish brown hair hanging over the broad shoulders of the thin frame. She was just about to look upon his face when she heard her named called – making her jump and lose the image. She turned with a curse word on her lips. She saw it was her sister; she had never been able to stay mad at her sister.

"Haylea… Mom says she needs a sprig of rosemary and some basil for the sauce she is making for supper this evening," said Sian breathlessly. She had run all the way from the house hoping to catch her sister before she left the market place.

Haylea nodded and turned from the figurines – suddenly having forgotten why she had been so intently staring at them. She walked to the grocer's cart across the street from it and asked the lady for the herbs. She was just putting the sprigs into her basket when she heard her sister exclaim with excitement that a fancy carriage had just entered the east gate. She turned and saw the grand vehicle her sister was speaking of being pulled by four beautiful white horses. A man dressed in forest green garments was in the driver seat. They couldn't see who was inside the carriage because the windows were blocked with burgundy curtains.

"Who do you suppose that is?" asked Sian.

"Probably some new lord come to lay claim to one of the empty estates in the west end," said the woman at the grocer's cart. "There is one that has been empty for close to twenty years that has just gone up for sale that is drawing much attention. The man that grew up there is a bit of a local celebrity – the wizard for the king."

Haylea had a strange feeling she knew who it was the woman was referring to, and not just by name as the locals did – like she knew him personally – but she couldn't explain why. It was a ludicrous thought, like the one she often got when she heard the king's name spoken or saw anything elflike – where on Ernel would she have ever been around an elf? As far as she knew they rarely ventured out of the forest.

"Probably," said the younger girl. She looked at her older sister then and said, "I have two dibs left, want to check out the carnival, Haylea?"

"When does Mom expect us home?"

"Not for another couple hours," said the younger sister, tugging on the older one's arm trying to get her to follow her.

"Alright."

Rall was just finishing up the piece of wood he had been chopping into smaller pieces as the sound of horse hooves rang through the air. He looked up and saw four beautiful horses with fancy burgundy tasseled bridles pulling a shiny black carriage coming up the street toward him. He guffawed. "Turned down the wrong street, you idiot," he said aloud as he wiped the sweat from his brow with his sleeve and started to go back to work.

The carriage driver pulled the reins to slow the animals and walked them gently up to stop just alongside the man.

Rall stood up again and set the ax on the ground beside the stump he had been using as a cutting stage. He supposed he could be civil enough to them long enough to direct them to the side of town they wanted. Perhaps he would be given a small purse for the helpful information.

He watched the driver get down from the seat and speak briefly to whoever was in the carriage. He could not hear what was being said but he guessed it was something to do with him since the driver kept looking over at him. After a final nod to whoever was in the carriage, the man turned and begin to walk toward him. He wiped his sweaty palms on the front of his trousers and tried to look anything but nervous and intimidated.

"Begging your pardon, Master Quinlan?"

"Uh… yes. May I help you?" said the man, uncertain how the man in the carriage would know him by name and more over why he would know him.

The driver bowed to him and held out a folded parchment with the king's seal melted into blue wax holding it closed.

Rall hesitated but he did finally put his hand out to take it – it was an insult and a crime, one punishable by a hefty fine, not to accept a notice from the king. He peeled the seal up gently, unfolded the parchment and read the words scrolled on it. It was a formal introduction of the lord inside the carriage, Aramis of Komac, and a request for an audience with said lord. His heart leapt in his chest, wondering why he would be receiving such a request.

"What say you?" asked the driver.

"Uh… certainly. I shall have my wife prepare cold drinks and a light entrée for the lord."

The man nodded then turned from him, walked back to the carriage, set down the steps and opened the door.

Rall watched him hold his arm out to assist the lord in exiting the compartment then he saw a large, young looking hand reach out and take hold of it. A very expensive looking jade ring was on the ring finger of that hand. As the rest of the man came into view he saw he was also large and young looking. He had grey velvet gloves clutched in his other hand. Rall watched him hand them to the driver as if it was the most interesting thing he had ever witnessed.

His eyes panned the rest of the lord then. He had bouncy brownish blond curls in a style that was much too long for his taste, hanging down to his shoulders. He was wearing a sky blue overcoat over darker blue leggings. Under the coat was a white ruffled tunic and a medium blue cravat was around his neck. He had a large and expensive looking sword strapped to his middle that hung down his left side to the top of his black knee high boots which were so shiny they could be used as mirrors. This told the simple man, whose boots were coated in mud, that this man did not walk anywhere unless he had to.

Rall was about to bow to the man, as was customary for someone of his class to do to someone of this man's class, when he got a good look at the man's face. He recognized that face.

Rall was having a hard time sitting still as he waited for his wife to come into the room with the drinks and nibbles. He knew it wasn't proper to speak before this offer of refreshment was given; he also knew it wasn't proper to shout down the hall for the woman to hurry up – though he was about ready to do both.

Aramis was having an equally hard time keeping still and keeping his decorum, still not used to the requirements of his new station in life. Uther had worked with him to try to prepare him, in the off chance Haylea's father wouldn't recognize him, so he would simply think he was a well-to-do lord interested in making a good bride of his eldest daughter. He could tell, by the look on the man's face as he stepped from the carriage, that he had recognized him instantly. He had promised Uther and Iligra he would follow custom either way so he was trying very hard to contain his anxiety.

"I beg your pardon, Lord Aramis," said Freena as she stepped into the room with a tray of iced lemon water, and a small plate of finger sandwiches and sliced vegetables.

Aramis stood and bowed to the woman then said, "No pardon needed, My Lady, I am not in any hurry so I beg you to take all the time you need."

"Th... thank you, kind sir," she said, more than impressed with how different he was than when he had arrived with their daughter a few months before. Her husband had been ready to run the boy through with one of the fire-place implements for touching his daughter and having the gall to speak back to him for how he intended to punish the girl for disobeying him and running away from their home then. He looked like he hadn't given up on this notion now yet either.

Freena set the tray down before the young lord then started to go to her usual chair. She stopped halfway there and kind of shifted between it and the tray, unsure if she was supposed to hand him the glass and offer him the food or not.

Aramis shook his head and said, in his own voice and personality, "Please, Mrs. Quinlan, Master Quinlan, let us dispense with these formal practices. I am essentially the same man I was when I returned your daughter to you before; I have simply learned recently that I am also the descendent of the lord of Komac. Though I now have an estate and the fortune that goes with it, I am still and will always be a simple blacksmith and cleric in my heart. And I will always be and am still deeply and truly in love with your daughter.

"I am hoping, if she has not already been betrothed to another, that I may request you now consider me as a proper suitor. I have brought along a bride-price that I am hoping will help to convince you my desires are true and that I can and will provide well for the both of you, your younger daughter, until she is wed, and Hay... Miss Quinlan."

Aramis knew Haylea's father was as much concerned with how his family would be viewed by the townspeople as he was with the wealth he so desired. He hoped convincing him he would be able to have both without any real effort on his part was part and parcel to getting his approval of his request.

Uther had offered to make it a decree by order of the king that Rall give his daughter to the young lord without a bride-price, which was well within the king's authority to do, but Aramis didn't want to take the girl in that way. He knew, for all the animosity her parents had felt toward him, it would not help Haylea to be estranged from them any more than his association with her in the forest had already done.

"But she is not..." Rall was about to tell the man that his daughter was no longer pure of body but he stopped when he remembered it was this man that had made her that way.

"Your daughter is still pure in mind, body and soul in my eyes and heart, Master Quinlan, I see no reason why anyone else would wish to suggest or feel the need to let it be known it is otherwise," said Aramis.

"You will promise to be good to my daughter?"

"Always."

Rall looked at his wife for a moment then back at Aramis and said, "Very well then. How do you wish this to be handled?"

Aramis wanted to say he wanted the wedding to happen this very instant, he was fighting his desire to run up the hall and the stairs to find Haylea and see if she would indeed remember him and how in love they were as soon as she saw him. He knew he had to do this correctly or he would be insulting her and her family's honor even more than he already had by having lain with their daughter and taken her virtue.

"I'm still in the process of getting my estate in order; I would need a few weeks to prepare. In the meantime I ask that you only tell Miss Quinlan that a young lord has requested her hand. You may tell her I am the lord of Komac but I must ask you not to tell her my name or anything about me."

"Why do you make such an odd request if you say you are deeply and truly in love with my daughter and you are so certain she feels the same for you?" asked Rall. He was beginning to suspect there was something not entirely genuine going on here.

Before Aramis could answer him the driver stepped into the room with a large trunk. He set it on the table before them and opened it. Inside was a large number of gold coins.

All of Rall's suspicions were instantly silenced. "I will do as you request."

It sickened Aramis that this man valued what was in the chest before him more than his daughter's happiness. He was glad that he now could afford to make this offer instead of another, who might not have been so kind to the girl. "I want Hay... Miss Quinlan to be made ready and be brought to my estate on the eve of the Summer Solstice."

"Yes, My Lord," said Rall, practically drooling over the sparkling coins he couldn't take his eyes off.

23

FAITH

Eonard lay awake as Nortus and Azure slept, both snoring quite loudly.

He knew he too should be getting some sleep but he couldn't. He was sure he knew where most all of his soul was now but that really was of little to no comfort. It wasn't going to be as easy to get the rest as it had been with Raspal, who had given him the piece he'd had more than willingly.

He believed, by the flashes of faces he had seen when he tried to locate the rest of his soul, other souls he was linked to in life, that were still in this realm, had the other pieces. If this was so, three of the people he believed had pieces he had no desire to be before again. He had no idea if he would have to use fight to get the pieces back or how to battle with them, if he did. He wasn't sure he was strong enough to fight them.

He jumped when he felt a shifting in the air – or what signified air on this plain. He sat up and looked around.

"Junt? Rius?"

"It is Rius."

Eonard had to believe this was their guide since he never appeared as anything other than a cloudy form. It could have just as easily been any spirit of the plain that might have overheard them speaking and decided to make use of them for its own purpose.

"It isn't time to be going yet, is it?" asked the elf. Junt had said that time moved differently on the plain but he was certain it had only been mere moments since they had stopped for what the spirit knight said would be several hours of sleep they needed.

"No, I wanted only to check on you."

This made Eonard a little nervous, and renewed his suspicions of the guide soul's intentions. If he *had* been asleep, like his other two flesh and blood companions, the soul would have been moving around them without their knowledge. Why would he want to do this unless it was for a nefarious purpose?

The soul must have picked up on the elf's nervousness because his form blinked a couple times as if uncertain of the danger to itself. "Please, Elf, I only appeared because I saw you stir. I mean you and your friends, and I will cause you, no harm. I swear it. I only wanted to make certain you were alright."

"I am... Well, I am as alright as I can be, given the situation I'm in," said Eonard. "I'm not certain I am strong enough to finish this... Especially if the other pieces are where I fear they are" He wasn't sure why he was suddenly being so candid with a soul that he had thought might be threatening them just moments before.

"We will get all the pieces of your soul back to you, Elf, no matter what it takes," said Rius with much conviction in the disembodied voice.

Eonard was surprised at the veracity in this statement – given his thoughts on the spirit just moments before.

"I mean to say that, as have your companions, in offering to be your guide, I am bound to see you safe as well."

The elf's abilities did not work as well on this plain as they did on Ernel but he got the impression the spirit had just said more than he had intended to. This also helped to make him feel a little more at ease though. He believed the spirit would not harm him. "I'm trying very hard to believe I will make it out of this but it is getting harder and harder to."

"Have faith," said the soul as it started to fade away again.

Eonard sighed deeply then lay back on the sandy surface that was the ground on this stop and closed his eyes. His brain was still running too fast, he didn't see how he would ever fall asleep. Without realizing it he was a sleep moments later.

The guide soul reappeared as soon as the elf's breathing became steady. He stood, or more like floated, over him for a few seconds then began to become more solid. A male body dressed in a tan woven tunic over brown linen trousers, in a style that hadn't been worn in close to fifty years, and a head full of bouncy dark blond curls appeared.

The all but solid spirit squatted down beside the sleeping elf and placed his hand so that he would be touching the elf's cheek if it were solid enough to. "Trust in yourself, Eonard. You have the courage, ability and capability to do what you must to regain your soul. I swear that I will do all in my power to make sure of it."

The young elf stirred a little, grunted and smiled then rolled onto his side and fell into a deeper sleep. One he would stay in until it was time to awaken so they could continue the journey.

The guide soul remained where he was a moment longer then slowly dissolved.

24

HEART
& SOUL

Eonard awakened with a start. He was still not used to seeing the bland nothingness around him, nor did he ever want to get used to it. He longed to see green grass, to smell the scent of flowers on the wind, to hear that wind rustling the leaves on a living tree. He closed his eyes and breathed in deep. He smiled as the soft scent of roses came to him. He also thought he could now hear leaves moving and the sound of a small babbling brook. He opened his eyes and caught his breath at the vision now before him.

At first he thought he had made the scene change by having envisioned it. He saw a cabin beside him that had not been in his daydream and realized they had apparently entered the world of another soul on the plain. He started to reach over to wake Nortus when the door to the cabin opened. The man that stepped from it was younger than Eonard remembered. He had seen the man only about a year before, or at least a year before in Ernel time. The man had been alive when he and Aramis left Windsor.

Donnor took a step off his stoop and stopped dead. There was an elf, a normal looking man and a blue skinned man lying on his lawn. He opened his mouth to tell them to get off his property when he got a good look at the elf. He searched his mind for his name. "You were a friend of my last apprentice."

Eonard stood up and said, heatedly, "Yeah. You know you almost broke my friend's spirit."

"I know... I am sorry, but he frightened me."

"I know, now, why you would be, but he did not and would not ever have used the herbs for anything other than the good they could do."

"If he were anyone other than who he was I might have been able to believe that... I know who his father and his grandfather were," said Donnor.

"Aramis' father was a good man."

"Not always... he was a follower of the order – willingly – in the beginning."

"What do you know of the order?" asked Eonard, stepping closer to his friend's former teacher.

Donnor did not answer this question. "What are you doing here? I thought you left Windsor?"

"You are not in Windsor anymore," said the elf.

The old cleric looked around and appeared to be suddenly realizing this to be true. "This looks like my cabin but... there should be a mill there," he said pointing to where the building set in relation to his real cabin in the real town on Ernel. "Where are we?"

Eonard wondered if Donnor knew that he was dead. He wasn't certain if it would do harm to a soul if it was told the truth before it was ready to accept it but he was inherently an honest being. He said, "This is one of the Plains of Vethe," as gently as he could.

"The plains of... you mean the supposed plains that souls that have unfinished business go to?" He guffawed and said, "I never believed in that."

"Be that as it may..."

"I... I remember a pain in my chest...one that would not stop... and calling for help but there was no one to hear me... I remember falling to the ground... just there," he said, pointing to the grass just beside where Nortus was lying. An image of Aramis' teacher became visible then, lying on his back, clutching the left side of his chest. "I... That was me dying? My heart stopped that day, didn't it?"

Eonard slowly nodded.

Nortus sat up then, as if he had heard someone calling his name. He looked at Eonard and the man beside him and said, "Hello, Donnor... I cannot say I am surprised to see you... nor am I pleased."

Donnor stepped back, all the way back to the door casing. He looked as if about to go back inside and slam the door shut. "Master Elgin?"

Eonard had not thought about the fact that Nortus would have been to Windsor before until that moment. He guessed he should have made the connection, seeing as he was Aramis' grandfather. Darius, Aramis' father, was the dark cleric's son so his wife, Leanne, would have been Nortus' daughter.

As if seeing all this connecting in the elf's mind, Nortus explained, "I apprenticed Donnor once. He was told, when the time came, he would extend that favor to my grandson. Which, the man did... for a time."

"You did not tell me he would know herbs..." said Donnor in his defense.

"There was a time you were not so afraid of them," said Nortus.

An image appeared of Donnor standing at the side of a younger dark cleric. Another man, on the dark cleric's other side, Darius, looked like an older version of Aramis.

"You were one of the followers too," said Eonard.

Donnor's spirit lost what little color it had then.

"Were you involved in attacking my home village... did you assist in taking my mother's lifeforce?" asked the elf, his voice getting deeper and his own color actually getting clearer and brighter.

Donnor did not want to admit it but he could already see that the elf knew. "Why are you here?"

"The dark cleric was raised from stasis. He attempted to take my lifeforce as he did my mother. It was spilled and came to this plain where it has become fractured. I believe I am here because you have a piece of it here."

"I have nothing of..."

"What?" asked Nortus, seeing an odd look come to the dead cleric's face. "If you have a piece of Eonard's soul I order you give it over."

"I did not know I was dead... I thought... I have been coming out here... for what I believe was every day... to tend my garden... I found something the other day... I did not know where it had come from... and did not want it on my property..."

"What did you do with it?" asked Eonard.

"I... I threw it into the brook."

Eonard went to the waterway quickly. "Where?" he asked. His eyes saw a sparkle under the water. He reached into it and was surprised how cold and wet it felt. He pulled his hand out and found a medallion like the one Aramis wore – that had also been worn by his father, Darius, and his grandfather, the dark cleric.

The dragon had come awake during this exchange and was now standing beside Nortus. The spirit knight and the cloud that was their guide were beside him.

The elf held the round medal out up, showing it to them.

The dragon and Junt had no reaction. Rius' form seemed to quiver slightly.

Eonard placed the medallion against his chest, over his heart, as he had the leaf Raspal had given him. It stuck to his chest and a light came from under it, as the leaf had. It then became transparent and was absorbed into his skin. The elf again fell to the ground and began to convulse. This time the others only stood back and watched.

Once the elf stopped thrashing, Nortus went to his side and performed a healing. This time it took hold even faster.

The elf stood up slowly then and said, "thank you."

Donnor only looked confused.

"As I said, my soul has been fractured. This was a piece of it," said Eonard. He turned to his companions and the guide soul and said. "I had a vision last night... or before we lay down to rest... I saw faces... I believe the pieces of my soul are with people I knew that are stuck on this plain."

"You say this as if it is a bad thing," said Azure.

"Some of them I would not wish to see again..."

"Mahki?" asked Nortus.

"Him, as well as the wizard Paitell and his follower, the one that held us in the camp, Helon."

"You will likely have to fight them for these pieces," said Rius.

"I know," said Eonard. He turned to Donnor again, uncertain what to say.

The man's form looked to the ground, not liking that way the elf was looking at him, and said, "I... I am sorry for how I treated Aramis... and for running him out of Windsor ... I am truly sorry." A bright light began to form around the man then. He looked at his arms and then back up to them. "What is this?"

"I believe you are moving on," said Junt.

Donnor opened his mouth as if wanting to say something but no words came out.

He became hundreds of points of light as Raspal had. They began to drift on the wind like flower seeds. Not long after the cabin, the garden, the grassy knoll they were standing on and the brook disappeared.

25

WOODEN CARVINGS

What passed for morning in the plain came quickly and only one of them felt as if they had gotten any sleep. With no sun or stars to use they had no idea how long they were supposed to have slept, though Junt said they had gotten more than five hours.

The spirit knight seemed eager to be moving this morning, which made the others anxious – this and that he refused to give a reason why no matter how many different ways Eonard found to ask.

"We must go as soon as you have eaten," was all he would say. His ethereal form seemed to be standing stiffly and he was looking away from them, in the direction they took as behind them, as if watching for something.

He was.

He didn't want to tell them, not wanting to frighten them – but they were being followed. By what, who or how many he couldn't say. The feeling he was getting said whatever it was it was something of great power that could mold and shape the plain, he was watching whatever it was doing this to the skyline behind them now.

The misshapen cloud the guide always appeared to them as kind of stepped from nowhere beside the dragon, making the blue man jump. "Are we ready to move?" he asked, seeming as anxious as Junt was.

Nortus was just putting the dried beef and cheese away as the spirit asked this. "I believe we are," he said, looking at the other two to make sure they were in agreement.

Eonard nodded.

The dragon only kind of grunted.

"Step closer together," said the cloud-form.

Jumping was a strange feeling – kind of like a cross between going through a magical portal – which they had all done before – and being stretched out to the very limits of being one body then being squeezed back together in a blink of an eye.

Eonard had no idea where the spirit was trying to jump them to but he was focusing all his energy on the bits of his soul – he couldn't explain just how but he could feel another one very close.

The flesh and blood companions kind of shivered as they stopped on the plain again. They all felt as if they had been plunged into a bucket of ice water, physically manifesting itself in shakes for the flesh and blood companions in the group. They all looked around, confused as to where they had landed. They had expected to see a desert-like scene, as they had when they stopped after the last few jumps, instead they were in what looked like it could be a store in any city on Ernel.

It had shelves around the edges and display cases in the middle with hundreds of different wooden carvings. There were simple geometric shapes like squares, pyramids and spheres, hearts and magical symbols, normal animals and mythical beasts, letters of the alphabet and numbers, any manner of flowers and trees and boxes with hinged lids. Some of the last had designs carved along their outsides, some were burnished or painted and others were left unfinished. A display case that also served as the sales desk was near the middle of the shop and a bench with carving tools, burnishing irons, jars of lacquer and stain, brushes and blocks of wood waiting to be made into more of the decorative items was set behind it. A half completed piece was setting on the center of the counter, waiting for the finishing touches – an egg, half cracked open, with a baby dragon emerging.

"What is this place?" asked the dragon.

Junt's transparent head was shaking and his face looked confused. "It is not unheard of for... what I would assume might have been the craftsman that had created these items in life, to have recreated his shop here but it is normally done among other spirits in one of the ethereal towns to allow for some interaction..." The view outside the windows showed them they were actually still in the center of the desert like expanse with nothing to either side of them.

They couldn't see Rius' face but they all got the impression he was just as confused. As was Nortus and the dragon. Eonard was not, nor was he paying any of them any attention. He was busy looking closely at the half finished piece – recognizing it.

They all jumped, even the two spirit forms flickered, when a man stepped from the back room of this shop.

This man jumped as well when he saw there was someone else there.

Helon Cetto had known he was dead when he first became conscious in this realm but he had not understood why or where he was. He waited for someone or something to come and tell him what he was supposed to do. When he realized no one or thing was coming and he wasn't going anywhere he began to look around.

He was shocked and horrified to see he was in a shop with hundreds of wooden carvings. He wondered if this was one of the so-called seven levels of hell.

He had always hated the tiny artistic forms; they bothered him on a deep emotional level. His mother had collected them so they were all over his house as he grew up.

She liked the tiny people doing miscellaneous tasks best though she had animals and other things as well. They all looked so realistic, like miniature living things. He had always felt like they were watching him and was certain they moved whenever he was alone in the room.

He had lost track of the number of times he'd had nightmares of them coming to life and attacking him with their tiny hands and teeth over the thirteen years he had lived with the horrid woman who claimed to have given birth to him.

He had forgotten this childhood horror until the day he happened on the elf they had held hostage in the camp of the brotherhood whittling on a piece of wood one day.

He had no idea how long he had been dead but each and every of what he thought must be considered days in this realm passed he found himself standing in the center of the shop just staring at all the tiny monsters, until…

He had been surprised and not so when he stepped into the shop this last day and saw the half-finished dragon emerging from the shell on the shelf. He hadn't known just how he knew but he knew it was somehow connected to the hated elf.

He had again been surprised and not so when the elf himself appeared in the shop.

"*You,*" growled Helon. "It is your fault I am here." He grabbed one of the carving tools from the bench and went at the elf, waving it threateningly before him.

Eonard didn't move, thinking Helon was no real threat to him since the man was a spirit and he was flesh and blood. He was beyond shocked and cried out in surprise and pain as the sharp and concave blade of the tool plunged deep into the flesh of his shoulder. He screamed in agony again as the end of the tool was ripped out of the hole in his shoulder – blood sprayed out with it telling them all it was very much a real injury and a vital vein had been hit.

Junt stepped forward without even thinking about it and grabbed the assailant that had just hurt the elf by the collar of his tunic. He tossed him across the room where he crashed into the shelves of wooden kitsch. Dozens of pieces fell on top of the stunned man.

"Blazing hell, how could he do that?" screamed Eonard, his hand was over the hole in his shoulder, trying, without much luck, to stop the blood that was exiting it in a rush.

Nortus went to him quickly.

"How come none of you made a move to stop him?" grunted Eonard as the cleric took hold of his shoulder and began to work the edges of the wound together.

"We didn't think it could harm you," said Rius, apparently answering for all of them.

Eonard heard Nortus saying the same chant he had heard Aramis say more times than he would have ever liked to. He squirmed under the man's hand as he felt the veins, tissue, muscles and skin reforming and his body becoming whole again – it was a strange itching and stretching feeling – very similar to the feeling of jumping actually.

Only a small indentation in the skin of his shoulder and a slight discoloration around it remained when the old cleric was finished.

"So if you didn't think he could harm me how was it he did?"

"Some in this realm can do anything they want… if they want it bad enough," said Rius.

Helon had recovered from being manhandled and was now coming at Eonard again, the sharp tool still dripping with the elf's blood was held before him, telling them all what he still wanted to do badly – none of them doubting he couldn't do it again.

Eonard quickly looked at Junt and asked, "Can I do him harm as well?"

"As you are of this realm now, yes, you can."

Eonard nodded and looked at the approaching man. No matter how angry he was he was still an elf so his need to preserve life if at all possible made him say, "I have no ill will with you, Helon," hoping to end this peacefully.

"You ruined all my plans. I would be immortal right now if not for you."

Seeing he didn't intend to stop and not wanting to feel the pain of being injured again, the elf threw out his arm, and used his magic.

Helon flew backward into the same wall. The shelves, tools and merchandise had miraculously reset themselves after he stood up; his body was now destroying them all again. This occurred several more times before the man finally stopped; seeming to realize it was doing him more harm than it was the elf.

"I wish you no harm, Helon," said the elf again, more adamantly.

"It is your fault I am here," Helon repeated, through clenched teeth. "And I know why you are here. I will not let you have it."

Eonard knew he meant the piece of his soul that had drawn them here. "*Give it to me*," he said, sounding very little like the usual kind-hearted elf. He was feeling a heat building in his middle that it took him a moment to name – anger.

"Over my dead body," growled Helon as he threw up his hand.

Eonard clutched his chest; he was suddenly unable to breathe. It felt like something was squeezing his heart, he could feel it struggling to beat but it was unable to. He fell to the floor hard.

Nortus and Azure both started toward them but Junt put a hand up to stop them.

Eonard forced his body up through the pain and threw both his arms out.

Helon flew back again, this time he wasn't stopped by the wall because that part of the shop had disappeared.

The cleric was a little dazed but unharmed. He stood up, brushed himself off and threw his hand up again, this time he closed his fingers as if they were around the elf's throat and he was squeezing.

Eonard could not get any air to enter his throat. He grabbed at the hands he could feel gripping it but there was nothing there. He started to panic. He knew he had to do something or he would be dead for real. He guessed his friends either weren't going to or couldn't help him – he hoped it was the latter. He didn't want to die so there was only one choice to him – it was either him or Helon. Going on instinct, he pictured the heart that would have been beating in the chest of the cleric if he were alive. He thrust his arms out and brought his hands together so hard and fast that the bang of his palms coming together echoed loudly.

Helon clutched at his chest and the look on his face went from anger to surprise to intense pain to relief in a split second. His image became transparent, broke into hundreds of bits and pieces, sparkling as if on fire, then turned to smoke and dissipated.

Nortus and Azure both looked amazed at what the elf had just done, Junt looked slightly envious. Rius' cloud like form was a deeper shade of gray, though none of them knew whether this was from amazement, jealousy or fear. None of them seemed eager to go to the elf's side to see if he was alright.

Eonard bent over, placed his hands on his thighs and puked. He didn't have much in his system so it was mostly only foamy bile. He began to gasp for breath, fighting the feeling that he was going to vomit again. Hot tears were streaming down his face; he was fighting not to openly sob. He had never killed a man before and even though this one was already technically dead and it was in self-defense he didn't like that he had been forced to this time.

Nortus looked at Junt, to see if it was alright for him to go to the elf now.

The spirit knight, guessing this was what was on the man's mind, nodded to him.

The old cleric gently put his hand on Eonard's back and asked, "Can I ease your pain?"

Eonard jumped, not realizing anyone had approached him. He shook his head quickly and stumbled away from him. He was angry none of them had tried to help him while he was being strangled to death. He wanted to shout for all of them to get away from him but he couldn't make his lips move to do it.

Thinking the elf was only upset that the man, Helon, had been dispelled before they could get the piece of his soul from him, Nortus said, "We will find you another piece, Eonard..." He had no idea if the elf could survive without all of his soul being returned to him. He looked at Junt and the cloudy form of Rius, hoping for confirmation.

Junt shook his head and the image of Rius kind of wavered a little.

The elf stood up straight then he stumbled back into the counter behind him. He suddenly lost his already-pale color.

"Eonard?" screamed Nortus.

The elf's image started to waver. He was disappearing and reappearing fainter each time.

Nortus and Azure started toward the elf, they stopped when his form became solid again.

"Is there a way to find the piece this man, Helon, had?" Azure asked desperately, looking at the spirits. He had a feeling this was the end of the elf if their answer wasn't yes.

Junt was about to say he knew of no way to. He stopped when he saw the elf turn toward the counter and start to go around it, as if searching for something.

Eonard could feel his lifeforce waning, just as he had when the dark cleric Mahki was draining it from him. He knew, by the sound of fear and uncertainty in the voices around him, that seemed to be coming from miles away, there was truly nothing any of his companions could do to help him this time. Everything around him was getting gray and blurry, the air was thick, the room was spinning and he was getting very dizzy. He could feel his throat closing off again, as if it was being squeezed again, though this time it was in panic rather than the magical forces the cleric had been using on him. He tried to call out for help but he couldn't speak, he couldn't get the muscles and bones of his face to work, his tongue felt like it was swelling up and his head was fuzzy and numb. He could hear Nortus calling his name and see him and his companions trying to get his attention but they seemed and sounded a great distance away from him now. He couldn't make himself respond to them even if he wanted to; his brain felt like it was turning into mush.

He looked around the fake shop desperately, looking for something, anything that would help him. His eyes stopped on the workbench behind the counter, on the item that was only half completed. He had carved one like it while Helon was holding him prisoner in the brotherhood's camp. He jumped when he saw it begin to glow a bright golden color, pulsating like a tiny star sitting on that countertop. He somehow made the muscles of his face respond, or at least it felt like he had smiled, as he quickly went to it. He lifted the carved baby dragon and held it against the skin of his chest, over his heart.

26

SURPRISES

Helon was floating in a void of nothingness. He didn't have a form anymore; he was now nothing but consciousness. He wondered if the elf had somehow found a way to disperse his essence and if he was now heading beyond – to heaven – or more likely in his case – hell. He smiled as he thought that at least he had hurt the elf.

He had acted without thinking when he grabbed the tool from the counter and ran at the hated elf. He had been surprised when he saw it embed deep in the elf's shoulder and saw the blood splurt out as he yanked it out, thinking he was dead as well. He had also been surprised when what was obviously another spirit grabbed hold of him and threw him back against the wall – he had thought he was only a ghost. The force of him hitting the wall had been hard and had momentarily stunned him but it hadn't hurt. He recovered quickly and stood back up, still full of anger and wanting to destroy the elf.

He was laughing inside his head as he heard the elf all but begging him to leave off, that he wished him no harm. His anger was the only thing keeping him going right now, there was no way he would ever leave off. He had thought how much he wished he could reach into the elf's chest and squeeze his heart, wanting him to feel the same horrific pain he had when Paitell had done it to him. He smiled as he did feel himself reach into the elf's chest, grasp his heart and clench it. It felt warm and squishy. It was also a little slimy, his hand started to slip off it so he squeezed it harder. He felt a heady rush knowing how close it was to bursting. He realized something else then – he could feel!

Not feel in the metaphorical sense, as in emotions, but physically. He could feel his hand, where it was touching the organ, the raised veins running along the outside of the precious muscle, and the warmth of the blood that was backing up as it tried to flow through it. He could feel himself becoming alive again with each slowing pump of the elf's heart. Something in his head was screaming that he could be alive again.

He watched the elf manage to get to his feet through what must be excruciating pain then watched his arm swing out and felt himself flying backward. This surprised him on two fronts that the elf was this strong and that he apparently had magical abilities. He hadn't known elves had any.

This time the back wall of the shop wasn't there to stop him so he smashed into the sandy nothingness that was this plain between spirit realities. He could feel the coarse and sharp grains digging into the skin of his face, arms and chest and taste their saltiness in his mouth. He got back to his feet, spit the grit out of his mouth and used every bit of strength and energy he had to grasp the elf's throat with waves of air. This time he could feel the softness of the elf's skin, the tautness of the muscles, the weak pulse as the blood ran through the veins under his grip and the airway compressing as he squeezed.

Again he could feel the elf's lifeforce entering his own chest. He could feel the shriveled heart in his own chest begin to expand and felt it trying hard to beat as it came to life again. He started to squeeze tighter and saw the look on the elf's face change. He watched him bring his hands together. His heart, which only moments ago had become alive again, burst. The pain of it was like nothing he could describe, it was worse even than having it done for real as Paitell had – that time it had been over instantly.

Everything around him disappeared in an instant.

Helon opened his eyes again, or become conscious of being awake again anyway. He had thought the elf had ended his existence on the plain. He looked around and caught his breath at the beauty surrounding him. He was beyond happy he was no longer in the horrid figurine shop. He wondered for a moment if this was heaven. He frowned as he looked closer at the scenery. Some colors seemed muted, others seemed brighter and more colorful than usual and everything was out proportion and a little out of focus.

He was looking out over a lake with a waterfall that was way too small to be kicking up the amount of white water it was making. The body of water it was spilling into seemed way too small to be being fed by it. What he thought was supposed to be a hawk was flying low over the water but either it was huge or the lake was actually more like a small pond. He grunted as he turned around. Before him now was rolling hills of tall, swaying green grass, beyond them were ice and snow covered mountains. He scratched his head at what he thought was supposed to be a castle. It was sitting on the top of one of the hills rather precariously. It looked like it might tip over and slide down the steep slope if a stiff wind blew across it. It too was out of proportion to the landscape around it – the trees nearest it looked like tiny saplings and flowers that he guessed were supposed to be near its walls looked gigantic.

He started to snigger, wondering how his mind had come up with this crazy place. He jumped when he heard a throat clear behind him. He slowly turned around and saw a man that looked like an older version of the cleric he had let go with the wizard, Darlyn Algier, what seemed like forever a go now. "Who are you?"

"I am Mahki, or the dark cleric, as I became known as for a short time. Who are you and what do you have against the elf?"

"The... the dark cleric?" said Helon. That would mean this was the man the brotherhood had been fighting so long and hard to bring back to life. The man that held the key to giving him what he wanted so badly. If he was here then Paitell must have failed. It was a sick bit of pleasure at the thought of this.

"You know of me?" asked the dark cleric.

Helon fell to his knees and all but kissed the ground before this man as he said, in a voice deep with reverence, "I am your humble servant, Master."

Mahki smiled at this. "Are you one of the men that tried to resurrect me?"

"Aye, I was."

"You were assisting... what was his name?"

"Paitell Tobac," said Helon, obvious disdain for the man was in his voice.

"Yes, that was him. I give him much praise for his attempts, though futile they were. Was the elf the one that killed you, sending your soul here?"

"No, not directly, but it was by his and his friends' hands that I fell from Paitell's graces and was not allowed to assist further in your raising."

"I see."

"What is this place?" asked Helon.

"This place is known as one of the Plains of Vethe. It is where human souls go when they are not ready to be reborn, in a manner of speaking."

"How am I still here? I thought the elf just destroyed me?

"This plain has a type of conditional law but it is beyond even my higher intelligence. I believe, in order to ascend or leave this place one must either come to terms with their death or have finished whatever business is keeping them from being ready to enter either heaven or hell. I can only guess that you are still here because your business is not done yet."

"If this plain is for human souls, why then is the elf here?"

"His soul was spilled as I was being dragged back here. The open doorway dragged it here as well."

"The elf said I had a piece of his soul. I refused to give it to him," said the man, feeling proud of himself.

"He was able to get it in any case."

"How?"

"Apparently he can feel the pieces. He has been leading his sorry band of helpers all over the realm trying to find them. He has overlooked more than one piece but he is more determined than I had anticipated. He will no doubt find them all, unless he is prevented from doing so."

Helon got a wicked look on his face then a look of misunderstanding. "I don't know how to stop him but I would do all in my power to if there was a way."

"There is a way."

"Tell me how."

"Come with me."

27

THE
DEFINITION OF INSANITY

Paitell watched a man launch himself at the Magnus then saw the obsidian sword in his hand. He could feel power emanating from the sharp blade from across the room. It was forged with an elemental magic that was more powerful than anything he, or any other wizard, would ever wield. He wondered if it was powerful enough to kill an immortal. The look on the old man, Nortus', face told him it could do the Magnus master great harm.

He was suddenly frozen in place. He watched the black blade penetrate the Magnus' chest as the two men tumbled backward into the cement coffin. Finally he started forward. He didn't particularly care if the master died but he couldn't let him die before he got what he deserved. He stopped when he heard someone call his name behind him. Everything else was forgotten then.

It was a voice he knew and had been waiting for.

He watched Darlyn Algier, a man he had hated for half his life, walk into the chamber and was a little taken aback by the air of dignity he had about him even though he was limping and using a cane. Their eyes connected and the blind hatred and jealousy he had felt for the boy Darlyn was when they were in school together returned in a flash. He could see it had for Darlyn as well, making him smile.

He watched his rival look around the chamber and heard him snort condescendingly then wave his hand and remove the spell holding the elder and young clerics and the elf as if wiping away dust and wanted to smack him.

He watched the young cleric run over to his friend and catch him before he hit the stone floor and the elder cleric run over to the man that had stabbed the Magnus, who was now lying beside the coffin with blood gushing from a wound on his head. Not a one of them was running out of the room, yet the three men of his own order, including his first officer, Brom, whom he had thought would stand with him through most anything, did run from the chamber, without looking back. He realized, as always, he was alone.

Why was it this impudent wizard, who had shunned any kind of relationship – including his own family – when they were in the Guild, had so many loyal enough to die with and for him now, yet he could not even find one that would even consider giving theirs for him? Even Brom, who he had thought was loyal to him, had left him to save himself.

A horrid and putridly sweet smell hit his nose, making it and his lip curl up. He turned to see the Magnus' body was ablaze and being consumed in magical flames meaning it was too late to save the man now. He wasn't terribly upset by it; he had all his equipment and could figure out the rest.

He turned his full attention to his only real threat.

"Hello, Paitell. It has been far too long," said Darlyn arrogantly. "I was surprised to learn you had survived, though not so by you having kept it a secret. I suppose I owe you a modicum of respect for having managed to elude the Guild and make us all believe you dead for so long."

"The Guild masters are ignorant bastards, fooling them was beyond simple," Paitell spat back. "None of them will ever know true power; not power like you and I wield, Algier. They fear you, you know? They have been just waiting for an opportunity to bind your powers; waiting for you to step too far over their line of tolerated transgressions. They still fear my memory and they will fear me again as well.

"Think of all we could do if we became allies. Remember the challenge our professor gave us at the Guild? It has been a contest between us from the start, hasn't it? I know you still have the same desire as I. If you do not interfere I will show you how to fulfill that desire. Think of all you could learn, all you could try, things that would take a lifetime to a mortal would be but a mere second's lesson to you. Even the Guild's combined efforts could not stop you then."

"Thomithy was a fool, he had no idea what true immortality is. It isn't this," said Darlyn, his hand sweeping the room. "True immortality is doing for others, and living on in history by having people remember all you did."

Paitell laughed hysterically to this, "You must be joking. You can't possibly believe that drat, Algier? How completely pathetic! What happened to the blazing bastard that used to berate me so constantly in school? I see your leg is hurt, tell me, did you also bump your head? No one will remember you or anything you might do after you are gone, except to say that you were a fool," he said as he grabbed the bag of herbs and the chalice full of a thin red liquid. "I will see *my* desires come to be; then *I* will be the greatest wizard to walk Ernel and you will be forgotten."

"I cannot let you have that," Darlyn said. He threw his hand up, intending to call it to him.

At first Paitell thought the wizard wanted the life force for himself, that he *was* still after the same prize after all, but the look of worry and concern in his eyes was not at the idea that he might lose out on it, it was that it would mean the elf wouldn't be able to be saved without it – again a shot of jealously raged through him.

This man had lost everything that should have ever meant anything to him and had been to hell and back, literally, from what Paitell had learned of his activities since leaving the Guild, why should he care so much about an elf? Why would he?

Darlyn Algier had gone soft. Paitell wanted him to be the miserable, arrogant, insolent boy he had been in school, the one that had battered him mentally and physically so many times that he hadn't wanted even to get out of bed some mornings, not wanting another day of the abuse. He wanted to return some of that abuse to him, so he could have the pleasure of defeating him now. If Darlyn was strong willed and caring of others he would not be so bothered by being defeated and he would not be so easy to defeat. He wanted him demeaned and demoralized, he wanted him devastated – he smiled as he remembered that he knew a way to break the man.

"I see now I should have taken you out at the same time as I took care of your family. It was so much fun turning your pathetic brother against you and your parents, and so easy. Your little brother was just aching for it, wasn't he?" Paitell saw another flash of emotion in the wizard's eyes then and remembered it, it had been the same lost look he had about him when he returned to the Guild after the trial and funerals of his family. For two weeks after Darlyn had been so preoccupied that Paitell had managed to get some of the instructors' attention. Sadly, it didn't last very long – Darlyn still had too much of their respect to be allowed to flounder too long and he had recovered quickly under their added attentions.

Paitell watched anger light in Darlyn's eyes then and knew he had hit the right button. He heard the words of a spell coming to the rival wizard's lips but wasn't able to counter it quite fast enough. He was thrust backward. He smashed into the wall hard and painfully. All the air exited his lungs in a rush – partly from surprise at the veracity of the attack, partly from the pain of hitting the rough rock of the wall and partly in anger as he felt his hand release the chalice. The vessel rattled to the floor, spilling the liquid inside it.

"*You idiot!*" he cried out then stepped away from the wall.

Even more anger burst forth when Paitell saw a look of pain in Darlyn's eyes as he realized he had just doomed his friend. He threw his hand up and hurled all his energy at the wizard, reciprocating with a spell of his own.

He watched Darlyn fly backward and smash against the edge of one of the golden doors and smiled. He knew the impact would do as much physical damage to him as it would mental. The wizard crumpled to the floor where he stayed, on his hands and knees.

He smiled sickly as he watched him trying to get up and was surprised he still had enough energy to levitate himself into a standing position. He saw the last vestiges of whatever humanity the man had gained in the last few years disappear from his eyes then and saw only burning hatred. *Good*, he thought. He felt another wave of anger and hatred burst in his own breast and readied himself for another attack.

He heard Darlyn begin the words to the spell he had sworn, at risk of being bound and expelled by the Guild masters' if he ever used it, *Balefire*. He raised his hands, knowing it wouldn't do any good. He didn't want to die but was pleased that at least he would have made the hated rival take himself and all his friends out as well when he did.

He jumped, as did Darlyn, when he heard someone shout out the wizard's name and saw realization of what he was doing alight in the man's eyes. He watched him draw the power of the spell back into himself, and knew he had to know it could kill him. Why would Darlyn Algier, who'd always thought he was better than everyone else, be willing to sacrifice himself like that?

He watched a beautiful woman step into the chamber and saw the look of love in her eyes when she looked at Darlyn Algier – not infatuation, or lust, or the idea of being with someone that wielded so much power, but true love – and wanted to scream at the unjustness of it. Her eyes moved to him then and the look changed to one of pity. He wanted to show her what that look would get her.

He looked at Darlyn then and watched his eyes shift to the woman and saw a rush of shame come over him, at having disappointed this woman. He wanted to laugh at how weak the wizard before him had become, the thought that a simple woman could stop him, then he saw the feelings the wizard felt for the woman and was more than jealous. His own eyes went back to the woman then and he knew something else that made him hate Darlyn Algier even more.

This made him angrier than anything the wizard had ever done to him. This man had taken everything from him as a child, always showing him up at the Guild, and now he had everything he wanted as an adult. This man and his friends had destroyed everything he had been working so long for, he had nothing left except the shame of having failed – yet again – he would not live with that label any longer.

Paitell began the words to the same spell Darlyn had just stopped. He knew Darlyn knew there was nothing he could do to defend himself and watched him step in front of the woman so she wouldn't get the full brunt of it. He felt the energy building in his middle as he finished the words and wanted to revel in it, as he had when he said the spell so long ago, but this time he was going to release it. He felt it move up from his belly, down his arms and start to leave his fingers and wanted to laugh that he would be the one to finally defeat Darlyn Algier.

Just as the energy started to leave him he saw a shaft of blue light coming at him from outside the room, from the other end of the tunnel. It hit the shaft of yellow light he had just thrown out and instantly destroyed it. The heated energy turned to flakes of snow and fell to the floor. He was about to ask who had the power to stop *balefire* when he saw a blue dragon in human form step into the chamber. "I saw the mountain destroyed," he said in utter shock.

The dragonman said nothing, only used the same spell Darlyn had used to thrust Paitell across the room.

It felt like someone was pulling him from behind as he flew through the air. He tried to stop himself but there was nothing to catch him. His leg hit the edge of the coffin and he fell back into it, landing on top of the still thrashing Magnus. The same thing that was destroying the dying cleric was now consuming him.

The scream he heard coming from his mouth didn't come close to the pain he felt. It was a shooting pain, coming from all points of his body, but hurt so much he almost couldn't feel it at all. It was like the feeling of being trapped in the balefire so long ago. Like then, he could feel his body being burned from the inside out and the acrid smell of his own skin and hair burning filled his nostrils.

He tried to pull himself out of the invisible flames and felt arms grab him from behind. He realized something was holding on to him. He thought at first it was the Magnus but the dark cleric had no arms anymore. The ghostly image of a regal man in splendid armor came to him then the image changes to another – to the face of a boy he had used and wronged that was now getting his revenge. He wanted to laugh at the irony of it and scream in anger that – yet again, Darlyn Algier had won. He tried to cry out for the man to release him but couldn't because he no longer had a tongue or a lower jaw to scream with. His final thought as his eyes closed, or ceased to see in any case, was the unfairness of it all.

Suddenly the pain was all gone.

Paitell opened his eyes and watched a man come from behind him and launch himself at the Magnus then he saw the obsidian sword in his hand. He was frozen in place as he watched the long black blade penetrate the Magnus' chest and the two men tumble backward into the cement coffin.

He started forward to help the master then stopped when he heard someone call his name behind him. Everything else was forgotten then. It was a voice he knew and had been waiting for…

Paitell let out an audible sigh and wondered how many more times was he going to have to relive this day?

Paitell watched a man launch himself at the Magnus then he saw the obsidian sword in his hand. He wondered if it was powerful enough to kill an immortal… and then thought, *not again…*

The fog cleared and the elf, cleric, dragon and two spirits stepped onto the cracked ground before the cave the dark cleric had been sealed in. Eonard hesitated for a moment then entered the dark opening. All but Rius followed quickly.

The cloud-spirit moved toward the opening then away from it several times as if trying to work up the courage to follow. Finally, it sped forward into the darkness and caught up to the others.

Eonard walked along the same path Helon had taken him, Torrin and Haylea what seemed like a lifetime ago now. The others followed, guessing he knew where he was going. He didn't especially; he was just following his instincts.

They came to a fork in the tunnel. The elf went down the opening on the right and continued to the door of the office Helon had taken him, Torrin and Haylea to, in which they were introduced to the wizard divine, Paitell Tobac. He did not enter it, only turned from it and walked the route the man had taken him and his friends to the opening over the mineshaft where Raspal had died. He retraced their earlier steps again from there to the hallway with the golden doors.

This time they were standing open and he could hear voices from the chamber they had been concealing. He slowly walked down the hall and saw his final moments on Ernel playing out before him, though he was seeing it from another perspective.

He felt Nortus step beside him and heard him draw in a breath and knew he was watching himself moving to help the fallen Phineas as if seeing it from someone else's eyes as well.

Though Junt had no physical form even he sounded like he had inhaled as he too was watching himself come from inside the coffin to hold the burning body of the dark cleric in the death claiming flames.

Azure had not come in at this point of the scene so he did not recognize it at first. A blue beam came from some-where behind him and he then knew what he was seeing. This was when the elf had lost his soul. He had entered at this point and dispelled the hateful magic the wizard divine that had tried to kill all of his kin had just thrown at the wizard, Darlyn Algier.

Eonard thought it was strange that the wizard divine, whom he could feel palpable waves of hatred rolling off didn't react to him or Nortus as they entered the chamber, even though he was looking right at them, He realized the man was not seeing them, he was seeing his version of his final battle with Darlyn playing out before his eyes and was reacting to the people that had been in the chamber that day.

The scene continued until Paitell was all but ash in the coffin on top of the dark cleric then began to play through again, from the point of Phineas entering the chamber with the black sword before him again.

The newcomers watched it play through a third time and realized the man was re-enacting his death over and over and over – Paitell had recreated his own hell of sorts.

Eonard felt a little bit sick but also a bit of satisfaction thinking the man would have to relive his defeat and manner of death over and over again like this.

"Can't he see us?" asked Azure, stepping within inches and waving his hand before the face of the man who continued to speak to Darlyn as if they weren't there.

"He senses a presence but he is unable to break his concentration to acknowledge us," answered Junt with much wonder in his voice.

"Excuse me?" asked a bewildered Eonard.

"He is too new to this plain to be able to do more than this one thing. He is using all his energy to relive this moment over and over, which leaves him none to do anything else."

"Why does he torture himself like this?" asked Azure.

"I would guess he is trying to figure out where he made his first mistake as if he might be able to go back and fix it and change the outcome," answered Nortus.

"That is ludicrous," said Azure; just as soon as he thought he understood humans one of them completely tossed out all his reasoning.

"That is, sadly, the human psyche," said Nortus.

The dragon was shaking his human looking head as he turned to the elf and asked, "Is a piece of your soul here?"

The elf shrugged and began to look around the scene.

Eonard was hoping it would give off an aura like the other pieces he had found had done but he didn't see anything like it. He started to say he didn't think there was one here when a sudden flash of bright light nearly blinded him.

He squinted his eyes and brought a hand up to block the golden rays as he saw his blood, or the man's recreation of his blood, in the chalice was shining much brighter than the muted colors around them. He hadn't seen the light before because it had already been spilled when they first arrived.

As the scene reset itself again he couldn't miss it.

"The chalice full of what is meant to be my blood and life energy," the elf answered as he pointed at it.

"How ironic," said Nortus.

"How do we get it?" asked Azure as he sniggered then groaned when the scene began to repeat itself yet again. He really didn't like what he looked like in human form and really didn't want to see it again.

"I am going to try to catch it as it drops the next time the scene begins."

"What if removing that element destroys his concentration?" asked Azure.

"Then I will fight him as I did Helon," said Eonard with no doubt or compunction.

Azure had no response to this.

Nortus only looked worried and sickly pleased.

Eonard stepped around the scene and got himself into place to catch the falling vessel. He willed all of his energy into making his hands solid enough to be able to. He caught his breath as it began to fall from the wizard divine's hand and put his own out. He felt the very edge of the chalice touch his fingertips but all he managed to do was knock it a little off balance.

It still spilled over and rattled loudly to the floor.

"Drats!" he shouted.

The elf stood still and waited to see if changing that element would bring Paitell out of his self-induced torment. The wizard divine gave no outward signs of having noticed. Eonard waited for the scene to replay itself again and again positioned himself to catch the falling cup. This time he did.

Without so much as a word to the others, or a second thought, he brought it to his lips and drank down its warm contents. He desperately wanted to have the energy the piece would give him in his veins in case this did awaken the wizard divine and he needed to defend himself.

It was thick, lukewarm and slightly salty tasting but not unpleasant. He felt a warmth flood his stomach and slowly move out to his extremities then the now-becoming-familiar convulsions raked his body and he fell to the ground with the glowing aura surrounding him.

Nortus, Azure and Junt all tensed, ready to keep Paitell at bay if he came out of his trance. Again, he gave no outward signs of having noticed.

It was close to two full minutes and half another run through of the scene before Eonard managed to get back to his feet.

He again looked at Paitell, who was still re-enacting the scene, and almost wished the man would awaken. The feeling of another piece of his soul now coursing through him was beyond exciting.

"Is there any more of your soul here?" asked Azure, seeing the chalice of blood once more in the scene and spilling again before them.

"No, it isn't bright anymore," said Eonard. The color of the blood was more brown than red now. A part of him had hoped this was the case as well but he knew that would be too easy.

"Should we do something to help the pathetic man?" asked Rius, sounding surprisingly compassionate for a spirit that supposedly had no connection to any of the people before him.

Eonard answered with a nasty sounding, "No. It is a just and fitting punishment to make him relive this day for all eternity. I don't want him to find any peace."

Paitell actually did sense the presence of five new elements to his scene and knew all but one of them was part of the very scene repeatedly playing out before him. He wanted to destroy them all but he could not make himself respond to them, even to defend himself.

That was one of the things he was most often reprimanded for at the Wizards Guild, his lack of discipline. He had never been able to do more than one thing at a time. Some very gifted wizards could perform spells while fighting, making potions, even sleeping, if they worked hard at it or were naturally gifted. Darlyn was naturally adept at all of these, which was yet another thing that made Paitell hate and resent him so much.

He watched the elf step up beside him and try to catch the chalice as it fell. He wanted to laugh at him and tell him it was nothing but smoke, it wasn't his blood, then he saw somehow it was. He wanted to stop him but he couldn't get his body to respond to the thought then the scene started over again and he no longer cared, consumed by his hatred of Darlyn Algier again.

He didn't react as the five left him to his torment.

Paitell sighed as yet again… He watched a man launch himself at the Magnus then he saw the obsidian sword in his hand…

He felt two more spirits enter the periphery of the scene but again could not and did not respond to them.

Helon laughed as he watched the scene playing before him. This was his first time seeing it so he was completely enthralled. He heard the man beside him harrumph and realized he shouldn't be laughing giving it was his death he was watching and laughing so hard at. He quickly stopped and cleared his throat, about to apologize, then he saw the man wasn't paying him any attention.

Mahki could not care less that the pathetic spirit was laughing at his fiery demise, he was upset that no one had even attempted to try to save him or cared that he was dying. Where was the loyalty he had garnered from his men once upon a time? He thought for a moment of leaving the even more pathetic wizard divine to the hell he had created for himself.

As he watched the scene reset itself yet again Mahki did stop it, not out of compassion but simple tiredness of having to see it again after already living through it. He stepped forward, waved his hand and the scene dissolved around him, the plain desert scene appearing moments later.

It took Paitell several seconds to realize and under-stand why the scene wasn't going to play through again, another few seconds to realize, that there were two other forms near him and a few more to realize and fully absorb who they were.

"Is this some new torture?" he asked aloud.

"My God but you are truly pathetic!" said Mahki, unsure if he wasn't just as pathetic for even considering using this and the other soul with him as anything other than lavatory paper.

Paitell started to drop to his knees as he realized the soul before him was not just his weak and sick mind conjuring his pain.

"Would you get your ethereal arse up!" spat Mahki.

With a guttural growl, Helon launched himself at the soul of the man who had killed him then, not even giving him a chance to get fully to his feet.

Because neither soul had been on the plain long enough to control much yet the first only fell through the second, coming to rest quite hard and ungracefully in the sand behind him.

Paitell was caught by surprise by both actions but he quickly recovered and began to laugh.

Mahki stepped forward, reached out, sunk his hand into Paitell's chest, grabbed hold of the man's imaginary heart and yanked it out, much as Paitell had done to kill Helon. It wasn't real and would not cause the spirit any pain but the affect and intention was more than obvious.

"Are the two of you quite finished?"

Helon had recovered and was wiping the non-existent sand from his conjured clothing.

Mahki turned to the wizard divine then and asked, "Do you wish to do more than relive this torture, Master Tobac?"

"Yes."

"Do you wish to wreak revenge on the elf, whom is partially responsible for your death?" asked the dark cleric.

"Yes."

"Do you swear your undying soul to do anything and everything I ask of you?"

Paitell hesitated for a moment, uncertain what the Magnus meant by this. He watched the man squeeze the non-existent organ. He fell to his knees and clutched his chest. The pain he was feeling was excruciating – worse even that the physical pain of actually having died a very painful death not too long ago.

Mahki stopped squeezing the thing that was now all but mush in his hands and smiled. He asked the same question again then, a little slower.

"Yes," said Paitell as he tried to rise. He knew he would be sorry for giving this promise but something told him it wouldn't be for long. Anything was better than having to relive his final moments over and over again.

28

A
MATTER OF REMEMBERING

Torrin and Phineas couldn't stop whistling and none of the others wanted to stop them. They were all feeling quite giddy with excitement and pleasure at having seen Eonard, knowing for certain that he was alright – though he was still far from better – and the information Raspal had been able to give them of the location of Jacobi's homeland had breathed new energy into the group.

They had quickly packed up and moved on – knowing it was a hard road ahead of them and a long one. They would be leaving the open road and going through untraveled territory to reach the mountains.

Phineas took point using the dagger he had gotten from the pawn shop when he was in the city, scoping out potential allies for the battle to reclaim the throne, to cut them a path, it never seemed to dull so he was expending very little energy to do it, meaning he wasn't needing to go slow. They lost track of the number of leagues they had covered by the time they stopped for the night, beside a small woodland pool.

Not knowing what kinds of animal life inhabited this part of the forest they set up a larger than usual fire and doubled up on the watches.

They weren't bothered by anything overnight but they had heard more than a few noises of things moving around them, which kept them all from being able to fully relax and made the morning came quickly for all of them – including the cat.

"What is the matter, Onyx?" asked Darlyn as he tried to get the animal to take some of the dried meat that was their breakfast.

The cat was slumped beside a stump. He only lifted his head, sniffed the bit of food, licked at it – halfheartedly – then laid his head back down.

Darlyn started to reach for him, intending to check to see if he felt hot. He stopped his hand halfway when the cat hissed at him. This upset Darlyn for two reasons – first, because it worried him and he didn't like how much it did, and second, because he hadn't been planning to bring the animal with him so he didn't like that the thing now seemed to be upset to be there.

He started to hiss back at it, deciding he didn't care what happened to the little ingrate beast, when his vision suddenly went blurry. It took the learned wizard a moment to figure out what was happening to him.

Darlyn was no longer in the clearing – at least not mentally – his physical body was still there and only looked to be asleep or deep in meditation to those around him. His mind was what he guessed was many years in the past by the items he saw around him, but he couldn't say how many or exactly where.

It looked to be a small workshop or laboratory – with herbs hung up to dry and various ingredients used for making potions in pots and beakers along shelves. He would guess it was either a small town doctor's shop or a fortuneteller's – someone who barely had enough magical knowledge to make a simple potion and then one with little to no real potency.

He was about to pull his mind back thinking he must have gotten drawn into someone else's sending by mistake when he saw a small black cat cross the room. He knew instantly it was Onyx and knew too that this must be some bit of his past that he was showing him.

'*What is it you want me to see?*' he asked the cat through their connected minds.

A small, bent over man hobbled into the room just as this thought came out.

Darlyn watched him walk over to the bench and begin to pull various bottles down from the shelf. He then got a black cauldron and began to put a pinch of this and a dash of that into the pot. The man turned around and went to the fire then. He took a cloth from a nail sticking out of the brick façade and used it to take hold of the handle of a pot in the pit. Darlyn saw it was black and was boiling hot when the man lifted the lid of the pot. His mind said it was likely pitch.

He watched the man bring the pot to the counter and pour about half its contents into the cauldron. The stuff began to pop, fizzle and steam as soon as it hit the ingredients in the cauldron. Darlyn couldn't move from where he was standing and he wasn't able to see around him to make out what those ingredients were so he had no idea what the man had just concocted.

He watched him took a small pipette and draw a bit of whatever it was he had just made from the pot then turn and call the cat to him. He watched Onyx run over to the man eagerly and begin to rub against his shin. He watched the man lean over, pick the cat up and hold him tightly under his arm then force the end of the tube into the cat's mouth and squeeze whatever it was down his throat.

Darlyn was trying to tell himself it was only some medicine the cat needed or was some sort of nutrients to keep it healthy but he knew better. He watched in anger, pain and horror as the cat began to convulse – obviously in great pain.

Darlyn's mind tried to scream out for the man to reverse whatever he had done to Onyx but he knew he wasn't really there so he couldn't.

The man was smiling as the cat writhed on the floor in front of him. The smile got bigger as he then said the words to a spell Darlyn had heard preformed more than once before but had never performed himself. Not because he couldn't, he had learned it his first year at the Guild – the course of study had been taught to the other students in their last year – but because he saw no use for it.

He had refused to perform the spell for his final exam – it wasn't a required course but it was a penalty against his credits. He had taken the penalty for this with pleasure – partly because he did not like seeing the effects the spell had on the unwitting creature it was performed on, partly because he didn't want to be in any of the creatures he had to choose from even for a second and partly because he knew he had more credits than any other student so it would not affect his standing – which was top of his and many of the classes of the near and distant past. He was hearing the words to a *transmogoration* spell – the spell that allowed an animal to be taken as a familiar.

Darlyn watched the man's soul leave his body and enter the cat and the cat's soul leave its body and just kind of drift into the corner and wanted to scream.

The next several scenes flipped past quickly – first he was slinking down an alley then he was sliding between someone's legs and entering another shop – what appeared to be a grocers' shop. He watched through the animal's eyes as it moved to the back of the shop, jumped onto a counter beside what appeared to be a person's waiting meal and proceed to vomit into the drink that was awaiting the person's return. A small bit of smoke rose from the drink then the contents of the vomit dissolved into the liquid. That would have been whatever the man had injected down the cat's throat before exchanging form with the animal.

He watched the cat jump down and get into the dark corner just in time for the grocer to miss him as he stepped up to the table and lifted the mug. He watched – again in anger, pain and horror and this time frustration – as the man then began to convulse as the cat had.

The bent over wizard's form then left the body of the cat, which having no soul inside of it only slumped to the floor, the soul of the grocer left his body and drifted upwards and the wizard's soul entered the body of the grocer.

The old wizard, now in the grocers' body, walked to the door of the shop and twisted the lock then he walked to the door at the back of the shop, stepped through it and climbed the stairs to the man's apartment above it.

Darlyn's mind didn't follow him up those stairs, he was stuck where he was because a small bit of the cat's psyche remained with its body – this bit was holding him there. He could hear what was happening above though.

He heard a woman crying and begging the man, that she thought was her husband, not to do what he was doing then screaming out in pain. He didn't need to be in the room to know what the man had just done – he had used the grocer's body to have his way with the grocer's wife.

The cat replayed several more of these types of occurrences for Darlyn before his mind was returned to his own body and he was back in the clearing in the present time.

The wizard came out of his trance-like state so fast that it startled the others. He didn't say anything to calm them; he only looked at Onyx and said, "Is he close?" He knew the animal couldn't answer him with words but the feeling it relayed to him told him the man was. He stood quickly and said, "I need to do something. I should not be long... Please remain here until I return."

"Now? Is it Iligra?" asked Cieri.

"No," was all the wizard said. He turned from them and opened a portal then looked at the cat and pointed to that opening.

Onyx stood up and quickly went through it.

"Please wait for me," Darlyn said again. His eyes locked on Torrin's for the briefest of seconds then he stepped in and the portal disappeared.

Darlyn found himself in an alleyway that was so far beyond dirty he couldn't say the *smell-inhibiting* spell fast enough, though the fact that he was gagging may have played a part in this. He had been in horrific places before, he had seen and smelled things few would care to even imagine but none of them came close to this.

There was something that looked like it once might have been a dog lying beside a barrel of what might have been blood. Likely the dog had been drawn to the carnage and was feeding off it. Whatever the case, neither was appetizing now.

A thick coat of brown and white hair remained on its back end but the front was only sinew and bone now. The sides of the wooden barrel were coated with mold, from the blood inside having seeped deep into the pores of the wood, further fermenting the stuff. The blood inside the barrel had long since gone rancid, now having a greenish tint and a skim coat of moss-like moldy slime on the surface. That surface looked to be boiling rapidly. It was swimming with fly larvae and maggots. More maggots were crawling along the rim of the barrel and all over the half dissolved carcass beside it. Flies were swarming over it all and were now getting in his face as well.

Onyx was already at the end of the alley waiting for him. He saw no need to linger on the horrible scene so he quickly moved away from it.

He didn't recognize the town he was in. He saw no sign of a castle or fort so he knew this was one of the many small villages that had cropped up between larger towns. It had barely more than ten houses. There was a large barn, a wellhead, a smithing stall, the equivalent of a town market place, a church and a park with a small garden and what had once been a fountain in its center.

He looked at the black cat that had brought him to this place and asked, "Is this the place you showed me in the vision?"

Onyx didn't speak, at least not with words, but Darlyn got the impression the cat had nodded.

"Lead the way then."

He followed behind the cat as it slunk down other alleyways – some in nearly as bad a condition as the first but most only piled up with rubbish and crawling with rats. Finally they came out beside a rundown shack of a building in the small market.

It looked like the walls were going to fall in at any moment and the shops to either side of it almost looked like they were leaning away from it, as if not wanting to touch it and catch whatever it was suffering from. There was no sign telling him what the shop was selling but the many bottles in the window named it an apothecary of sorts.

The cat didn't use the door, which was barely hanging by one hinge, instead he went through a crack between two boards that made up the outside of the sad hovel.

Darlyn waited a second to see if anyone inside would react to the cat's entrance, when he heard none he stepped forward. He hoped Onyx would have spit a warning at him if there was danger to him inside.

Surprisingly the remaining hinge made no sound as he pulled the door open. It was all but rotten so it was very light. He hesitated to enter, not wanting to be surprised, to let his eyes adjust to the darkness inside and again to listen for the occupant to acknowledge they had visitors. He heard nothing except a clock steadily ticking and wind whistling through the various openings in the boards along the exterior.

He recognized the place as the one in the cat's memory – except that it was even messier than it had been then. The meticulous wizard couldn't imagine staying in the place for long and the thought of trying to work in the conditions was ludicrous. Potion making required all but pristine conditions – even a fleck of dust could skew the intended results.

He saw many of the same bottles as he had in the vision, still lining the shelves; them and pots, pans and burners were covered in a thick layer of dust. It didn't look like anything had been disturbed in many years.

"There is nobody here, Onyx. Why did we come here?" Darlyn asked the cat, unable to hide the annoyance creeping into his voice.

"Who is there?" came a scratchy voice from further in the building.

Darlyn jumped and readied himself with a defensive spell.

A bent over form in brown strips of cloth that might once have been a robe, stumbled into the opening between the room Darlyn was in and one in the back. The form was hunched over so he couldn't gauge just how tall it might be standing upright, nor if it was male or female – the voice could have been either sex, and thus didn't know if it posed a viable threat to him.

Onyx arched his back and let out a hiss that made the hairs on the back of Darlyn's neck stand up.

"Midnight? Is that you?" asked the scratchy voice.

Onyx hissed again.

"I wondered where you got yourself off to… I thought you had up and disappeared on me, or gone off to die," said the thing, breaking into dry raspy laughter.

Onyx hissed again.

The thing stood straighter then and brought a stump of a foot out, intending to kick the cat. "You ingrate."

Darlyn said the words to an *immobilize* spell and the form's foot stopped in mid-swing.

"Ah, brought me a wizard, did you?" asked the raspy voice.

Darlyn looked at Onyx, who was still arched up – all the hairs of his back standing up. Could the cat have lured him here as some form of inducement or apology for having up and disappeared on his original master?

The form before him lowered the hood that had blocked its face from the wizard then. Darlyn saw it was a man that looked to be close to seventy birth years. He had long, stringy hair that was even more transparent than his had been after his battle with the book several months before.

The form waved its hand and the air holding its foot still disappeared then it brought itself up straighter to show it was a man of about six paces tall. He seemed much wider than the hunched form had appeared and not nearly as frail. The beyond white skin of his face was pulled so tight that there wasn't enough elasticity for a wrinkle to form. His brown eyes were set deep in his skull and looked dull and wasted, until they locked on Darlyn's blue-gray eyes.

"I know this face," said the man. "You are older now but still have the arrogant look of a boy that thinks he knows more than anyone else after having learned half as much."

Darlyn remembered a man from his past saying this to him on their first meeting – nearly twenty years ago – in a far different setting. "Professor Thomithy?" asked the wizard.

"It is. And you are Darlyn Algier."

"I thought you were banished from the Guild and your powers were bound?" said Darlyn. If this was so he should not have been able to perform the spell he had witnessed him using through the cat in the vision or dispel the one he had just placed to stop him from harming the cat a moment ago.

Thomithy laughed heartily to this.

The sound of the cackles went deep into the younger wizard's soul and made a chill run up his spine – he had only heard one thing he would consider worse.

"There is no way to completely bind a wizard, Darlyn. That was your one failing; you do not see anything beyond the end of your own desires."

Darlyn spit at this, sounding very much like the cat had a moment ago.

"So… have you followed my instruction and come now to tell me how it is done?" asked the old wizard.

"Sorry?" asked Darlyn, not certain what instructions he was referring to – wondering if the man was now senile.

"Have you become immortal?"

Darlyn smirked and said, "I know how to, but I have no desire to be immortal any longer." He was about to tell his old professor that he would not tell him how it could be done when he watched him wave him off as if he could not care less.

"Makes no never mind… Why are you here then?" asked Thomithy.

Darlyn was confused, another emotion he was not used to and did not care for, "You don't want to know how to become immortal?"

"Perhaps, if I were twenty years younger. I would not want to be trapped in this frail body for the rest of my days. Would you?"

Darlyn nodded in agreement. He wanted to know more about the man's claim that a wizard's power could not be completely bound. "The Guild masters were adamant the binding process is total and complete. How were you able to counter it?"

"Still have a one-track mind, I see. I always knew if I needed a problem solved you were the one to put to task to solve it. You never give up until you have your answer."

"So give me this one," barked Darlyn.

"Why, might I ask?"

Darlyn again hissed, as sinisterly as the cat had.

"I have heard much of your exploits, Young Master Algier. Do you have something even more indecorous you wish to delve into and are worried the Guild will come after you?"

"Answer the blazing question!"

Thomithy actually took a step back from the anger in the younger wizard's voice. "I see power has softened your disposition," he said sarcastically. "You will have an answer to your question when you tell me why you wish to know?"

Darlyn actually had to stop and think for a second. Why *did* he need the answer so badly, he had given up his pursuit of dark knowledge, hadn't he? "I am only seeking more knowledge. As you imparted in me at the Guild – *knowledge is the ultimate power*," he spit.

"Ah, you *were* paying attention during your studies then… I always got the impression you felt my classes were beneath you. At least those I taught to the regular student body. You paid close attention in our private sessions, didn't you?"

"I answered your question, now answer mine."

"After one more of mine."

"I will not play blazing games with you, Old Man!" shouted Darlyn. He was about to throw a *manipulate* spell at the man, to make him speak. His hands went to his throat as it suddenly pinched off. He could still breathe but that was all he could do.

Thomithy had a sinister smile on his face. "You did always speak so ill to your elders, Young Master Algier. I will release the air around your throat if you will promise to not try another spell on me."

Darlyn didn't want to make that promise, he really hated to go back on his word, but he wasn't liking the feeling that with a simple thought his throat could be closed off entirely and he apparently was defenseless to prevent it. He nodded his head quickly.

The air was released then.

Darlyn brought his hand up and rubbed the outside of his throat, this did little good in relieving the itchiness on the inside of it. "How did you do that?" he croaked out.

"You are still just a student, Darlyn. You may have reached master status in ranking but there is much you will never know."

Darlyn hated the man standing before him, for many more reasons than just the rivalry he had encouraged between him and Paitell – that had resulted in the death of his family – but he wanted to know this man's secrets more. "Will you teach me?" he asked in a raspy and shaking voice.

29

BOX
OF TREASURES

Eonard was felling invigorated as they moved to the next place he thought a piece of his soul might be. They were looking at the ornate gate of a well-to-do town when the fog of *jumping* cleared.

The elf could not make out the name of the town.

Nortus recognized it, having been there recently, "Lancarst?"

Isn't that where Haylea and Darlyn are from?" asked Eonard.

Both Nortus and Junt nodded.

"Oh, gods, no," said Eonard. He knew the pieces of his soul had gone to people he knew and he knew the wizard was still alive... He quickly moved into the city.

Nortus had figured out what Eonard was thinking as well. He was not certain he could forgive himself and knew Aramis would never forgive him if their thoughts were true.

Azure and Rius' cloudy form followed the elf and cleric, curious what they knew and was not telling them. Junt was reluctant to go under the gate, not wanting to be back in the town he too was born in.

Nortus was about to tell Eonard that Haylea's house was on the east side when he saw the elf seemed to be walking with purpose, toward the west side of town. He hoped maybe they were wrong then.

Eonard was following the feeling he had come to associate with the pieces of his soul, praying it was being held by anyone other than who his mind was screaming. He knew the girl had stayed in town but he had no idea if Aramis might have joined her after he and Nortus went through the portal. He found himself standing before a large house that had a for sale sign in front of it. It didn't look like a place he imagined the girl having come from.

Junt stopped a little back from the elf and cleric. He looked like he was going to be sick, if a spirit could get sick. "This was my… my former master's house."

Eonard turned to him and said, "Darlyn isn't dead." He realized he didn't know this for certain. Time moved different on Ernel and he had not thought Donnor, who he had seen alive and well only a year before, would be dead.

Junt could not give him an answer and neither could the others.

Eonard slowly started up the walk and entered the house. He could see it had been nicely furnished in its day. He saw nothing but covered furnishings in the two rooms that opened from the foyer. There was a grand set of stairs that went up to the next floor and an open door showing a less grand set leading to a basement under the house. He had a feeling what he was looking for was in the basement.

He walked down the steps slowly, the wizard's name on his lips. At the bottom of the stairs he found a large pile of boxes. He did not see anyone around those boxes. "Darlyn?"

A small glow began to come from out of one of the boxes, in about the middle of the stack. Eonard went to it and, with Azure and Nortus' help, moved the boxes to get to the one that was giving off the light. He saw it was marked as having come from Darlyn's room. He slowly opened it and found some of the man's childhood possessions, including a very intricately carved wooden box. It was this wooden box that was glowing.

He looked around and called out for the wizard again. He noticed Junt was hovering near another pile of boxes. He started to ask him if there was something there he needed to see.

The spirit knight's image blinked as if he had just been startled and he actually looked around in panic for a moment. He seemed to realize someone was watching him then. He turned from the pile of boxes and walked over to the elf. "What did you find?"

Eonard was about to ask if Junt was alright when the glow before him became brighter. He picked up the box and opened it. Inside was an amber stone like the one Darlyn had given the elf to call him to get him when he was ready to rejoin the quest and a necklace with a black stone hanging from it. The amber stone was what was giving off the light. He knew this was the piece of his soul. He picked up the stone and held it to his chest. He shook a little but didn't fall into convulsion this time. He smiled as his image became even clearer.

Nortus went to him and performed a healing – he smiled as well and said, "You are getting stronger."

Eonard nodded and looked back into the box. He lifted the other object, uncertain why it would be in the box with the piece of his soul. He got an image of the wizard as he took hold of it.

Junt let out a sudden breath and said, "Last year, I tried to help heal the wizard after he was injured retaking the castle in Hundertmark. A part of him had come to this plain. I returned here to find it and return it to him. I was not able to find all of it… That must be the piece I was not able to find."

"So the wizard is not dead then?" asked Azure.

"This piece of him was and was apparently strong enough to have caught the bit of the elf's soul and hold onto it," said Junt.

"Can we get it back to the wizard?" asked Nortus.

"I do not know," said the spirit knight.

Eonard closed his eyes, squeezed the charm and imagined it going into the wizard's body. A light came from around his hand and he convulsed. He did not fall to the floor because Azure was holding him up. He opened his hand and smiled as he saw the charm was no longer there. He did not know how but he knew he had just returned that missing piece of soul to Darlyn.

30

MASTER
& NOVICE

"Try again," the man barked.

They had been trying for more the five hours now. Darlyn was beyond frustrated. He had never had so much trouble learning a spell before – was this truly so much more advanced than him.

"*Concentrate!*"

The younger wizard was about ready to tell the older one to go to the Plains of Vethe but he didn't. It was his failing not the older wizard's. He suspected because his insides were all but mush right now he would have a hard time controlling the new power; the forces wouldn't want to respond to him when he was exhausted and was emotionally unstable. He was not one to give up though. "Give me a moment to rest," Darlyn spat, wiping sweat from his forehead.

"Yes, always did give up too quick," said Thomithy just under his breath. "That was why I preferred Paitell."

This angered Darlyn more than most anything else he had endured in the last year. He screamed out the words to the spell.

Thomithy fell to the floor writhing, his hands clawing at his throat – at hands that weren't there.

Darlyn smiled evilly – a smile he hadn't used in close to a year – it felt sickly good to his fevered mind. He only watched with great pleasure as the man lay dying before him.

Onyx began to hiss at him then, like he had his previous master.

Darlyn started to shoot the same spell at the cat, angry that he would dare threaten him. His eyes fell on the thing as he started to speak the words – the look of fear in the animal's eyes made him catch his breath. He came awake. He heard the sounds of the man that was seconds from being dead before him then. He waved his hands to release the air that was binding his windpipe.

The man lay gasping for breath in a pool of sweat for several minutes. Finally he went up on his elbows and said, through a voice that was all but gone, "I knew it was in you somewhere. You cannot always make yourself that mad to cast the spell though. You need to practice so you can do it even in your happiest mood."

Darlyn was shocked, he had just tried to kill the man and all he heard in his voice was admiration.

"Now, try again on the cat."

"No!" said Darlyn.

"You did not mind doing it on me?"

"I care for the cat."

"Very well. There is no love lost for me either. I do not think I will survive another attack like that from you so I will find you another body to train on then." With that the man, less than gracefully got to his feet then disappeared from the shack.

The older wizard returned a moment later with a frail looking woman. She was dressed in rags and looked as if she hadn't seen a bath in years.

"Most of the people of the town have relocated; others, transients and the like, have since moved in, in their place. I have found them most useful to my own testing of spells."

"That is inhumane," barked Darlyn, shaking his head and backing away.

The older wizard took hold of the woman's head and turned it so her face was facing the younger wizard.

Darlyn was shocked to see the blankness in her eyes. She was not but a shell. "What is wrong with her?"

"Too much tragedy, I would guess. I tried to reach into her mind when I first found her but all I got was screaming. She truly could not care less what is done to her now." To prove this the older wizard took a candle from the shelf beside him and held the flame to her hand. She didn't even flinch as the top of the fire lapped at her palm.

"Still…" started Darlyn.

"Do you wish to learn or not?" challenged Thomithy.

Darlyn knew he would hate himself for this but he would worry about that later – in a lot of ways this would be a better fate for the woman than what she was obviously suffering from. He drew in a deep breath, blew it out slowly, cleared his mind and said the words to the spell again, this time aimed at the defenseless woman.

She didn't even move to try to free her closing throat. She only stood gagging for breath.

Darlyn released the waves quickly.

"Very good, you are as fast as ever."

"What is next," barked Darlyn fighting the need to vomit.

"How about a spell to get rid of the white in your hair, I remember well how upset you got when you got your first blemish."

"I am fine with my hair just the way it is. Tell me how you reversed the binding spell."

"Later, next we try *transmogoration*."

"NO. I do not need to learn that little trick. Tell me how you fought the binding."

"*Transmogoration* first."

Darlyn had no desire to try the spell but he wanted to know the other spell badly so he nodded.

"Do you remember the words?"

"I do," said Darlyn. He looked at Onyx, who was backing away from him and hissing even more viciously now. "I must do this, Onyx."

The cat stopped and sat down as if understanding his new master.

Darlyn said the words he had memorized as a child, in case his instructor had insisted he prove he could do it. He felt his consciousness enter the cat. Onyx's, in turn, was pushed out. The cat's soul was now a shadowy form in the corner. The younger wizard's physical body was just standing stiff in the place he had been, staring as blankly as the woman before him was.

It took Darlyn a moment to understand what he was seeing. Apparently a cat could see in more colors than a human. He finally was able to get his eyes to adjust to the scene before him. He looked from the dead eyes of the woman to those of his own human body and realized why the woman was blank then.

"That was far too easy, Boy," said Thomithy.

Darlyn began to panic then. He tried to get his mind to speak the words to reverse the spell but he couldn't. He remembered how the instructor that taught this course at the Guild had told the students that had refused to attempt the spell, if they chose to learn it later in life that would have to practice reversing the spell with a trusted ally – one that could do it for them if they could not – before their first attempt to be sure they could reverse it when ready to return with no ally available to them. He had not learned the reverse spell or practiced it with a trusted ally nearby because he never intended to use the spell.

He couldn't believe he had been this gullible. He watched in horror as the older man's body went limp and his eyes went dull then he saw his own body begin to reanimate.

"Aaahhhh," the man said in exaggerated pleasure as he looked down at the body that was more than half his age. "I was so tired of being that pathetic woman, or the stray bat or rat I could catch. You see, Darlyn... or should I call you Midnight now? The people of this gods-forsaken town learned too quickly what I was doing. They drugged me and left while I slept, leaving me with nothing but this shell," indicating the woman – who had sacrificed herself by taking the sleep agent, "and that old body to live in. They tricked me much as I just did you.

I needed a new body and I did not want to be a woman. I had planned to leave this city and find myself a suitable… host, I suppose you would call it, when you so conveniently stepped in here."

This is how you achieve immortality, Darlyn. When I tire of one body I will leave it and enter another, younger and stronger body – thus I will never die." The man began to run his hands over Darlyn's body then, "Nice. You have kept yourself in good shape, considering the things you have suffered through." He turned to the mirror beside him and continued, "I am not sure I care for the hair but I will get used to it."

Darlyn tried to speak, to tell the man what he thought of this, but all that came out was a hiss much as Onyx had uttered just before.

"Now, now. I can throw you out in the cold if you like? Let you live on the insects and vermin you catch. I have no desire to leave you in that form; I am not entirely evil, Dear Boy. I have enjoyed getting to feel needed again so I will assist you in the spell you cannot speak now. I will give you a choice, my old body or the woman's."

A deep growl came from the cat's throat this time.

"Very well," said Thomithy through Darlyn's now sneering mouth. "I'll choose for you. I have many questions of you, as to what you have been up to, that you cannot answer as the cat. I need to know all about you and your life up to now so I can assume it. At the right time I will let it be known who I really am – the Guild will never see it coming! Until then I will enjoy being a somewhat valued member of the wizarding community."

Darlyn watched his lips begin the words to what he could only hope was the spell to reverse the *transmogoration* then his consciousness left the cat and began to drift around the room. He had no idea which body the evil wizard would choose to put him into and had no way to stop him from making the choice. He felt himself becoming solid and realized it was the woman's body.

Onyx's mind then reentered his cat body and slumped to the floor in exhaustion.

Before Darlyn could do anything to counter the situation the older wizard said words he had never heard before. A feeling much like the one he had when the cleric, Helon, had used an herb on him that supposedly blocked his powers washed over him then. He began to panic as he realized this was a true binding, he was now powerless and stuck in this woman's body.

"I am hungry; I never had much appetite before. Go to the kitchen and get me some of the soup over the fire while I acquaint myself with my new body," said Thomithy through Darlyn's lips. "And take my old body out of here. It's ruining my appetite."

Darlyn couldn't get beyond hearing his voice being spoken by another or the arrogance he heard in it. Had he sounded like that? He was a little dazed as he tried to make the woman's weaker muscles respond to him. He took a step, then another, then another, getting a feel for the new body. He placed the woman's hand on the forearm of the older empty body and walked with it to the front of the small shack.

Darlyn stopped the empty body shell by the door then turned to a cruddy mirror on the wall and looked at the face his eyes now saw from. He guessed the woman had been in her early thirties when Thomithy emptied her. Her hair was shoulder length and was so dirty he couldn't tell what color it was supposed to be. He didn't dare wash it to find out – it would likely all fall out if he tried to. She was deathly thin, he could feel her bones sticking out from her skin and a general feeling of nausea as well. Her eyes were a dull brown and her face was gaunt and tinted yellow from lack of proper nutrition. He moved her lips a little and found teeth that were rotting in place and a tongue that was covered with sores.

"This... uhhh..." her voice was beyond raspy, "this will not do," he said. He tried for all his might to clear his/ her, throat but couldn't get enough phlegm to do it. He reached for a full waterskin on the counter beside him and started to take a drink from it.

He had it inches from his/ her, lips when a thought came to him.

His eyes scanned the counters and shelves around him/ her, trying to remember the scene as it had looked when Onyx had first brought his mind here. He saw a lot of containers with fluid in them but couldn't see the one he was looking for. He jumped and let out a high-pitched squeal as Onyx jumped onto the counter beside him.

He watched the cat sniff at one near the back.

"Is that the one I want?" he whispered to the cat.

"My stomach is not getting any fuller," Thomithy shouted from the other room then.

Darlyn had no idea whether this trick was going to work or not but he had to try. He took a cloth hanging beside the fireplace, used it to take hold of the hot handle of the pot hanging over the fire and set it on the counter. He took a bowl that was filled with dust and ladled out a healthy portion, not even bothering to empty the dust out first. He then took the bottle the cat had indicated and poured half its contents into the soup and stirred it up. It didn't appear any different; he hoped the thick soup would mask the taste of the potion.

He had to do this quickly if it was going to work.

He took hold of a knife on the counter beside the pot, turned to the empty body that had been the wizard, Thomithy, and slit his wrists parallel to his veins, from his wrist to the cusp of his elbow. The shell did nothing to stop him. Thick blood began to empty from the cuts, dripping down the arms to the floor. This wouldn't kill the empty man right away but it would soon enough.

Darlyn looked down at Onyx and said, "Get as far from here as you can, I don't want him to be able to enter your mind." It seemed strange hearing his words in a female voice.

Onyx mewed worriedly then darted through the crack between the boards he had first used to enter the shack.

Darlyn whispered to any God that wished to humor him, "Please let this work!" then took hold of the bowl of soup and went back into the other room.

Thomithy was staring at Darlyn's naked body in a full-length mirror when the man in the woman's body stepped in. He was running his hands over the muscles of his chest and smiling.

"I bet the women find you quite attractive, don't they? Do you know how long it has been since I was with anything other than that shell you are now inside of?"

Darlyn had to fight the woman's body from vomiting then. His/ her skin felt like it was going to crawl right off his/ her body. "I brought you the soup," he said, sounding almost as arrogant in the female voice as he ever had with his own.

"What is with your leg though? Hurts like hell. I will get used to it." said Thomithy. He didn't even bother to dress; he only walked over and sat down at the small table. He took a large spoon of the soup and blew over it – the steam moving away from it like the smoke of a lit cigarette. He took it into his much younger mouth, chewed up the bits of vegetables then swallowed it down. He took another and another, smiling after each bite. "Ooh, yeah. That is good. I haven't been able to taste anything in years."

Darlyn, in the woman's body, said nothing, only watched with anticipation.

Thomithy was near the bottom of the bowl before there was any kind of reaction.

Darlyn watched his hands go to the side of his head and heard a moan escape his lips. His blue-gray eyes locked on the dull brown ones of the body Darlyn was now inside of then.

"What... did... you... do?" came from Darlyn's lips in an angry hiss then his body slumped over and Thomithy's consciousness left it in a cloud.

Without a second thought, Darlyn pulled the bottle with the other half of the potion out of the pocket in the front of the woman's smock and drank it down. He had to fight not to puke it back up; it tasted like horse dung. His wasn't diluted with soup so it worked much quicker. His mind left the woman's body and quickly re-entered his own body. He didn't have time to enjoy being back inside it now though.

He watched the essence of Thomithy trying to find his original body – this had been part of Darlyn's plan – the man had bound the woman's flesh so in her body he wouldn't be able to perform magic, in his old and frail body he could.

Darlyn followed the cloud into the first room, as did the female's body, and watched the essence float over the now dead body that had been Thomithy's. The essence quickly went into the woman's body then, before it was dispersed on the winds.

Darlyn didn't even give the older man the chance to take a breath in the woman's body. He took the same knife he had used on the man's old body and sliced a deep gash in her throat – slicing halfway through her esophagus.

Thomithy gurgled as blood poured from the wound for a moment then the woman's body slumped to the ground, dead – the older wizard's mind now trapped inside it.

Darlyn hadn't seen this; he had gone back into the back room quickly and grabbed his clothes and weapon. He did not to take the time to get dressed. He fought the urge to stop and take a bath, sickened at the thought of what the older man might have done to his body while he was out of the room then ran back to the front room. He moved past the lumps on the floor and grabbed the lantern from beside the door. He tossed it into the center of the room and ran out the front door.

It was only moments before the ramshackle building burst into flame. Being nothing but old, dried up wood it was only minutes before there was nothing but a blackened rectangle of ash left on the ground the building had once stood on. Sparks flying out from the blaze caught the buildings beside it and soon that side of the town was ablaze.

Darlyn pulled his clothing back on as he watched the destruction then he turned and called out for Onyx.

He didn't come.

A panicked thought came to him – he wondered if in worry for him the cat had re-entered the hut or had chosen to hide out in one of the buildings now becoming ash fast before him. He prayed if this was so his death had been swift and painless.

He was just about to open a portal back to the others when he heard a meow from behind him. He turned and smiled as the black cat, covered in dust and cobwebs from wherever he had chosen to hide, leapt from the road and landed in his outstretched arms.

He quickly said the words to open a portal but nothing happened. He panicked – had the binding Thomithy had done been on his soul rather than the woman's flesh? He started to say the words again when a sudden pain burst in his chest. He clutched the left side, over his heart and fell to the ground convulsing. An image of Eonard came to him then – he wasn't sure if it was the actual elf or just a memory of him at first.

"I found this bit of your soul while looking for mine. I figured you might like to have it back," said the elf.

Just like that, the pain was gone – as was the pain he had grown used to in his leg. He felt invigorated – like he had slept the sleep of the dead for weeks, or was twenty years younger. He smiled, called the cat, who was now hiding in the shrubs across from him, back to him then swirled his arm and opened the portal with no effort.

Torrin, who had the watch, jumped when the portal opened across from him, Knowing who it was already, he quickly calmed and sat back. He watched the cat walk over to a stump across from him and flop down as if exhausted then the wizard do the same.

"Where did you get yourself to?" whispered the warrior.

"Just had some unfinished business," said the wizard cryptically. "Is there a river or water source close by?" he added.

Torrin saw a strange and unpleasant look coming to the wizard's face – as if not liking the feel or smell of something. "Yeah, about four spans east."

Darlyn said the words to an *illumination* spell and a tiny orange ball of flame appeared by his head. "I will not be long."

The cat followed the wizard.

Torrin shook his head at them then went back to polishing the sword he had taken to using when he realized his grandfather's sword was gone.

31

THE BETRAYER

Eonard was feeling good as he and his companions broke camp on what was their ninth day on the ethereal plain. He knew he still had a long hard task ahead of him so his pleasure was a little bittersweet.

He had five pieces of his soul back but there was no knowing how many pieces it had been broken into, he could feel the last bits trying to break up further whenever he tried to reach them in the odd darkness the plain was made up of.

He knew the bits of his soul were being drawn to people he had some connection to in the living world. Giving that Helon and Paitell each had pieces, it was likely the dark cleric would have a piece of it as well. That man's soul had been on this plain for decades and likely knew all the tricks of how to manipulate it to his will. This meant he needed to find all the pieces he could before they met, and that he needed to practice manipulating this plain as best he could while the others slept. He had a feeling the dark cleric knew he was on the plain and that he would do anything he could to keep him from getting all of the others pieces first.

He had gotten the feeling they were being watched from almost as soon as they began to move but he had thought it was either the clerk – journalizing their plight for his recounts – or their odd spirit guide – now he was sure it was neither of them.

"Where to?" asked Nortus, looking from Eonard to the guide soul.

"Gather around me," the elf said without explanation.

The others did.

Eonard wasn't sure how he did it but they didn't jump as they had the others times they had moved on the plain, this time they more only shifted.

They were now standing in the middle of a re-creation of a road in the center of a town three of them knew well.

"Where are we?" asked Azure.

Junt was looking around them, not recognizing the place either.

"This is Windsor," said Rius.

Nortus and Eonard looked at the cloudy form in confusion then.

Rius didn't say anything to explain how he would know the town Eonard and Aramis had grown up in. He also didn't explain himself when his cloudy form began to move toward the small cottage the two had grown up in.

"Rius?" Eonard called out.

The cloud didn't stop.

He was becoming solid, taking on the shape of a man of average height with a wide body and broad shoulders, wearing a cleric's robe. Bouncy brownish blond curls began to appear on his head and a tight beard formed on his chin. He looked back at the men he had been guiding as his hand reached the knob to the door.

One of the companions recognized him.

The others stepped inside the cottage then.

It was warm and smelled of baking bread. The sound of someone humming was coming from a room in the back.

Nortus and Eonard were frozen in the center of the room, Azure and Junt were just inside the doorway and Rius was walking toward the humming.

The sound got louder as the woman making the bread appeared in the doorway opposite them.

She was a little on the short side and wide in the middle but pleasantly so. She had loose and bouncy reddish brown curls on her head and pink on her cheeks. She was wearing a brown fitted gown with a white apron over the skirt, both were dusted with white powder – flour. She was carrying a small tray with several small cactus plants on it that she had just watered. She jumped when she realized she had company.

The men had all frozen when they realized she was coming into the room they were in.

Her eyes went to the two at the door first. She wondered what a dragon in human form was doing on the plain. The other was a spirit from this realm. She didn't recognize them but felt nothing but wonder and a little bit of confusion coming from them – no threat to her. She shifted her eyes to the two in the center of the room. She knew them both though they were older than when she had last seen them. One of them made her quite happy and a little sad to see, the other quite angry – she would deal with them in a moment. Her eyes continued to the last in the room and she dropped the tray.

The pots of some of the plants exploded, sending the planting medium and the tiny plants spreading across the floor, others managed to land on their bottoms with only a slight thud.

The man that had appeared to the companions as only a cloud up until now took the steps between him and the woman's soul in a quick step as if intending to catch her as she started to follow the plants.

Leanne began to scream and push the soul away from her.

Eonard threw his arms up and the soul that had been their guide was thrown away from the spirit of the woman that had raised him. "How dare you try to harm her," he shouted. He started to bring his hands together to disperse him as he had the soul of Helon when Leanne and Nortus both screamed for him to stop.

The elf looked from the old man, whom he had thought he could trust, to the only woman he had known as a mother with confusion. Why wouldn't they want the man's soul dispersed?

The man got to his feet and looked directly at the elf then.

It took a moment for who Eonard was now looking at to sink in, the man looked like a younger version of Mahki or an older version of Aramis – which meant…

"Darius?" Leanne asked. She was on the floor on her knees – Eonard had thrown the man away from her before he could catch her.

"I am sorry. I am so sorry," the man said, looking from her to Eonard and back.

"Why didn't you tell us who you were?" asked the elf.

"Who is he?" Azure asked behind them.

Junt only shrugged.

"He is the one that brought me to your time to live with his wife and son," said Eonard, unsure how he was still standing – feeling dizzy and a little bit betrayed.

"I am. I am Darius MaComber, son of Makhi, father of Aramis, son-in-law to Nortus and husband of Leanne," said the man.

"But the clerk said you had to be an impartial guide," said Junt.

"I knew you would not allow me to guide you if you knew, and Nortus would have known me if he had seen me as myself," said Darius as his eyes moved to the face of his father-in-law.

"You tricked us," spat Eonard.

"Not intentionally."

"You are working *your father*, aren't you? You have been trying to lead us to him this whole time," spit Eonard.

"No!" Darius said adamantly.

Eonard didn't hear this. A yellow glow was beginning to appear around one of the tiny cacti on the floor, one with a tiny pink flower on the top of it, like the one he had been thinking of when he first became aware he could manipulate the waves here, and another was coming from under the collar of the robe of the man he was about to thrust his building anger at.

Darius looked down at his chest and drew in a deep breath. He removed a medallion like the one his father and his son had, with an open book and a mortar and pestle – his family's clerical symbol. "I didn't know."

"He has had a piece of the elf's soul this whole time?" growled the dragon.

Darius took the chain from around his neck and started toward Eonard with it. "I would never have kept it from you, I swear. I didn't know I had it."

Junt dissolved and reappeared before the spirit cleric. "You will not harm him."

Darius was frozen, his hand outstretched with the chain and medallion dangling from it.

"Release him," Nortus, Leanne and Eonard said in unison.

It was the third person's request that made the knight step back.

"I swear to you, I do not mean you any harm. I spoke true when I said I felt my father reenter the plain and truly do wish to help you disperse him forever."

"Why?" asked Azure.

"He destroyed all that meant anything to me," said the man as his eyes went to Leanne, who was cleaning the dirt, broken pots and plants from the floor.

Junt looked at Eonard then.

The elf nodded and stepped forward. He took the chain from the man that he had always thought of as his savior and placed it over his head – he was praying that had not changed. The round pendant was warm on the skin of the center of his chest. Like the other bits of his soul it began to glow brighter as did the rest of his body. As before he began to convulse and twist up. When the shocks had subsided, he bent down, his eyes on the small cactus that the woman was beginning to pick up that was also glowing.

He wasn't sure he could go through the onslaught again right away but knew he needed to – he could feel Mahki breathing down his neck.

Nortus could see this was what the elf was about to do; he stepped forward and said, "No, Eonard. You need time to recover."

"I don't have it," said Eonard. "May I have the cactus with the pink flower?"

Leanne looked at him strangely and asked, "Why are you here, Eonard? Father?" Her eyes took them all in. "Are you all dead? What is going on?"

"Mahki was resurrected by an evil wizard, hoping to be given the… gift of immortality as payment. They took Eonard, intending to use his blood in the ritual. In the course of the attempt his blood was spilled. Mahki's soul was sent back here and Eonard's soul was dragged along with it. The plain has broken it up, trying to disperse it since it does not belong here. We have been trying to find the pieces," said Nortus.

"What just happened?" asked Leanne, still trying to get a grasp on what was going on. "You looked to be in great pain, Eonard."

"Darius had a piece of my soul and I believe the cactus is another," said the elf, his hand still held out for it.

Leanne passed it to him then.

"Thank you," said the elf as he closed his hand around the plant.

The tiny spikes on the side of the plant sunk into the skin of his palm, making it sting. Blood began to drip down from the dozens of puncture wounds. He continued to squeeze the plant until it began to bleed the water that it had just sucked up into itself. The light began to glow from it and the elf again.

He convulsed again and this time fell to the floor. The double hit to his system left him in a semi-catatonic state – unaware of anything happening around him and unable to react to anything that might happen.

Just as Eonard began to writhe the door behind the dragon burst open, knocking the blue man to the floor in a pile.

The others turned to see what had caused the strange occurrence to see three men in the doorway.

"Hello, my son," said Mahki; a very pleased smile on his handsome face. "I thank you for leaving so easy a trail to follow."

32

OUT
OF FABLES

Torrin was getting more and more anxious each day as they climbed higher and higher up the mountain range Phineas said was the Ashgroth Mountains. He had been searching for any sign of elves, which he thought would be leatherleaf trees, but so far all he saw was towering evergreens. He was standing on an outcropping of granite jutting out from the side of the ridgeline, watching the second sun going below the peak above them as Cieri came up beside him.

"We are not far behind him, Torrin. We will get your sword back."

"He has had enough of a jump on us that he is likely already among his people again. If they are anything like the Silver and Brown elves we will never find them."

"We have a Silver elf with us and a wizard who is not likely to give up very easily."

Torrin wanted to continue to argue but knew he couldn't. "Thank you," he said as he bent down and kissed her.

"There was a pond a few spans to the south of us, want to go take a bath together?" she asked him with a sly smile.

Phineas was just coming up the path with their dinner as the female warrior said this. He smiled at the lovers' backs as they started down the path behind him. He continued on to their campsite, plopped himself down in front of the fire, pulled out one of his knives and began the arduous process of skinning the rabbits he had managed to snare just after setting up the camp.

Darlyn hadn't noticed either of these happenings, he was writing feverously in his tiny notebook, wanting to record every detail of what had happened between him and Thomithy days before. He had the first watch this night and should have been getting what he could for sleep to prepare for it but his mind was working too fast to be able to shut it down.

Sangas was equally as oblivious of the happenings around him. He too was sitting beside the fire, with his legs crossed, his hands folded together in his lap and his eyes closed, deep in meditation.

The first two jumped when the third suddenly opened his eyes.

"We are not alone," said the Silver elf.

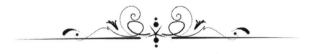

Torrin and Cieri didn't spend long bathing; they had not been able to be together since leaving Cutter so almost as soon as their clothes came off their bodies met.

The male warrior carried the female one to the edge of the bank, where a large patch of moss had taken hold. He was just getting himself positioned over her and was just leaning down to kiss her when about ten figures stepped from the trees around them.

Neither Torrin nor Cieri were especially modest but they hadn't expected to have an audience so they quickly stopped.

The men around them were dark skinned, dark haired and had tattoos over various parts of their faces and the bits of skin showing through the beaded vests they were wearing. Leather bands around their foreheads made their pointed ears even more prominent. None of them looked upset at having disturbed the couple, each had a long bow with an arrow notched.

One of the dark elves stepped up to them, set the very sharp tip of his arrowhead on the left cheek of the warrior and said, "Off the woman and get dressed."

It wasn't long after Sangas' admonition the three men at the camp began to see figures stepping from behind shrubs and trees all around them, each holding a long bow with an arrow notched.

Darlyn had thought at first of using an *immobilize* spell but he guessed by the similarity of Jacobi's tattoos to these men's that these were the fabled Green elves they had been seeking. It would do them little good to make them immediate enemies so he let the words to the incantation dissolve from his mind. He wanted badly to speak to them himself but knew it was best to let Sangas, a fellow elf, make the first contact.

One of them motioned for the silver haired elf to stand.

Sangas did so.

The three jumped again as ten more of the Green elves, escorting the barely dressed Torrin and Cieri, came into the clearing.

"Why are you in our forest?" asked one of the elves, one that looked to be quite old by the wrinkles that were causing the facial tattoos to looked pinched. This was said to Sangas.

"We are in search of an elf named Jacobi. He took an item that did not belong to him that we are looking to retrieve."

"Are you accusing an elf of thievery? Elves do not steal!"

"I too am an elf; I know elves do not typically steal... I also know some have taken on the ways of... the outsiders." Sangas had to speak delicately of the fact that most elves saw human contact as wrong, that it was their evil minds that had corrupted the elves and caused the break of the three races so long ago, not wanting to offend the humans he was traveling with either.

"Are you prisoner to these… *white skins*?"

"No. I am a companion."

The elder elf gave him a look that relayed his dislike of the thought without him needing to speak it. "I do not know this elf you call Jacobi. Do you know which sect he is?"

"No. We tracked him to this area. Is there a council we can meet with that might offer us help in finding him?"

"What is it this Jacobi is accused of taking?"

"A sword that belonged to my grandfather," said Torrin as he pulled his tunic over his wide chest.

The elf made so sign of having heard the warrior, his eyes still locked on the Silver elf before him.

Sangas repeated what Torrin had just said.

"All this for a sword?"

"Not just any sword, this was one of the swords forged with help from Dwendlyn and was used in the Torge wars," said Sangas.

Dwendlyn was a legendary half human half elf that had gone to work in the human lands as a swordsmith. He used his magic to fortify and strengthen the weapons he forged. He was commissioned by Conath Hundertmark to assist seven of the most powerful wizards of the day to forge seven swords, one of which was given to Kentril Radric.

"All the swords were found and destroyed," spat the Green elf.

"All but this one was," said Torrin.

Sangas hissed for the warrior to hold his tongue then said, "I too know what has been told to our peoples about the swords but this one is still whole and was taken from the human warrior without his permission."

The elves brought their arrows up and all had them aimed at them again.

Sangas said as forthright as he could, "We do not mean you harm".

"Is that why you have three white skin warriors and a powerful white skin magic-user with you? Did you come here looking to take the sword back by force of arms?"

Sangas wanted to believe they were truly hoping it could be done without force but he knew Torrin was ready to do whatever was necessary. The Silver elf could not tell even a half-truth.

The elder elf took his silence as answer and motioned them to go with them without telling them whether they were their prisoners.

Short of starting a fight that would certainly mean at least one of them getting injured or worse and likely losing the chance to connect with the fabled elves, the companions decided to cooperate.

They were taken through a veil much like the Silver and Brown elves used to hide their domains and led to a large open field. There were several small mud and thatch huts surrounding a large pavilion of sorts. Young elves of both sexes were playing around them and older elves were either working around a large bonfire or were in the process of making a new hut on the far side of the field.

"Is this where we will find Jacobi?" asked Torrin anxiously.

Sangas knew the Green elf would not respond to Torrin so he asked the same question.

"There are settlements like this all throughout this valley. The elf you seek is not a member of ours."

"Do you know which he is?"

"I do not know the name," said the elder elf.

"How far is it to the next?" asked Torrin.

Sangas knew the warrior was anxious, and that he couldn't speak to him about holding his tongue here, but he hoped the hard look he gave him would get the point across.

The man looked angry at the unspoken scolding but did hold his tongue.

Sangas again asked the elder elf the same question the warrior had.

"We cannot allow you to roam our lands."

"I am not interested in roamin'…" Torrin's voice was getting deeper and his posture was getting stiff.

This time Sangas did speak to the warrior, though it was in barely more than a whisper. "Please, Master Radric, this process of reacquainting with the Green elves is going to be delicate enough." He then looked back at the elder elf and said, "Please forgive my human companion, he is anxious is all. I assure you we only want the sword returned; we do not wish any of you any harm."

The elder elf looked about to order the elves around him, who all still had arrows notched in their bows, though they were aimed at the ground, to bring them back up and loose them but he didn't. "We will take you to The One in the morning. The One will be able to tell you where to find the elf you seek."

33

SACRIFICES

The dark cleric threw his hand up quickly, stopping Darius, Leanne and Junt in mid-step. He could do nothing physically to the dragonman or Nortus, being flesh, but he didn't need to. While he was incapacitating the spirits his companions had gotten to Eonard, who still lie on the floor of the ethereal cottage, unconscious from getting two pieces of his soul back back-to-back.

When Azure and Nortus saw Paitell had his hand positioned over the elf's chest, ready to plunge it through the skin to tear his heart from him, they stopped themselves.

"What a happy reunion, yes? It is too bad your son, my and Nortus' grandson, Aramis couldn't have been here. I do so wish I could have gotten to know the boy, he seemed so much like you when you were younger, Darius."

"Go to blazing hell," shouted Darius, his image got brighter from the expel of heated energy.

"In case you haven't noticed I am already there," said Mahki with a sick smile on his face.

"This place is neither heaven nor hell," said Junt.

"To some it may be a place somewhere between the two but to me anywhere but being alive is hell," spit Mahki. He noticed a strange light in the spirit knight's eyes as he said this, as if he agreed with him. He put that tidbit to the back of his mind; he might be able to use that to his advantage later. "Make this easy on yourselves and come with me willingly."

Nortus started to say he would die first. He stopped as he saw the first inch of Paitell's fingers plunge into Eonard's still only half solid chest, making the elf squirm. "We will go without fight," he said, looking at the others to be sure they understood and would comply as well.

"Very good. Paitell, take hold of the elf, the rest of you gather close to me."

The others did as they were told.

The feeling of jumping on the waves of the plain washed over them all. When it cleared they found themselves on what was supposed to be a grassy knoll.

"Alright, First thing, Spirit Knight, open a portal back to Ernel, the dragon wishes to return to it." Mahki knew he could control Nortus with the threat of harming the elf but he didn't trust the dragon – he didn't know if he was loyal to the elf just as its protector race or to this particular elf – the latter he could manipulate – the former would mean he'd only feel a fleeting pain at having lost this one. He couldn't take the chance or the risk.

"I will not leave the elf," spat Azure.

Paitell was ready for the dark cleric's cue so he again began to plunge his hand into the elf's chest without a word – deeper this time.

Eonard moaned in pain and began to struggle in his trance-like state.

Nortus turned to the dragon and said, "Go, Azure."

The dragon was still going to refuse; the look on the elder cleric's face made him turn to Junt and nod.

Junt wanted to refuse to do this, knowing they would need the dragon to help them fight what the evil cleric was going to do but he knew of no way to stop this. He waved his hand and a small opening formed, they could see through it to a field of green grass.

Azure had to force himself to step through that portal; he did so without looking back.

Mahki was smiling quite sickly as he waved for the spirit knight to close the portal then for them all to go into what was supposed to be his castle.

The blue man stepped into the middle of the field in the middle of nowhere. He looked behind him just in time to see the portal to the Plain of Vethe they were on disappear. He threw back his head and screamed a howl no human throat could ever make then shook himself all over, in a flash of blazing color he was back in his natural form. He spit out a sheet of ice that froze the ground and trees before the beast then spread his wings, pumped them once and leapt into the air.

The frozen trunks exploded in a rain of splinters and sharp leaves as the icy blast of those powerful wings hit them.

The room the dark cleric led them to was misshapen, like the outside was. The ceiling looked to be very high in some places and only a few feet from the ground in others. A portrait of what was supposed to be Mahki as a younger man was by the doors. It made him look as if he were a giant compared to the items behind him.

There were several ghost-like shadows moving about the room that didn't seem to react when they entered it. These were other souls Mahki had collected and put to work for him. Most were barely arrived so they hadn't learned how to control the waves and he had bound them to him so they now could not reach out to the realm unless he gave them permission to.

He directed his *guests* to a large chamber that was supposed to be the great hall and motioned some of the servants to his side "Hold the spirits," he said to them, pointing to the forms of Junt, Darius and Leanne.

The forms moved around the three, surrounding them, in essence walling them in.

Mahki had no way to physically bind Nortus but the continued threat to the elf should keep him in check, as well as the threat of sending him back to Ernel as the dragon had been if he didn't cooperate.

The dark cleric was uncertain how best to hold the elf. He was half living and half spirit. He had never dealt with this before. He motioned for Paitell to chain him to the wall and hoped it was enough – as long as the elf remained unconscious it certainly would be.

"What are you planning to do?" Darius asked, through clenched teeth, seeing the elf hanging helpless before him.

"I am planning to do essentially the opposite of how I found myself here, Son."

Leanne, Darius and Nortus looked confused by this response. Junt was shaking his head furiously.

"It is forbidden," the spirit knight snapped.

"By whom? There is nothing in this realm that can harm me," said the dark cleric.

"I will not let you harm Eonard, Mahki. You may be able to hold me at bay as long as you are only threatening him but I will not remain that way if you do more," said Nortus.

"I know this, Old Man, which is why I will be dispatching you first."

"You cannot dispatch living flesh," said Junt.

Mahki walked over to Nortus and reached forward with his hand, the fingers went around the man's neck but since they weren't solid they didn't close on any flesh, only went through his neck to meet and clasp into a fist behind him. The man didn't seem surprised by this, because he wasn't, it was meant merely as a show to the others that he already knew this. "There is one here who can though."

The three spirits and Nortus looked confused by this; the elf was unconscious and the man had already sent the dragon away, the only two with them that were flesh.

Mahki didn't answer their inquiry. He walked over to the elf, grabbed a hold of a handful of hair and yanked his head back hard.

Eonard came awake with a start. He saw the man before his face and felt panic well up inside him. He couldn't make his arms move to defend himself, which made him panic more. He moved his eyes and saw Paitell and Helon behind the man, both looking very pleased and excited. Nortus was standing stiff in the center of the large room, and Leanne, Darius and Junt were surrounded by what he guessed were shapeless souls. He did not see Azure anywhere. He wanted to ask what was happening but all that came out was a mournful sounding moan.

"You are still weak from getting more of your soul back, elf. If I had come a few minutes later than I had you would likely be able to overpower me. As long as I complete my intended task quickly you will be unable to do me any harm."

Eonard fought to make any part of his body work – he could not.

Mahki laughed sickly then looked over at Nortus. "I learned the last time I was here that if a soul was to find a way to reach living flesh they can take that flesh over, sort of like a wizard doing a *transmogoration* spell. I could not use the dragon and I was uncertain whether I could use the elf... at least not until I saw what Helon had done to him in their meeting. Since he is half living and half dead..."

Eonard realized what the man was implying by that even not having heard the exchange of moments before. "NO!" Eonard shouted, finally finding his voice.

Nortus was shaking his head as well.

"I give you a choice, Nortus, I will either take your lifeforce and release the elf, or I will take the elf's and kill you. Either way you will cease to be."

"You say you will release the elf? Do you mean he will not be harmed?"

"NO, Nortus," Eonard said again, trying with all his might to get his body to respond to him.

"I will allow him to return to Ernel. He has most of his soul back." Mahki took something from a pocket in his robe. It looked like a small bag, very much like the one he had produced in the cavern that held the herb he had used to take the lifeforces from the elves. It was glowing a golden yellow, telling them all it was another piece of the elf's soul. "If he swears before all of you that he will not harm me in this or the upper realm once I am back among the living I will give him the final piece."

"You will do this if I do not fight you?" asked Nortus.

"I will," Mahki said.

"NO," said Darius, "He can't be trusted."

"You know me well, Nortus, have I ever lied to you about anything?" asked Mahki, angered that his own flesh and blood would slander him.

"You were always arrogant but painfully honest," said Nortus.

"Please don't do it, Father," begged Leanne.

"There is another way," Junt said.

They were all drowned out by Eonard's plea. "Don't do it, Nortus."

"I must Eonard. Aramis needs you," said Nortus.

Mahki was smiling sickly now.

Paitell and Helon both looked confused; how was the dark cleric becoming alive again and allowing the elf to go unharmed going to give them the revenge he had promised them?

Mahki stepped away from Eonard and said, "So, what is it to be, Nortus?"

Nortus lowered his chin to his chest, took a deep breath and said, "I will…"

"This is not what you promised me," shouted Paitell, even in spirit form the anger was enough to make spittle form and spew from the man's lips.

"I was told I would have my revenge," shouted Helon only a little less angrily.

Mahki waved his hand and both of the spirit men flew backward a few feet.

Neither man cared what became of the other's soul, nor of the other's desire for equal part in the revenge, both only knew they were about to be cheated of their part of it – they acted together only because they knew neither had a chance against the man alone.

They launched themselves at the dark cleric.

They took Mahki unaware, having already dismissed them from his mind. The force of their anger made them both quite strong. One of them began to rip his ethereal flesh from his body as the other plunged his fingers into his chest, trying to rip out his ethereal heart.

The others only watched this; for once they were actually rooting for Paitell and Helon.

Mahki struggled under the onslaught, he screamed out in pain and anger then threw his arms back.

The two spirits flew from him.

If he had been living flesh he would be dead, his heart now on the floor before him and half his skin and muscle torn from his right side, but since he wasn't... He shook briefly then the heart that was beating down on the floor dissolved and the flesh that had been ripped from his body reformed.

"*You dare*?" he screamed in a voice that was beyond angry. His eyes looked to be on fire as they moved from one spirit to the other. He didn't speak a word, only pointed one hand at one of them and the other at the other. He brought the fingers of those hands together to form two fists and squeezed.

The form of Paitell, on one side, and the form of Helon, on the other, began to writhe and convulse then. It looked like they were being turned inside out; their images were becoming all distorted and gray. Neither man could scream though both had their mouths open and their faces were wrenched as if they were trying to.

It lasted only a few seconds then what had been the two male forms become thousands of bits, like ash, blowing around the room. Those bits landed on whatever surface they were near for a split second them dissolved and disappeared.

Mahki turned his still blazing eyes on the other three spirits then, "Do you three want the same?"

None of them said anything.

"I will do as you ask," Nortus shouted. His eyes were on Eonard's as he said this.

Eonard was going to shout no again when an image of the old man formed in his mind.

Darius watched the elf go limp in the restraints; he couldn't imagine how he would be willing to just let Nortus give himself over like this. He didn't know how he did what he did next but he did.

The spirit that had once been a man grunted and lunged forward, knocking the wisp of smoke that was his guard out of the way. He was screaming a very living sounding death cry as he launched himself at his father. He knew there was a good chance he would be like the two spirits he had just watched being dispelled mere moments before but he was not going to let his father harm the elf if there was any way to stop him.

"Stop him but do not harm him, Mahki. I will not fight you," said Nortus.

Mahki wanted very much to show his son what he thought of him trying to destroy him again but he wanted to be living flesh even more. He waved his hand but only to stop the advancing form in mid-launch.

Darius was now frozen, several inches off the ground.

Nortus turned to Junt and Leanne then and said, "Do not fight this, please. I cannot let him harm Eonard. By doing this the elf will have his soul back, we will have all fulfilled our reason for coming here."

Junt wanted to say not this way but he only nodded.

Leanne was in tears.

Darius was still fighting to move.

Eonard was still hanging limp, uncertain if he could allow what he knew was coming next to come, even though knowing it was the only choice they had.

Mahki looked at each of the people in the room, seeing none of them were going to stop him, he stepped over to Nortus.

Nortus removed the medallion from around his neck, it had a protection spell on it, no one, not even a spirit, would have been able to physically harm him as long as he wore it. He let it drop to the floor – the heavy thing making no sound as it landed was very loud. He opened the front of his robe to show a once muscular chest, now sunken with age, then pulled a knife out of his pocket. He closed his eyes and, without a word, plunged the blade into the left side of his chest, into his heart.

Mahki's ethereal heart was beating hard and fast and he was getting a little dizzy with excitement and anticipation. He watched the blood drain from the wound in the chest of the man, who was somehow managing to remain standing, and saw the glow beginning to build in the wet opening to his heart. This was the moment he was waiting for. He reached forward and plunged his hand into the opening.

Unlike the spirit bodies of Paitell and Helon, or the half spirit, half living flesh of the elf, none of which produced any blood, lots of it poured from the wound and the heart that was in the hand of the dark cleric when he pulled it free with a squishing pop sound was real.

The others watched this act in horror and disbelief. It was over and done with before any of them could barely take a breath.

Nortus' body slumped to the floor but, like the metal medallion, it made no sound. He didn't feel it either, dead long before he reached it.

The dark cleric paid it no attention as he brought the still beating heart to his own chest and pushed it inside it. He had a look on his face that might have been a smile or a grimace.

It was in fact both.

Mahki fell to his knees in excruciating pain as the organ began to beat inside him. He wanted to laugh, at his triumph and that he had finally gotten his revenge against Nortus, but at the moment his body wouldn't let him. The blood flowing out of the real organ changed the ethereal blood in the ethereal one to real blood, which pumped out through the ethereal veins, making them real again too. The same action moved outward through the sinew, tissue, muscles and skin to make his body living flesh again.

He let out a final anguish filled scream that changed to a sick guttural laughter, it echoed through the cavernous chamber and through the hearts, both ethereal and real, of the others in the room.

Mahki's skin was once more peach colored, his hair once more blew about naturally and his eyes were seeing the world for real instead of the distorted view he had as a spirit. He climbed to his feet, less than gracefully, not used to the weight of living flesh and bone yet, and looked around him as if unsure where he was at first.

It all looked familiar but wrong.

His eyes took in the ghostly image of his dead son, whom he had stopped in mid-lunge halfway across the room, then his dead son's dead wife and the spirit knight still being held by his ghostly servants, all crying over the loss of the old man lying in a pool of blood. He began to laugh.

He remembered now that he too had been dead but he was no longer. A smile, one that was beyond pleased and evil looking, spread across his face then, making his actually quite handsome face look very ugly. He was about to tell the pathetic audience before him that he was now going to make them watch him kill the elf as well. He only got about halfway around when something sharp stabbed him in the lower back.

He looked down to see the very tip of a blade protruding through the skin of his stomach. He felt the warm blood flowing from the wound there as well as the one on the other side of it on his back; the organs that had just come back to life and were now skewered by the blade were bleeding more of the fluid inside of him. He couldn't grasp what was happening.

He finished turning around and found the elf standing behind him, not on the wall, in the chains, as he had been. "How?" he croaked.

"Nortus sent me a vision; he said the only way to kill you was to do it once you were living flesh. He had to let you kill him to make you that way so I could then kill you," said Eonard. The reality of the statement hit him then. He was fighting back a fresh round of tears he wanted to shed for his best friend's good grandfather. He had no idea how he was going to explain to Aramis that he had, in essence, killed both of his grandfathers.

"NO!" Mahki shouted. "Not like this, not here, not by you... Not by an elf."

Eonard took hold of the tang of the dagger and yanked it from the now living flesh of Mahki's back. It came out without any effort.

Mahki began to gurgle then as blood poured from his lips. "You cannot... Not an elf..."

Eonard stepped back, holding the dripping dagger before him in case he needed to use it again.

The light came from around the wound, just as it had when the man's other son, Phineas, had stabbed him in the chamber in the cave, telling Mahki his soul was leaving his newly-made-flesh body. He wanted to scream that he would not accept the fake life on this plain again – this wasn't anything he was going to have to worry about.

Eonard waved his hands and the ghostly forms that had been guarding Junt and Leanne dissolved then Darius was able to move again. They both went to Nortus.

The elf pointed his hand at Mahki, brought his fingers together in a fist and squeezed them tight, just as he had watched the man do to Paitell and Helon moments before. The image of the dark cleric began to shrivel and convulse as Paitell's and Helon's had then it became nothing but bits of ash-like dust and dissolved into nothingness.

Eonard dropped the bloody dagger, which made no sound as it hit the nonexistent stone floor, then took two leaping steps and fell to the ground beside Nortus' dead body. He pulled the old man into his arms and began to cry.

Darius took Leanne into his ethereal arms and held her as they watched the elf wailing in lament.

Junt only stood stiff.

When Eonard had cried himself out he looked up at the three spirits standing around him.

Leanne left Darius' arms then and went to the elf's side. She couldn't touch him, since he was solid and she wasn't; she put her hand on what would be his shoulder if she could have and said, "He did this for you. He knew, ever since I was a child, this day would come... He had foreseen it."

Eonard looked at Leanne. He wanted to tell her she was wrong but he couldn't. He watched her go back to Darius. He wanted to ask her to stay with him, needing her comfort like she had given him when he awakened afraid from a horrible nightmare he couldn't remember as an elfling – one he now knew had most often been seeing his real mother die, but he knew he couldn't.

The husband and wife brought their ethereal lips together in a kiss then they both began to become bits of bright light like Raspal had.

Eonard looked at Junt then, waiting for him to do the same. He didn't appear to be about to. "Your mission is completed, you can now go on too, can't you?"

Junt said nothing, he only walked over to where the dark cleric's soul had been and lifted the bag of herbs that was the last bit of the elf's soul. He walked back to the elf and handed it to him then waved his hand to open a portal back to Ernel.

Eonard was beyond confused. "Are you staying here?"

Junt said nothing.

Eonard looked into the knight's eyes then and had his answer; he too had a piece of the wizard, Darlyn's soul. "You must return it."

"I know," said Junt.

"Why?" asked Eonard, unsure if he should trust the spirit knight.

"I needed it to be able to help you."

Eonard wanted to argue this but he couldn't. "You will return it now?"

"I will." The spirit knight motioned for the elf to step through the portal, back to the living world.

Eonard hesitated but did step through. He turned to the opening and waited, wondering if the spirit knight had lied to him. He saw the portal shrinking and thought he had, then, at the last moment, the knight stepped through it.

The elf looked down at his body, he expected it to be old and frail feeling, as it should be if he had come back the age he was supposed to return as, which would have been his actual age.

"I thought this might happen. You have essentially been reborn to this body," said Junt.

Eonard was pleased to hear this and confused at the same time. "I was reborn?"

"In order for you to be brought to the current time your soul was taken from your body in the past and put into an elflings body in this time."

"What happened to the soul that belonged to the body I was given in this time?"

"It was born already dead, only an empty shell. It was meant only for you to inhabit and live inside."

There were far too many questions to ask from that. Eonard shook his head and sat down where he was.

"We must find Master Algier," said Junt.

"Let me take in the last bit of my soul and rest, then we will go to them," said the elf.

Junt bowed and stepped back.

A deathly loud cry filled the valley they were in then, making the elf clamp his hands over his ears and fight not to vomit.

The knight was unaffected except in worry of the elf. He began to look around for what was making the sound.

A blue streak shot from the sky above their heads then came to rest on the ground a few spans from them. The sound of scales clicking into place and the whistling sound of a long tail whipping back and forth filled the void the dissipating shout left in the elf's head.

"Azure?" the elf asked once he was sure he could open his mouth without his innards spewing out.

"You are back?" boomed from the beast's throat.

Eonard put his hands to his ears again, to block out the sound.

"Avert your eyes," said the dragon.

A bright light filled the valley, then a loud boom filled it; the dragon was gone and the blue human-like figure was once more before them. "Is the dark cleric dispelled?"

"He is."

"Where is Nortus and the other two spirits?"

"Leanne and Darius found redemption and dispersed. They had been reunited, which was what both had been searching for," said Eonard, a slight warming filled his middle at the thought that love could continue even after death.

"Nortus?"

"He had to sacrifice himself in order for Mahki to be killed. Mahki took Nortus' heart and made himself living flesh, which allowed me to stab him, then I dispelled his soul."

"He is destroyed then?"

"He is destroyed."

"What of you?" Azure asked the spirit knight.

"I have a task that I must complete."

The dragon didn't question him, he only looked to the elf and said, "What now?"

"Junt and I must find the wizard, Darlyn Algier."

"He is in Hundertmark, yes?"

"No, he is looking for the Green elves. One of them took a sword that belonged to another friend of mine. They were going to try to retrieve it from him."

"The Green elves are the ones Skyfire took the dragon eggs to," said Azure.

"If you wish to accompany us you can retrieve them."

The dragonman nodded.

"First though." Eonard took the bag of herbs, opened the waterskin on his belt, poured the contents of them into the water and drank it down.

Again he began to convulse and glow but he didn't mind since this would be the last time.

34

THE
ONE

True to his word, the five companions were awakened at first light by one of the Green elves in this clan and taken to the elder that first spoke to them. He and all the others in this clan were waiting for them inside the large pavilion at the center of the settlement.

The floor at the west side of the structure had been covered with animal skins and a small stool was set in the center of these, on this stool sat the elder. He motioned the younger elf to go to his place then the outsiders to step before him, so they would be standing between the bulk of the elves and the old elf.

"Are we being brought to this elf they called *The One* today?" Torrin asked Sangas, just over a whisper.

Sangas whispered back, "I am not certain."

The elder elf turned to Sangas and said, "Tell the white skins to hold their tongue. We do not allow *white skins* to speak to The One."

Torrin looked, and was, put out by this. He started to open his mouth when Cieri placed her hand on his right arm and Darlyn placed his on his left.

Sangas bowed to the elder and said, "They will hold their tongue, Shani."

"Are you willing to take the punishment if the large white skin does not?" asked the elder.

The quick jump told the others the Silver elf had not expected this. "I am." Sangas said slowly.

"We will leave when the second sun reaches the mountain top," said the elder, pointing to a high peak beyond them.

If Darlyn judged right that meant in about an hour. He whispered this to the others.

"That is acceptable," said Sangas. He bowed again to the elder then motioned the others to do the same.

They did so quickly.

The elf that had first gotten them took them back to the hut they had spent the night in. He said nothing to them only stopped by the door then turned and trotted away.

"Are we to assume they will come for us again when it is time?" asked a frustrated Torrin as he watched the elves going about what he guessed was their usual day; as if not even noticing them there.

"We are to. I must implore you, Master Radric, as the clan elder said, The One will not listen to you if you speak. They distrust white skins, as they call humans, even more than the Silver and Brown elves do. He would be killed if he responds to you, even if by accident."

"So I am expected to keep my mouth shut?" asked the largest of them.

Phineas began to chuckle at this, which made Cieri as well and brought a slight curve to the wizard's mouth.

Torrin gave them an indignant huff, "I *can* do that. What is this punishment you will have to accept if I do not?"

"I will be tied to a post which has been driven deep into the ground, they will tie the end of a line around my tongue, the other to an arrow and shoot it into the rear end of a horse, this will then send the horse running away, which will wrench my tongue from my mouth," said Sangas with no emotion, as if only stating a fact.

"Blazin' cripes!" said Torrin.

Onyx was laying across the wizard's left forearm and the wizard was slowly running his right hand down the cats back as he said, "I can bind your tongue if you require it of me... it would not be permanent."

"I *can* hold my tongue," said an indignant warrior.

"I'll keep the words to the spell on the tip of my tongue, just in case," the wizard said to the Silver elf.

Sangas nodded.

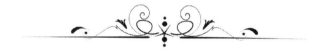

The Green elves did not tell the companions where they were going only motioned for them to move. At times they began to wonder if they were only being taken deep into the woods to be left behind, lost in the unknown forest. Finally, after about five hours, they began to see lines of smoke, telling them they were approaching another settlement but they did not know yet if it was the one where their spiritual leader resided.

A large, lush green, valley opened up in the center of the forest. There was only one hut in it, though it was twice the size of the ones in the first elder's settlement, and a large rectangular wooden pavilion. A stone fire pit was at one end of it and several animal skins were on the floor before it, telling them this was the side *The One* sat.

The elder elf, who Sangas had called Shani, motioned all of them to stop and wait as he approached the large hut. He stepped to the opening of the hut and shook a line of hollowed out rocks; the wind blowing through them made them sound as if they were ringing.

The others were about fifty feet from the hut so they couldn't make out the words but they could hear someone speaking inside.

"What is he saying?" asked Torrin.

"The One is typically a she," said Sangas.

"Oh," said the warrior. He wasn't against females leading, Cieri was one of the highest ranking soldiers in his royal guard, assigned with direct protection of the king, but he still wasn't used to it.

It was close to ten minutes before Shani came out, looking a little frustrated. He said nothing to the group waiting, nor did he motion them to follow him, he only walked toward the pavilion, to a stone archway set up beside the structure. Hanging inside the arch was what looked like a long curled up tusk. It had either been hollow when it was cut from whatever animal it had come from or it had been cored out. He placed the small end of it to his lips and blew into it. A long, deep and hollow sounding reverberation came from the horn. It didn't sound loud enough to be heard by anyone other than those before them.

"What now?" asked Torrin.

"Now we wait," said Sangas.

"More waitin'?" said the warrior.

"The Green elves are apparently deeply into pomp, Master Radric," said the wizard.

"Pomp?"

"If you mean they follow and take their rituals very seriously, in this you are correct. All elves have rituals that we follow, they may seem to be strange and unnecessary to you but to us they bring organization to the maelstrom that threatens to take us daily. Some of the Silver elves, who have had more contact with your race, feel they are unnecessary now as well but the elders of our race are trying to reinforce them in hopes that they will see our ways are better for our souls' survival.

"The Brown elves are more slowly losing their rites as they become more aware of the outside world but it is happening with them too, more so now that they have begun to converse with the Silver elves.

"The isolation of the Green elves has allowed them to hold onto their beliefs with less worry."

Torrin nodded and said, "So, now we wait."

They waited another three hours then they began to see other elder elves stepping from the forest surrounding the valley. Some had younger elves with them, likely acting as escorts, all with arrows notched. Some were alone. None of them acknowledged the companions as they passed them and walked to the pavilion.

"These are?" asked Torrin.

"The elders from each of the Green elf clans... their leaders."

The young elves stayed outside of the structure, the elder ones stepped forward. They each stopped beside a cored out rock that was set beside the archway holding the dangling tusk horn. It appeared to be filled with water, or something else that was colorless, even Sangas could not say for certain what it was. They each stuck the first two fingers of their right hand into the liquid then brought them to their forehead and ran them from the edge of their scalp to the bridge of their nose then kissed the ends.

After this they stepped onto the raised floor of the pavilion, each removed the animal skin that had been wrapped around them like a cloak, spread them on the floor before the fire pit, forming a semicircle around the fire pit, stood beside them, and waited.

Movement in the doorway of The One's hut brought the companions' eyes back to it, they watched as an elf that made Corinitsia, the seer from Sangas and Eonard's village, whom had seemed so old, look like a child, step from it.

This elf was beyond old and moved like it. She was wearing a thin tan robe that hung from her like a tent and dragged on the ground – threatening to trip her. She barely lifted her sandaled feet, the scraping sound of the bottoms against the packed dirt of the path to the pavilion seemed far louder than it should to their ears. She was slouched over nearly parallel to the ground. A younger elf was holding her forearm, which appeared to be nothing but bone with a draping of skin, but she wasn't supporting her, more directing her.

She was stopped by the same rock pool as the elders had; she too dipped the first two of her twisted fingers into the liquid and brought them to her forehead. She turned toward the five companions as she did this, giving them a full look at her face, which made all but Sangas draw in quick and surprised breathes – she had no eyes.

"Many of our most revered are… handicapped, as you would call it… We believe they have been altered to better follow the spirits' wishes. She is not driven by what she sees only what she hears. It is said only one that is blind can see if one is lying."

Darlyn nodded; even without being blind he had known this to be true.

"So, now what?" asked Torrin, as he watched the blind elf being led to the furs before the fire pit.

"Again, we wait."

The stance the warrior took up told them all how little he wanted to do that yet again.

It took the old elf woman several minutes to get her robe just the way she wanted it, since she couldn't see the folds she had to do this with her hands. She seemed to be trying to get both sides to lay perfectly the same. Each time she adjusted a wrinkle Torrin would expel air. Each time he would expel air she would stop and turn her face in his direction. Finally Cieri took hold of Torrin's arm and spun him around so he was looking at the forest instead of the old woman and her ministrations.

It was another few moments before she seemed satisfied with the arrangement of her robes and had brought her face up. She motioned to her assistant who was now holding a long thin pipe. She took the pipe in her wrinkled hands, sucked on the thin end of it and expelling the smoke, as if she had all the time in the world.

"What is she doin' now?" asked Torrin.

"She is cleansing her soul."

"Cripes, this is gonna take a lifetime..." snapped the big man. A hard look from Sangas and Darlyn made him stop.

He knew it wasn't polite to disregard another race's cultural beliefs but he was on a time constraint; Jacobi could have already done the sword harm and all of this would have been for nothing.

It was several puffs later before the old elf woman lowered the tube and brought her head back forward. This was the cue to the others, who had been standing still before their furs, waiting.

They bent their legs and sat down on their knees, all facing The One. In unison, they bowed, bringing their chests forward so they were against the tops of their thighs. They remained in this position until the woman said to rise.

"Who is it that required this meeting?" asked the old elf woman's beyond scratchy and raspy voice. It sounded eerily similar to the hollow sound that had come from the horn.

"It was I," said Shani.

"Why did you require this meeting?"

"To ask of another of our race."

"Clarify."

"One of ours has been accused of taking that which does not belong to him. He was sent out for his Tsiaga."

"His Tsiaga was taken without belonging to him?" asked the old elf woman.

"It is believed to have been."

"Elf warriors know they must win the Tsiaga, it cannot be taken," said the woman.

"I cannot answer that," said Shani.

"Is there one here who can?"

Torrin started to step forward but Cieri and Darlyn's hands on his arms and Sangas shaking his head stopped him.

Shani looked over at Sangas and nodded his head once.

Sangas repeated the gesture and stepped forward. He stopped at the cored out rock, did the same as he had watched the elder elves do then stepped forward. He stopped before The One, and stood in a place that would close the circle of elders.

"Who is this, he smells wrong," said the woman, wrinkling her nose up. She then spit a glob of phlegm on the flooring beside her.

"He has been traveling with white skins," said Shani.

The old elf woman hissed. "Why does he do this?"

Shani couldn't answer that, he motioned to the Silver elf to do so on his own behalf.

"May I have your consent to speak?"

"First you must be purified," said The One. She motioned for her assistant to take the still smoking pipe to the new elf.

Sangas bowed to her, took the pipe and began to take long slow puffs, blowing the smoke out through his mouth. It tasted woody but wasn't unpleasant. He didn't stop until The One nodded and motioned to her assistant, telling him his scent was now acceptable to her.

"Who are you?"

"I am Sangathanis of the Silver elves, Picani Sect. I come before you with the white skins. It is our hope you will consent to offer us assistance in finding the Green elf we seek so that we may retrieve the item he has taken."

"The item belongs to the white skins?"

"It does."

"What is the item?"

"A sword forged with help by Dwendlyn."

"Then it is elfish; it was not stolen, only returned."

"It was given to my grandfather," grumbled Torrin.

All eyes and The One's sightless face turned to the white skins standing on the edge of the trees, to the face of the human warrior that had dared to speak.

Darlyn waved his hand quickly, without a word.

Torrin tried to speak again but all that came out was air. He couldn't move anything but his head so he couldn't even stomp to show his frustration, and he certainly couldn't storm over to the pavilion and ring the neck of the elf that was deciding the fate of his grandfather's sword. He turned his head and looked angrily at the wizard. He didn't need to be able to speak to rely what he would have said if he could have.

Darlyn shrugged his shoulders then motioned to Sangas.

"It was entrusted to the king of Hundertmark and in turn given in form of a commission to a man in the king's army; therefore it was no longer elfish property," said Sangas.

"A thing does not cease to be elfish just because it is in the hands of white skins," the woman snorted.

"Be that as it may, it was given in good faith to the human warrior who used it in many battles against many Torge in the war of the beast," said Sangas.

"It was used *by* this white skin? It defended him against harm?"

"It did."

"Then it had bonded to him... It should not have been taken by an elf unless it was given to him by the bonded one's own hands," said the old elf. "Was it?"

"The bonded one was killed in the fort during the same battle. His spirit rose and gave the sword to his grandson," said

Sangas, indicating the still magically bound warrior off to the side.

"Has it been used in battle by him as well?"

"It has. I watched it defend him well in battle," said Sangas, remembering how majestic the man had looked as he wielded it from atop his horse in the battle to put Uther back on the throne.

"It was bonded to him then. He did not give it willingly to this elf?"

"He did not."

"Who is it accused of taking the sword as Tsiaga?"

"An elf named Jacobi," said Sangas.

"Which clan claims this elf?"

None of them made any outward sign of knowing the name.

The One moved much quicker than her age and frail body should have, getting to her feet. Her voice seemed to have even more authority to it, booming deeply, as she said, "It will be learned."

One near the far side of the circle shifted then.

The woman's head turned to face him. "Cambi, you know this elf name?"

The elf she had called Cambi bowed, then said, "I did not lie. He is no longer one of my clan. We do not claim him."

"Why is this?"

"He has been tainted."

"Explain?"

"He is Pyisthta."

"That is a harsh accusation; one that has only once been claimed in my three hundred years," said The One in great disbelief and displeasure.

The other clan elder's intakes of breath said none of them could believe it either.

"It was not given lightly. He had more than just the sword from the white skins... he tried to use them to turn us."

"What was his punishment?"

"We banished him."

"You will take the Silver elf and the white skins to your clan, together you will find where the Pyisthta is and retrieve the sword that had bonded to the white skin."

The elf, Cambi, glared at the four humans then nodded and said softly, "I will do as you require."

With that, The One motioned her assistant to come forward, take her arm and direct her back to the hut she had come from.

The elders that had not been given a task stood, lifted their furs, wrapped them back around their shoulders and went back the way they had come. Shani and Cambi were the only two that remained.

They walked over to the humans and Silver elf together.

"I will leave you to return to my clan now," said Shani. He bowed to Sangas and brought the first two fingers of his right hand to his lips then to his forehead.

Sangas did the same to the elder.

Shani then turned and left without a word or any acknowledgement to the humans.

Cambi did not give the customary departure greeting to the elder elf, nor the customary greeting gesture, which was the same as the departing gesture, to Sangas; showing how unhappy he was that he was being required by The One to do this. He only turned, walked to the group of elves he had come with and disappeared into the trees.

Without explaining what had happened – knowing the elves would not slow their trek for them – Sangas waved the others to follow them.

35

HEDGING
HIS BETS

"What is this Pyisthta?" asked Phineas as they followed the trail the elder elf was leaving them; though he wasn't waiting to be sure they were following it. He knew Torrin also wanted to know but he was refusing to speak, still upset that Darlyn had felt it necessary to bind his tongue.

"Loosely translated to your tongue, it means blood traitor."

"Which means," asked Torrin, his desire to know the answer outweighing his anger and stubbornness now.

"By bringing items from your world into theirs he has broken one of the elves most sacred edicts. The only thing worse would be to use any of those items against an elf."

"So they banished him?" asked Cieri. "The word and how they reacted seemed to imply a harsher punishment would be required."

"They didn't feel his stealin' my grandfather's sword warranted more than that?" said a frustrated warrior. Torrin was going to say a disfigurement and then banishment would have made him happy but a hard look from the wizard stopped him.

"Banishment would be seen as quite atrocious to an elf, am I correct?" asked Darlyn. He knew the stigma a wizard was given for banishment; it was sometimes worse than physical pain, which would eventually heal. He was always fascinated by the various forms the races had found to punish wrongdoing. Some could be merely a defacing of sorts, like a stripping of title and rank in the clan, others were far more permanent and painful.

"Yes, Master Algier, the shame of being banished would be far worse than death, which is over quickly."

Torrin still couldn't understand the concept as being similar but he let it drop.

"There is only one worse punishment. An elf that has done the worst wrong is made no longer an elf."

The look on the four humans faces were the same – confusion.

"They would have made his ears rounded, like yours … would have made him… appear human."

"Why was banishment all he was given, The One seemed to find this a lot more horrendous a crime than Jacobi's clan elder did and seemed to have expected more," said Darlyn.

"I can only speculate, but I would say it is because of his place in the clan… He might have been the son to a second elder or promised to one of the daughters of the elder."

"I'm sorry I almost got your tongue ripped out," said the warrior.

"You did not."

"What?" asked Torrin, wondering how the man could be so complacent about what he could have faced.

"I only said that to try to keep you from speaking, knowing it would make it harder for you to… The worse they would have done was ban me from speaking to The One, which I chances are will never have the opportunity to do again in any case."

"What?" stumbled Torrin.

The others broke into laughter at the joke.

Torrin guffawed and gave them all dirty looks.

The small settlement the elder elf, Cambi, led them to was the same style as the other elf settlement had been – a grouping of mud huts with a wooden pavilion in its center. The only difference was this one was by the edge of a steep cliff. There were ladders hanging down the cliff face, leading from cave holes in that face to the ground and bridges linking them across the cliff face. Like the others, this one had a stone arch beside the pavilion of The One and like that one it had a tusk horn. This one was smaller and let out a much higher pitched sound when Cambi blew into it.

It was only moments before the elves that had been going about their normal duties began to come forward and gather in the structure.

Cambi took up his place in it then said, "Does any know to where the Pyisthta went?"

There was no answer but one young elf girl near the back quickly looked down.

Cambi motioned her forward but she shook her head.

"Now, A'Shanti."

The girl did come forward then.

She looked to be about sixteen in human years, which would put her about fifty in elfish years. She was wearing a black and white sheepskin like top that barely covered her nicely sized breasts and short skirt that showed all of her muscular legs. She didn't have as many tattoos as the older women around her; she had only a small scroll on her right cheek, just below her eye, and one that covered the left half of her stomach and she was wearing none of the jewelry the other female elves around her wore. She was fairer skinned than the other elves and had much lighter hair, which made her stand out. All of the other females were attractive but she was beautiful.

Later Sangas would explain to them that just as a male warrior of the Green must prove his worth with his Tsiaga, a female elf must prove her worth as a wife, and in A'Shanti's case, an elder's wife since she is Cambi's oldest daughter. She would not get the rest of her tattoos until she was wed. He suspected the reason for the lack of jewelry but wasn't ready to voice that yet.

The girl was clearly shaking as she stepped up, "Yes, Father?" she asked.

"You know where he went, do you not?"

A'Shanti' wanted to say no but she could not lie to her father. She bowed and said, barely over a whisper, "He is by the second waterfall."

"Why did you not tell us he has failed to adhere to the punishment?"

A'shanti' only shook her head.

"You will take the elf and white skins to him."

The elf girl got a panicked look on her face then and started to refuse.

"It is required by The One," her father barked.

A'Shanti' nodded then and stepped back.

Cambi turned to and acknowledged Sangas and his companions for the first time then, "It is nearing darkness, you will be taken to the place he is believed to be at first light."

"Thank you," said Sangas.

Cambi's hospitality apparently didn't extend far enough to acknowledge this. He turned from them and went to his hut, which was larger than the others and nearest to the pavilion.

One of the younger male elves came forward then and led them to a smaller hut near the path they had come in by.

"Why was Cambi so harsh to his daughter?" asked Cieri once she was sure they were alone.

"I think it is because she was Dyan'A to Jacobi," said Sangas.

"This is?" asked the wizard, already suspecting he knew.

"Betrothed to him."

"How did you reach that conclusion?" asked Torrin.

"Her willingness to risk banishment or worse by seeing him, which she must have done to know where he was, implies it."

"Is that why he seemed so angry with her?" asked Cieri.

"By disgracing himself, Jacobi has disgraced her and through her has disgraced her father."

"She wasn't involved in his theft though," said Torrin.

"It is a form of guilt by association," said Darlyn. "If theirs is anything like some of the other tribal cultures I have read about, she is now considered damaged goods and will not be offered to another."

"Which means?" asked Torrin.

"Master Algier is correct. She will not be considered to have reached womanhood and will never be allowed to bear children if she is not wed." He paused a moment to let the gravity of that statement sink in. "If I am reading the situation correctly, Jacobi would have become the next elder if he had been able to fulfill his Tsiaga. Cambi has no male children, which would mean it was A'Shanti's responsibility to bear him an heir to become elder when her husband was no longer fit to be – in denying him this she too has disgraced her father."

"How do you know he has no male children?" asked Phineas.

"They would have been standing to his right," said Sangas.

Torrin was wishing now he had never found the abandoned fort, spoken to the spirit of his grandfather and been given the sword. He didn't want to be the cause of all this discontent. "Is there any way to reverse this, tell them I loaned Jacobi the sword, perhaps?"

"That is a very honorable intention, Master Radric, but in this case it sounds as though he has taken more than just your grandfather's sword therefore, unless you can get each of the other people he has taken an item from to say the same it will be a moot one."

"So he was hedging his bets?" asked Phineas.

"In a manner of speaking."

"Do you think he is going to be willing to give up the sword, and other items, without a fight?" asked Torrin.

On this Sangas could only shake his head.

36

HIDING
IN SHAME

The next morning the elf girl, A'Shanti', was waiting outside the hut for them. She was dressed much as she had been the day before, again with no jewelry.

Sangas had explained to them that he thought this was because she was no longer allowed to. They would be seen as a symbol of womanhood and beauty – because of Jacobi's betrayal she was no longer seen as either to her people.

Torrin wanted to apologize to her, feeling some of this was his fault – if he hadn't been so proud of the sword and hadn't bragged about it so much maybe Jacobi wouldn't have decided it was the item he wanted to use to claim as his Tsiaga. This of course wouldn't cover the other things he was said to have taken. Torrin had not heard of any other thefts in

Hundertmark so the elf must have found the items before they were captured and taken to the camp of the followers, before Torrin and he became acquainted.

A'Shanti' kept her head down as she said, "Are you prepared? The traveling will not be the easiest." She never looked at any of them and said this facing Cieri.

Sangas whispered that she is not allowed to speak with a man.

Cieri shook her head then nodded to him. She looked to each of the others before saying, "We are prepared."

The elf girl wasn't wrong, it was some very rough terrain and there was no obvious rhyme nor reason to the path she took, sometimes seemingly choosing what would be a harder climb over the sharp and jutting rocks that were littering the ground before them than she needed to. They were beginning to wonder if she was just leading them deep into the woods to disappear on them when they began to hear the sounds of the waterfall.

She motioned them to slow as the forested and rocky hillside she'd had them scaling opened to an open vista of a wide and raging river. It was crashing down the side of the mountain to a valley hundreds of spans below.

"Is he camped out up here?" asked Cieri.

"He is at the bottom," said the girl sadly, "near the second waterfall."

Torrin could hold his tongue no longer. "I am sorry that you have suffered because of what Jacobi has done."

The girl looked shocked the male warrior had spoken to her.

Sangas stepped up to him and said softly – which was actually more like screaming to be heard over the sound of the waterfall. "She is not allowed to speak directly to a male until she is made full woman... and since she will not be now..."

Torrin sighed sadly and decided this warranted the loss of an inch of his braid when they were stopped for the night.

The climb down to the bottom of the waterfall was actually easier than the climb to the river had been. A vine had been laid out along the side to hold on to as one climbed down the sometimes slippery rocks. Still, because they had to go only a few feet then stop and rest to allow the others to come down to them and move a little further down, stopping again, it took most of the rest of the day.

"I think we should wait and come upon the man in the light of day," said Darlyn as he helped Onyx get dried off. The cat had been trying to catch a fish in one of the small coves beside the river and had slipped and fell in, getting nothing but wet for his efforts.

The young elf girl looked nervous about this but said nothing.

Phineas felt a little guilty thinking it but as soon as he was sure he could speak to the wizard, warrior and Silver elf without the girl hearing, he said, "She may think to slip away and warn Jacobi."

The others had thoughts of this as well, which was why Darlyn had cast a spell over her so that her tracks would glow with phosphorescence if she tried to get too far ahead of them and Torrin had encouraged Cieri to stick close to her.

There was no sign that the girl, who had taken to her blankets as soon as the sky began to darken, had even left the camp to relieve herself once the first sun began to show through the trees.

She didn't move to go down to the cove to get cleaned up, even though Cieri offered to go with her, thinking she might be frightened to do it with men she didn't know so close – Sangas later explained that this was another bit of her punishment. She was essentially invisible to the clan now so she was expected to bathe by herself – though it was partly the fact that she did not know the men with her that had stopped her.

She took them along the side of the river to where it became a small pool and pointed to a moss covered patch in front of a small cave opening cut into the side of the cliff beside another smaller waterfall.

They could see a line of smoke telling them he was there now.

"How do we want to approach this?" asked Phineas.

"I think it would be best to sneak up on him and take him by surprise," said Torrin. He turned to Cieri then and added, "Can you stay here with the girl?"

The female warrior didn't like it but she did nod. She knew that the girl wouldn't be comfortable with any of the men and they couldn't leave her alone for risk of her warning Jacobi.

Torrin motioned Darlyn and Phineas to approach the site from the back side while he and Sangas came from the river side.

Cieri was anxious to be in on the action, she was taking her frustration out on a stick of hard salami she was slicing for their meal, they had decided they didn't dare risk a fire – Jacobi might see the smoke and get spooked – it was the female warrior that got spooked though, as the elf girl spoke to her.

"What will they do to Jacobi?"

"I cannot lie to you, Child... it will depend entirely on what he does."

"I do not think he will give the sword back without a fight... It has taken too much from him."

"We are sorry if he gets hurt in this but it was wrong of him to take the sword."

"I told him the same."

"Are you going to get in the way if we have to do something drastic to your Dyan'A?" The female warrior knew she would do anything to keep Torrin from coming to harm.

A'Shanti's face screwed up then. "I did not choose him, he was chosen for me."

Cieri wasn't sure what to say to that.

Jacobi had been on edge since the day before, since the last time A'Shanti had come with food and wine. He had been expecting her to come from the forest at any moment but she had not yet. He wondered if he had been too harsh with her and had frightened her off – she always was a little too soft for his liking – or if she had been caught.

He actually preferred Shayl'A, A'Shanti's youngest sister, but A'Shanti was the clan elder's oldest daughter. If he wanted to be the next elder he had to choose her. He would perform his duties to her as required to make an heir and have his pleasure with Shayl'A.

Jacobi had imagined the reception of his arrival, with the sword of Dwendlyn in hand, would be the opposite of what he had found. His soon to be father-in-law had smelled the white skin on the blade as soon as he took hold of it and wanted to know if he had killed the man to obtain it. He had thought of lying, of making up an elaborate battle where he had won the sword but the elder had known, from his hesitation he had not.

He had showed them other things he had collected, though they had only been as back-up – he had thought the sword would be more than enough – but all of the items only frightened the elder.

Cambi knew they were all from the white skins world and didn't want their taint on the clan.

Jacobi knew, from other clansmen that had failed the Tsiaga that the punishment could be harsh but none of them had been intended to replace the elder and bear him heirs. He had thought he would be given another chance but they had banished him – he was told if he was ever seen by one of their clan he would be made to look like a white skin and sent away and if he attempted to return after this he would be shot dead with as many arrows as could pierce him and taken to the white skin's soil so his body would not taint their soil as it rotted.

He had gone willingly, knowing the elder was fast becoming frail – there was another way for him to become elder, besides marrying his eldest daughter – he would go back in a few weeks and challenge the old man to a contest. He would use the sword of Dwendlyn to kill the elder. In doing so he would not only become the elder in his place, he would then have his Tsiaga since the sword would have defended him and would then be bound to him.

He heard a sound behind him. He knew it wasn't A'Shanti, she always came from the river side. He started for the sword, thinking it was an animal on the hunt. He stopped as he heard the whispers of a spell being spoken. He moved his hands to a scroll beside the sword instead. He didn't know exactly what the spell on the scroll was but he knew it was for defense. He knew the wizard, Darlyn, would not keep a scroll that would conjure something innocuous.

Darlyn hadn't meant to make a sound, he was normally adept at keeping quiet but a bird fluttering suddenly in the shrub beside him had startled him. He stopped his movements, as did the cat, staying close to his feet. He looked at the back of the man they were stalking. He didn't appear to have heard the sound. The wizard began to whisper the words to an *immobilize* spell then he froze.

He watched the man lean forward and lift up a rolled up scroll. The elf unrolled it quickly then began to say the words on the scroll. Darlyn recognized them as ones he'd written himself, he hadn't even known the scroll was missing. He waited, hoping the elf wouldn't get the inflection right to make the spell work. As he watched the words disappearing he knew otherwise. He cried out, "Stop, you do not know what you are conjuring!"

It was too late; the words had already been spoken and had begun to manifest themselves in the air around them.

Several portals opened and tiny hideous things with huge yellow eyes, razor sharp teeth, sharp claws, black scales, pointed tails and leathery wings poured from them.

37

HELL'S
SPAWN

The things that came out of the portals the Green elf had just opened with the spell he had invoked were creatures known as imps. They are related to fairies and sprites but instead of being essentially good, though mischievous, these were everything evil. They were only about six tines from the tip of the tiny horns on their heads to the tip of the claws on their extended feet but their teeth and those claws did as much damage as the same twice their size would have.

They did not play favorites, attacking the elves as much as the humans. Their speed and smaller size made them hard to stop. They clung to their hair, bit and clawed at their bare skin and shredded the cloth of their sleeves and pant legs.

Torrin found the side of the wide blade of his sword did better than the edge. It was mostly only knocking the flying pests out for a second or two but it kept them from doing more damage for a few seconds anyway.

Darlyn was trying to get his hands free to cast a spell to send the creatures back to their domain but the things were hanging off his arms, clawing at his chest and were twisted in his hair so he couldn't concentrate long enough to say the words.

Onyx had one on his back, its claws dug into his fur, as if it was riding him. Others were flitting just outside the aim of his claws. He was doing better than the others in taken the imps out. He had managed to catch a few of them, which were lying dead or were flinching in their death throes before him.

Phineas was having a little luck with the shorter blade of his dagger though it was not much use against the sheer number of tiny creatures.

Sangas was all but defenseless to them, having only a bow and arrows as weapon. He was using the palm of his hands to bat the things away but this only seemed to anger them more.

Jacobi had about a dozen of them following him. He paid them no heed, he had grabbed the sword as the last word of the spell was leaving his mouth and was running for the edge of the path by the river they were beside.

Phineas saw the Green elf was getting away. He started to call out to warn Torrin when he suddenly convulsed and fell to his knees.

Cieri came running out of the shrubbery on the upper bit of the path, beside the Silver elf, having heard the commotion and Darlyn's shouted warning.

A'Shanti was behind the female warrior but she was staying well back, unsure what to do to help or who to help. She too saw Jacobi trying to get away. She started to go to him, wanting to try again to get him to give the sword back willingly. She took two steps then was blasted backwards by a large portal opening beside her.

Darlyn, Sangas, Torrin and Cieri saw the magical opening that looked to be an ancient stone archway and wondered what hell's spawn was coming out of this one – if its size was any indication it would be the imps' master.

A man with blue skin and a wild mane of darker blue hair stepped from it.

Azure was shocked at the scene before him. He began to blast the tiny black sprites out of the sky – freezing them in flight. Each one he hit smashed to the ground and broke into tiny pieces as if they had been glass. He wanted to blast the entire cove but could not; the companions would also be in frozen bits and pieces on the ground then.

The imps, as if picking up on this began to stay closer to the companions.

Darlyn realized this was the blue dragon that had taken Eonard to the Plains of Vethe. He was about to ask about the elf when he was pushed hard from behind by strong hands.

Phineas wasn't sure which hurt worse, the claws of the imps that had converged on him while he was incapacitated or the feeling of being turned inside out – scarily it was a feeling he knew. He had a moment to realize that this was Junt entering him then the spirit knight was just as quickly leaving him – making him feel he had then been ripped outside in again.

Junt hadn't intended to leave the man's psyche so quickly, knowing the discomfort and pain it would cause, but he had seen an imp about to plunge the dagger Phineas had dropped during the convergence with him into the back of the unsuspecting wizard.

The blade entered the spirit knight's shoulder instead. It didn't enter him as it would with living flesh but he obviously more than just a spirit when it didn't simply fall to the ground.

Darlyn turned and saw the semi-solid knight with a knife sticking from his shoulder and was shocked – partly that the spirit was solid enough to harm and that he had just taken a blow that would likely have killed the wizard.

"I am sorry, Master Algier, I betrayed you… I needed the power to see the elf safe."

The look on the wizard's face relayed his confusion perfectly.

The knight held a small item up to the wizard.

It took Darlyn a moment to recognize the figure as one of the small charms he usually carried in the pockets of his person – a protection charm. It was a figure his brother had made him the day he left to go to the Guild and he had used as a vessel to hold the protection spell.

"I used this to hold a bit of your lifeforce... I took it from you while Master MaComber was trying to heal your leg."

"What?!" barked Darlyn, unsure if he should be angry or grateful.

The wizard didn't have a chance to be either, or to speak again. An earsplitting shriek that made every hair on his body prickle, his stomach twist into knots and his brain feel like it was trying to swivel up in his skull to escape the noise that was filled his head sounded from around him.

The others in the clearing also felt this strangeness – even the imps – stopping them in mid-fight for a moment.

Eonard was stepping from the portal just as the dragon was screaming out. He understood the meaning of it without needed it to be verbalized – it was pain and fear. He saw the opening of the cave was beginning to collapse from the energy being in turmoil around them. He knew what was inside that cave.

Eonard saw Azure heading for the opening of the cave and started to go to help him when he heard a scream beside him. He was surprised to see a young elf girl being assaulted by a dozen tiny black imps.

He used his ability to control the elements to wrap the things flitting around the girl with air. They all fell to the ground, their wings bound. His eyes locked on the beautiful face of the elf girl as he offered her his hand to help her step over the downed over-blown insects. The world around him suddenly stopped.

The girl's eyes were frozen on his face as well. She had never before seen anyone with so beautiful an aura.

Eonard started to ask her name. He jumped when she suddenly burst into tears and looked down as if she had done something wrong. He was about to ask about her odd reaction when he heard another scream came from the dragon, reminding him what he had been doing.

He turned from the elf girl and motioned to the sides of the cliff. He weaved the air around the walls on the outside of the opening, to shore it up then shouted for Azure to let him know it should be safe enough to enter.

A'Shanti was staring at the unknown male elf before her in awe.

Torrin, Phineas and Cieri were standing in the center of the clearing with their backs to each other, unsure which direction the next attack of tiny shredding claws were going to come from. None came. It appeared the imps had all been incapacitated, destroyed or had fled into the forest to find easier prey now.

Torrin saw Eonard holding his hands up and effort on his face, as if he was holding the mountain up then a blue skinned man and the elf girl, A'Shanti, coming out of the fast crumbling cavern with two spotted eggs each in their arms.

Phineas knew the blue skinned man was a dragon. He guessed the eggs he was moving were likely dragon eggs. The former marauder also saw the back of the Green elf with Torrin's sword disappearing down the path beside the river. He shouted to Torrin and pointed.

Torrin and Sangas ran up the path after the Green elf.

Phineas and Cieri went to help the dragon and elf girl save the eggs.

Darlyn turned from the spirit knight, deciding he would deal with him later. He started to follow the warrior and Silver elf, who were running after Jacobi, when the stone hanging from a leather cord around his neck began to hum.

The stone was linked to one he had given Iligra – one she was to activate when she went into labor, to call him home. His son wasn't supposed to come for three more days. He felt an odd sensation in his chest then. He hoped there wasn't a problem with his lover or his child. He looked around, unsure what to do.

Eonard saw the pained look on the wizard's face. His eyes connected with the man's. There was no need for words; Eonard had read the man's thoughts with the simple glance. He sent, "Go, I will tell them," to the man's mind.

There was a day having an elf communicate with him in this way would have worried Darlyn, now he was only glad for it. He called out to Onyx. The cat ran to the wizard and jumped into his open arms. He nodded to Eonard then opened a portal and disappeared.

38

TSIAGA

Eonard dropped to the ground, exhausted, when Azure came out and said he had the last of the eggs. The elf was paler than usual – opening a portal, fighting the imps and then trying to hold up a cliff had left him with very little of the life energy he had just gotten back. The rampant energies of the spell Jacobi had read had subsided now so other than a few rocks shifting and some loose debris falling over the edge of the opening every few seconds, the cave walls seemed stable again.

The elf girl went to her knees beside him, wanting to help but unsure how to.

Phineas and Cieri ran to his side as well. They were both uncertain whether to touch him or not as well.

"Where is Nortus?" asked Phineas. He looked around for the older man, who could heal the elf. He was wondered if he had gotten injured in the fight with the imps.

Eonard only shook his head.

Azure walked over to the humans and elves and said, "Master Elgin was killed in the battle to destroy the dark cleric's soul."

"My fath... Mahki is destroyed then? For certain?" asked Phineas. He knew none of them held his parentage against him but he still was sickened and angry to think his own blood could have done so many horrid things.

"He is," said Azure. He turned to Eonard then and waved his hand over the elf's body.

Eonard felt a warm tingling throughout his extremities then all the sore and tight muscles loosened and a sense of contentment swept over him. "Thanks," said the elf.

Torrin and Sangas came back up the path, having lost the Green elf in the forest.

"Are you hurt, Prince?" asked Sangas.

Eonard shook his head.

Cieri told them what the elf had done.

"Why didn't Darlyn help you?" asked Torrin as he looked around for the wizard.

"He had to go back," said Eonard.

"Go back? Go back where?" asked the warrior.

"To Hundertmark."

"Iligra?" asked Cieri, a worried look coming to her face.

Eonard nodded, looking a little gray as well.

"You are back? Does this mean you were able to get your soul back?" asked Torrin.

"Yes. It's a long story that I will tell you when we too are back in Hundertmark. Now we need to finish your mission," said Eonard.

Torrin was about to say he didn't want the sword back, it had cost him too much. He stopped when he noticed the strange look on the elf's face. "What is it?"

"Jacobi is trying to claim his place as elder of his clan."

The young and beautiful elf girl beside Eonard drew in a quick and frightened breath, as did Sangas, both knowing how the Green elf would be doing it.

Eonard's eyes went to the girl's. He locked his hazel eyes on her green ones. The girl quickly looked down, realizing what she was doing. Eonard said softly, "You do not need to avert your eyes, A'Shanti, you have done nothing wrong."

The girl jumped when he said her name. She opened her mouth then closed it and again looked down.

"She cannot speak to you, Eonard, or to any man, except her father. She has been prohibited to speak since she is not yet a woman," said Sangas.

"Why?" asked Eonard, confusion and anger in the simple word.

"Jacobi was her Dyan'A. He was named a Pyisthta'," said Sangas.

"If he kills your father he will be clan elder," said Eonard.

The girl didn't speak but she did nod her head; tears streaming down her face.

"You do not want to marry Jacobi," said Eonard.

A'Shanti looked up quickly, she wanted to deny this, it was seen as ungratefulness if one didn't accept who she was betrothed to, but she could not lie. She nodded slowly.

"Will you lead us back to your village?" Eonard asked the girl.

A'Shanti wanted desperately to speak to the beautiful elf looking at her. His aura was shining a bright yellow color – it was the purest aura she had ever seen, only one step away from being completely pure, white. She couldn't make her tongue do it. She could deal with losing the respect of her father and her clan but she felt she would be devastated if this elf ever looked upon her with shame in his eyes. She looked at Cieri and said, "I will."

A'Shanti started down the path Jacobi had made then looked back and said, being sure she only looked at Cieri, "This path would take him to the village."

"Cieri, stay behind us, with the girl," said Torrin. "You sure you're up for this, Eonard?" The elf was looking better since the dragon performed the healing of sorts but he was thinner than the warrior remembered him being.

Eonard nodded.

The dragon man, human men and male elves broke into a run, leaving the women behind them.

Jacobi kept looking back, expecting to see the warrior or one of his companions on his trail but he didn't. He knew they wouldn't be far behind him though. There was no way he could fight them alone.

This path he was following would take him back to the village of his clan; the place of his birth, the place he had grown up, the place his parents and sister still lived, the place he was meant to be the elder of, the place he was no longer welcome.

He slowed his step as he came upon the edge of the trees surrounding it. If he was seen entering the village he would be shot.

He watched the happenings before him – the elves were going about their daily activities as if his being no longer among them meant nothing. He saw his own mother hanging a rug out to be beaten, laughing and smiling with the other elf mothers doing the same, as if any other day and felt anger well up inside him.

He remembered how other elves that had been banished from the village had been treated; they were quickly put out of the clans' prayers and forgotten. He couldn't believe his own mother could do this.

He saw Cambi walking toward the wellhead with two buckets. There was no one near him; if he could get to him without anyone seeing him he could challenge him.

Jacobi took a tighter grip of the two handed tang of the sword, brought it over his head and ran out of the cover of the trees.

He made no sound, not wanting to alert Cambi, whose back was to him. He came up behind the elder elf and brought the sword around quickly – the length of the blade caused him to overcompensate. The edge of the blade stuck on the poles on the sides of the well.

Other elves close by heard the sound of the sword hitting the wood. They shouted out for everyone to defend the elder.

Ten young elves ran over and formed a semicircle around the wellhead and the two elves.

"I will be the next elder, as is my birth right," spit Jacobi as he fought to get the sword blade out of the wood. His anger was so strong that foamy spittle had formed around his lips.

The companions didn't stop at the tree line as Jacobi had; they already knew what they would find and wanted to prevent it.

They found just what they had expected – the younger elf had the older one pinned to the ground. His right foot was on the elder's chest and the sword was held over him, about to plunge it into his chest.

Eonard started to weave air to stop Jacobi, as he had done to the imps and to hold the cave walls. He saw that he didn't need to; the Green elf was already struggling to make the sword move. He knew Torrin, Phineas and Sangas did not have the power to do this, he looked to Azure but he seemed just as confused as they were, telling him it wasn't him doing it either.

"You will accept my rule," shouted Jacobi. He started to plunge the blade downward, ready for the exertion he would need to force it through the elf's flesh and bone. He grunted loudly but not from this effort. It was because it seemed the sword was frozen in mid-air – he could not make it move. A sound behind him made him look over his shoulder.

He saw Torrin, his companions and the blue man crashing out of the forest. He twisted around, intended to bring the weapon up in front of him. It did not follow his hand. He shouted, "I will not give it back."

Torrin realized the magic in the sword was preventing the elf from using it. He pulled the sword he had been using since Jacobi had taken the one was he holding from him and started forward, intent on taking the sword back. He froze when he heard a female voice shout out, "Stop!"

The eyes of the companions, the elves watching, Jacobi and the downed elder all looked to a spot on the opposite side of the clearing. They saw The One, being assisted by the younger elf woman, step out. It had been the elfish spiritual leader that had shouted out.

She walked over to the companions far faster than her blind and frail body should have been able to, or her assistant seemed to want her to.

"It must be done by an elf," said the woman clearly.

Sangas started forward then stopped, realizing, without The One saying anything, that it was not his destiny to end this. He turned and looked at Eonard – The One was also facing him, though her empty eye sockets could not see him.

Eonard wasn't sure who this old elf woman was but he could guess she was like the seer of his and Sangas' village. Unlike his human companions, seeing only skin over where her eyes should have been didn't shock him. The feeling that she still saw him was a little disconcerting though. He wasn't sure what she was expecting him to do but he guessed the sword was fighting Jacobi because he had no right to use it.

The half Brown, half Silver elf prince walked over to the darker elf he had thought of as at least a good acquaintance – though Torrin had spent far more time with him while they were in the brotherhood's camp. Jacobi was still trying for all his worth to get the sword to move, still trying to make it plunge through the elder elf's heart. Eonard reached his hand forward and grasped the blade; he was surprised to feel it move easily as his hand pulled it free.

"No!" Jacobi said through clenched teeth.

"You are not going to harm this elf," said Eonard.

Jacobi was shocked and angered when the other elf was able to lift the sword with ease. "No. I *will* be the next elder!"

Cambi was trying to get to his feet now, wanting to get away from them both. He didn't want to find out if this new elf was only looking to finish what Jacobi could not.

Eonard had no intention of wielding the sword against either elf.

Jacobi fell to his knees then. He had not intended his life to turn this way. He cried out, "I cannot live with the shame. I beg you, take my life."

"I have already killed one friend today," said Eonard. He turned from the two kneeling elves – one trying to get away from them, the other in shocked disbelief and walked back to his companions. He had the sword held before him, the tang on one hand, the blade on the other, as if presenting it to Torrin.

Jacobi's eyes cleared. This elf refusing to finish him was an insult worse than being called a blood traitor. He made no sound as he drew his dagger and started toward Eonard, intent on stabbing him in the back.

A'Shanti saw this. She drew in a breath, ready to scream a warning.

Eonard heard her warning, even though she had not said a word. He swung around, brought the huge sword around and plunged it deep into the darker elf's stomach – the blade showing about four inches out his back.

A shocked and pained look came over Jacobi's face. He tried to say something but all that came out was blood. A strange smile came over his face as he placed his hands around the blade. He stepped backward, pulling it from his body, and fell to the ground, dead.

Eonard wasn't as shocked as he once might have been that he had done this or that the other elf had reacted that way –

he had become a little jaded it seemed. He started to wipe the blood from the blade with the sleeve in the crux of his elbow, not wanting it to be dirty when he handed it to the warrior. He stopped when he saw movement beside him. The One was walking toward him. He thought at first she was going to be angry with him – unlike the others around him all of whose thoughts were flooding his mind with gratitude for having saved their elder – he could not hear hers.

The One took the sword from Eonard's hands. The blade was as tall as she was but she held it like it weighed nothing. She placed her other bent up hand on his shoulder. With only a little pressure, she pushed him to a kneeling position.

Eonard wasn't sure what she was about to do – even with the direct contact, which should have opened a channel between them, he could not read her thoughts. He couldn't tell from her face whether she was pleased or angry about what he had done – it was completely stoic. He watched her raise the sword and start to bring it toward him. He thought for a moment she was going to slice his head off with it.

The One did bring the sword toward the elf's neck but she stopped it and turned the blade on edge when she was within inches of it.

Eonard closed his eyes and clenched his teeth, trying to ready himself for what was to come next. He could hear A'Shanti, Torrin, Cieri, Phineas, Azure and Sangas all about to shout for her to stop and saw them all moving to stop her. He sent them all a quick message to not fight this.

It was hard for them all to comply but they did.

The One brought the razor sharp blade to the side of Eonard's face, set it on edge and touched it against his right cheek.

Eonard jumped as the cool feeling of the metal and the sliminess of the blood coating it touched his face but he didn't move away from it.

The One slowly pulled the blade toward her but she didn't slice the elf's flesh, instead she wiped some of the blood off the weapon onto his cheek. She moved it to the other side of his head and did the same to his left cheek. "You have fulfilled your Tsiaga. You are now a man." She motioned him to rise then.

Eonard was stunned speechless, as were all the humans, elves and dragon around him. He was shaking a little as he stood up.

The One held the sword out to him as he had been holding it – in presentation to him.

Eonard took it from her and said, "Thank you, but I do not want this."

She said nothing, only nodded.

Eonard was disoriented but he got the impression she had already known this. He knew somehow that the sword was now his to do with as he pleased. He turned then and again walked toward Torrin.

Torrin and Cieri both looked a little shocked and amazed at the elf they had thought they knew.

Phineas only had a smile on his face.

Sangas and Azure looked awed and impressed.

A'Shanti was completely mesmerized.

Eonard slid the bloodied blade through the cusp of his sleeve to clean it, as he had been planning to do before The One's demonstration, then stopped before the warrior. He smiled at him and said, "This sword belongs to you rightfully, Torrin Radric; wield it well and you will be victorious."

Torrin was choked up for a second. He was almost afraid to take the sword, afraid it wouldn't let him take it. He reached for it and was pleased, and relieved, when it lifted off the elf's hands with ease. He brought it up so the blade was vertical then kissed it and said, "I will," in a voice a little deeper than usual.

Eonard was about to say he was glad that was finished and he wanted to go home. He suddenly turned around and felt anger burst inside his breast.

A'Shanti had started for her father, to help him off the ground, as Eonard was walking toward Torrin.

Cambi shouted, "Do not touch me!" as he shoved his daughter back.

She fell to her butt in shock and pain when he pushed her away.

Shocked breaths came from the Green elves watching this.

Eonard went toward the elder elf, "Why do you do this to your daughter?"

"She is no longer my daughter."

Another shocked breath came from the Green elves still watching and a hurt breath came from A'Shanti.

Eonard walked over to the girl and put his hand down to help her up.

A'Shanti started to shake her head at the beautiful elf's offer. She did not want him to be shamed by offering her his assistance. She knew she shouldn't look at him, even more so after her father's admonition, but she couldn't help it. Her eyes went to his. She expected to see shame in his eyes, as was in her father's and would be in the eyes of all of her clan behind her. She saw only caring and compassion in them. She wiped her tears and did take the hand.

Cambi spit on the ground then on his daughter and said, "You are Kint'oo"

Eonard had never heard the word before but he knew what it meant by the thoughts the other elves her having – it meant she had committed the ultimate shameful act and now would be made to look human – it meant in their eyes she was no longer an elf. He waved his hand toward the ground and the elder elf fell to his knees. "She has nothing to be ashamed of."

The One came forward again then and said, "She *is* Kint'oo *unless* an elf man is willing to take her in union."

The girl's chest hitched and tears flowed down her cheeks unhindered.

Eonard heard '*No elf in my clan will have me now*,' play in the girl's mind. "I will," said Eonard, "if she will have me."

A'Shanti brought her red face up to him quickly, uncertain if she had heard right.

"He is not of the clan," shouted Cambi.

"I have declared him to be," said The One. She looked at the girl then and said, "Do you accept him as your Dyan'A?"

A'Shanti wasn't sure what to say at first, she had never seen this elf before this day but somehow she knew he would never harm her. She looked into his eyes again then said, "I will."

"It must be performed by midnight."

39

NEW LIFE

Darlyn had no idea to what he would be returning and was beside himself that he was doing it while his companions were in the middle of a battle. He was certain, if they survived it, they would understand, he hoped he would see them again to prove this.

He found a group of guards in the courtyard when he stepped from the portal. He only recognized one of them; the one Torrin had left in charge in his absence.

"Master Algier," said Nasir, going down on bent knee before him.

"Why was I summoned?" Darlyn asked, surprised by the anxiety in his voice. He was usually better at masking his moods – wanting to appear always outwardly calm.

"Master MaComber used the stone. Lady Iligra has been in labor for close to ten hours. He was concerned for her mental state and felt you should be by her side."

"Take me to her," said the wizard as he set the cat on the ground. He knew if Aramis had done this he had good reason.

The castle was abuzz with activity, much livelier than Darlyn had ever seen it before. He was surprised how many of the staff smiled at him as he passed them and started to bow to him, unlike a year before when they would have never looked upon him or would have immediately gotten out of his way. He nodded to the ones who only nodded and waved the others off with a mumbled, "No need."

He was led to the center floor, the one his suite was on, to the doors of it. He found Mari, the woman who had helped nurse him back to health during the battle to reclaim the castle and after his leg injury, and the king, pacing before the doors.

"Darlyn," said an excited Uther. He ran to the wizard and threw his arms around him. Not even thinking that a few years before this would have gotten his skin flayed from his body, while he was still alive.

Mari went to him quickly as well. She waited for the king to dislodge himself then took the stunned wizard's hand and kissed it. The wetness left behind was as much from the tears on her cheeks as her lips.

Their reactions made his heart clench – certain it was for bad reasons. "Is…" Darlyn couldn't get his voice to work or his lips to say the thought on his mind.

The door before them opened then and Aramis' head appeared in the crack. "I thought I heard you arriving," said the cleric. He opened the door more, grabbed the wizard's shoulder and pulled him inside.

Iligra was in the center of the bed she and the wizard had shared for about a year. She was pale, covered in sweat and her hair was plastered back. Her stomach was even larger than it had been, showing clearly through the tautness of the thin bed sheet covering her. Her eyes were closed and she made no sign of realizing anyone had entered the room.

"Is she...?" Again Darlyn couldn't get the thought or the words out.

"She is asleep at the moment... or more like passed out," said Aramis.

"Is there a problem?"

"No." said the cleric quickly. "She is having a hard time of it mostly only because this is her first. She is fighting to stop the birthing because she wanted you here but she refused to call you back, knowing you were needed by Torrin... She is a very stubborn woman."

Darlyn smiled to the last, that was part of what appealed to him so much about her. "May I go to her?"

"Please," said Aramis, as he wiped his damp forehead with his already well-used sleeve. "I need to get cleaned up a bit. Convince her that now that you are here it is time."

"I will do my best," said the wizard.

Darlyn didn't even wait for the door to close before he went to the bed and sat down beside the woman.

The wizard touched the skin of his lover's cheek gently. He ignored the clamminess of it and smiled as her eyes fluttered open.

Iligra had been dreaming that Darlyn had returned to her and was beside her so she didn't react when she opened her eyes and saw him there.

"It is truly me, Iligra," said the wizard as he leaned over and kissed her damp forehead.

Now the woman believed her eyes. "Darlyn?"

"It is me."

"Does Torrin have his sword back?"

"I would suspect he does by now," said the wizard as he pulled the blankets higher up on his lover's naked chest.

"You don't know for certain?"

"I got the call of the stone before he did."

"You need to go back then," said the woman as she started to get up.

Darlyn's strong yet gentle hand held her down. "I need to be exactly where I am. Aramis says you are refusing to let my child into this world."

"I wanted to wait for you," said the woman, suddenly weak again.

"Stop waiting. I am here now."

With that the woman's stomach contracted and she shouted out.

Aramis came running through the door seconds later, slamming it in the face of the two waiting in the hall. He threw the blankets of the lower portion of the bed up and shouted, "PUSH!"

40

HELLO
& GOOD-BYE

Another portal opened in the castle courtyard about five hours after the one the wizard returned through. There was only one guard there, the one on duty, since it was not expected. He started to go to the alarm as he watched several people step through the opening then stopped when he recognized four of them and was staring in uncertainty at one that was blue skinned and haired – especially when he saw clouds of steam, that turned to flakes of snow that slowly drifted to the ground exiting his nostrils.

The man dropped to his right knee, brought his fisted right hand to his left breast and said, "My Lord, Captain Radric."

"About your duties," said Torrin.

"Aye, sir," said the soldier. He stood and started back to his post.

"It is good to be home," said Torrin in a deep voice. He wrapped his right hand around the hilt of his grandfather's and now truly his own sword then took Cieri's hand in the other and motioned the others forward, starting toward the doors into the castle proper.

Sangas went with him, eager to see Uther.

Phineas went with him, eager to see his nephew.

Eonard, and A'Shanti, turned to Azure.

The guard stopped halfway back to his station and turned back around on hearing the booming voice coming from the blue skinned man. He was now frozen in fear and staring in shock.

"I must return to the eggs. For all they are not in immediate peril of the cave collapsing, thanks to you, they are still in danger. I must move them to a safer location, one where they are protected and can remain until they hatch."

"How long will that be?" asked Eonard.

"For some only another twenty years, others will be longer."

"Do you need help?"

"I thank you for the offer but the shells have already been tainted by human hands... elf hands have less of this oil but... I mean no disrespect by this statement but the oils of your and human skin break down the calcium on the eggs' crust... some of the eggs might already be too thin to support the dragonlings inside..."

"I understand," said Eonard. "Will you return when you have relocated the eggs?" asked the elf.

"I must remain with the eggs and protect them until they hatch and then I will need to feed and protect the dragonlings until they are able to hunt and defend themselves."

Eonard knew that would mean better than fifty years, since a dragon ages even slower than an elf. He would still be alive but none of his other companions would be. "Will you return to me when that is done?"

"I will," said Azure. The dragonman went down on his right knee and placed his hand over his heart. "It has been an honor serving you once again, Prince Eonard. Remember us in retellings of your story so that future generations of elves and humans know we are no danger to them."

Eonard waved the dragon up and said, "I will. You will be remembered as a hero and your kin will be seen as nothing but good and noble creatures. The honor was truly all mine. Safe journey to you and may all the dragons survive until hatching and then grow and thrive, creating future generations of your kin."

Azure stood, bowed to the male elf then to the female elf standing a little behind him then he walked to the center of the yard, so there was nothing near him, and transformed back into his natural body.

The blast of the transformation blew the hair on the elves' heads back and the helmet from the head of the guard, who was now jumping up and down that there was a real-life dragon before him.

Azure let out a rumble from inside his mouth, getting used to using his dragon vocal cords again, flapped his long and graceful wings a few times, shook the fur around his neck and shoulders out and rattled the blueish green mottled scales back into place then bent his knees and launched himself into the air. He went straight up for several spans then circled above the castle twice. He hovered over it for a moment then turned to the north and started back toward the forest, to where the eggs were.

Eonard looked at the guard who was still up-in-arms about what he had just witnessed. He waved his hands to wrap calming air around the man. He settled down then and went back to his post. The elf sniggered a little, remembering there was a day that would have been him, then offered his arm to his wife and entered the castle.

Uther had been telling the chatelaine what he wanted prepared for the dinner welcoming the wizard's baby to the world when the doors behind him opened. He jumped when he saw who it was then squealed with delight and told the woman, "Triple the portions and get to it!"

"Welcome home!" said the king happily. "Were you successful?"

Torrin pulled the first few inches of the sword from his scabbard and said, "I was."

"How is Iligra?" asked Cieri.

"She is resting at the moment. Darlyn is with her and the cleric is tending to her well… She was fighting the birthing…" The king turned to Sangas then and said, "Will you stay with us for a while?"

Sangas wanted to return to his people to tell them their prince was alive and well but it could wait. He bowed his head slightly.

"Excellent!" said Uther. The king started to wave them further inside when the doors behind him opened again. It took him a moment to believe his eyes. One of them he knew, the other was a female elf of outstanding beauty he had never seen before. "Eonard?"

"Hello, King Uther," said the elf as he started to go down on his knee.

Uther was before the elf with his hands on his shoulders, pulling him back up, before he was more than a few inches from the floor. "You do not need to bow to me, Emperor Eonard."

"I am not…" Eonard started then stopped. He realized he was, for all no formal ceremony had been held. "I am only Eonard to you."

"And I am Uther to you," his eyes drifted to the elf girl who was trying to hide behind Eonard.

"You do not have to hide away," Eonard said kindly to the girl. "You are my equal."

A'Shanti looked about to shake her head; if she had been married to a clansman of her tribe she would have been expected to stay behind him.

"You are my equal," said Eonard more adamantly, trying to make her believe him.

A'Shanti nodded then and stepped forward, though she kept her eyes lowered.

"King Uther Hundertmark, may I introduce you to my wife, and empress, A'Shanti," said the elf with great pride and pleasure.

Uther looked shocked for a second then a wide smile broke his lips. "Another thing to celebrate! It is a pleasure to make your acquaintance," said the man as he held his hand out to take hers.

She put her tiny hand in his and blushed as he leaned forward and kissed it, not used to the human custom.

The doors behind them opened again then and the wizard, with a bundle in his arms, and the cat as his heels, walked proudly in. He passed the bundle to the female warrior, who was now in tears.

Cieri began to coo at the beautiful baby boy in her arms. Torrin was bent over her shoulder making goofy faces at him.

She passed the wizard's son to the king then.

"Do you have a name for him yet?" asked the king, also cooing at the boy. The baby's eyes were turned to him but he wasn't really seeing him.

Darlyn's face screwed up for a moment, "We had never discussed it. She didn't think it proper to name him until we saw him, so we could choose a name that suited him."

"We will wait to make the formal announcement until you do then," said the king as he held the bundle back out to his father.

Darlyn smiled once more as he took the boy back.

41

RESERVATIONS

Leonard was as pleased as the others at the new addition to the wizard's family and said all the appropriate sentiments but he couldn't enjoy it as much as he would have liked to. It took all of his energy not to rush through the castle to find Aramis and all his energy to keep him from running away from it and Aramis. He wanted badly to see his friend but was equally afraid to.

How was he going to tell him he had killed both his grandfathers? He knew he would be happy – as happy as one can be to lose an ancestor – that Makhi was dead but would he be able to handle Nortus' death?

The elf hadn't intended to invade the older cleric, Nortus', thoughts but the man hadn't kept them buried very deep. He knew all Nortus had done to his friend and how upset Aramis was with him when he left. He also knew the man had not intended to return from the Plains of Vethe from the start.

He knew he had been trying to keep the bonds that might have formed between him and his grandson from forming in hopes of making his loss easier on the young man.

Eonard also knew Aramis well enough to know it would hurt him even more not having gotten to know the man as his grandfather instead of only an eccentric cleric and for how the relationship had been at the end.

He had to find a way to explain to his friend that Nortus had seen too much, been through too much, that he had been living on borrowed time for a long time and that he had died the way he had wanted to – not many could say that.

The king had directed them to the great room, so they could sit and talk over drink and food, which was being hastily set up around them. The elf kept looking at the doors, waiting for his friend to walk out. He jumped every time they opened then felt a rush of anxiety build again – waiting for the next one through to be him.

He froze in uncharacteristic fear when they finally did open to his friend.

Aramis' hair was tousled, more than usual, and he looked in dire need of a good night's sleep and a bath but he had a smile on his face.

The young cleric saw his uncle first.

Phineas didn't feel out of place but he was keeping himself well back of the activity – forever a loner.

"Uncle," Aramis said happily as he went to him.

Phineas took his nephew into his arms and patted him firmly on the back.

"I have some things I need your advice on at the castle," said Aramis quickly – he actually only wanted some friendly company there – not looking forward to returning to the cold stone structure alone.

He didn't get to hear his uncle's reply because he was suddenly swept into the strong arms of the warrior then he was laughing and trying to breathe at the same time.

"It is good to see you again, Aramis MaComber!"

"Alright, Torrin, alright, I need those organs you are squashing."

The warrior dropped him then and stepped back.

Cieri came forward and kissed his cheek gently. "Can I see Iligra?" she asked.

The cleric nodded. "She is only about half awake. She refused the sleeping tincture I want her to drink. Try to get her to take it before you go."

"I will," said the woman. She kissed her lover then walked quickly out the doors.

Aramis looked back at Torrin and asked, "Did you get the sword back?"

Torrin pulled it from its sheath and said, "I did, thanks to another of our friends."

Aramis waited for an explanation.

The warrior only smiled and stepped aside so the cleric could see the others in the room.

Aramis nodded to Sangas, whom he had never really had a lot of contact with, and smiled at the wizard, holding his newborn child. He was standing beside the king, who looked proud enough that he might have been the father himself. His eyes then moved to two others.

The cleric had never figured to see his friend, Eonard, again and thought that if he did manage to return he would be different – that he would be as the age he should have been – so when he saw the elf – looking no different really than when he last saw him – he didn't believe his eyes. He thought he was only seeing him because he wished he could be there with them too. He watched the smile he knew all too well cross the elf's face and him nod his head and saw Sangas was looking at him too and began to allow himself to believe it was not just a ghost or his imagination.

Eonard wasn't sure what he was seeing in the eyes of the man he had considered his brother and was his best friend – mostly confusion he thought, or hoped. He tried to get his feet to move, to walk over to him but he couldn't. He felt his heart clench, not liking the fear and anticipation he felt looking at the person he loved more than any other and being afraid to go to him, and the fear and anticipation he felt coming from the person he loved more than any other.

"Eonard arrived at just the right time to save our butts," said Phineas.
"Eo… Eonard?" Aramis asked, still afraid to let himself believe he was seeing him. He watched the elf start walking toward him.
"Hello, Aramis," said the elf slowly.

The two moved at the same time, coming together in a tight embrace in the center of the room.

They, as well as most everyone else in the room, were fighting tears as they separated.

"I have so much to tell you," said the elf.

"As do I. Are you whole... I mean... The dragon said your soul needed to be returned to you... did it, was it?"

"It was. I am *whole* again and very much alive."

"How is it... I know an elf ages different than a human but... you look the same age as when you left."

"The spirit knight, Junt, said your father had to take my lifeforce from my body and use a... a shell, for lack of a better word, of an elf's body in this time to bring me forward as he did. He said the timeline was restored when I left the solid world and I was essentially reborn into this body again when we returned."

"I would have been pleased to see you back at any age but..." Aramis waved his hands to indicate all of the elf standing before him. "I am even more that you are as you are."

Eonard nodded, pleased as well. He had not wanted to essentially lose out on more than a hundred years of life by skipping from sixty in elf years to one hundred and fifty in a matter of days.

Aramis' eyes took in a beautiful elf girl who had followed Eonard across the room and was now standing a few feet behind his friend. He couldn't miss the look in her eyes, which were glued to Eonard's every move.

Eonard smiled then and stepped back, motioning the girl forward. He held his hand out to her and brought her to his side as he said, "This is my best friend and brother, Aramis MaComber, Aramis this is A'Shanti Lorraine."

"Sister?" Aramis asked tentatively.

"Wife," said Eonard proudly.

Aramis was shocked and happy all at once then he smiled and said, "I am getting married as well."

Eonard didn't know how his friend could have fallen for another so quickly after Haylea so he guessed it was an arranged marriage. He hoped, for both his friend and his intended, that it was an amiable coupling. "Is she here?"

"No, Haylea is still in Lancarst. Her father is bringing her to my estate later this month…"

Eonard smiled then. "So, her father saw the error in his thinking?"

"Sort of – my now being a lord and offering him a bride-prize helped."

"She must be beside herself," said Eonard.

An odd look came over Aramis' face then. "She is still under a spell Nortus placed on her to make her forget me. Iligra says it will dissolve as soon as she sees me again."

"How is it living in a castle?" asked Eonard, feeling guilty for changing the subject but not ready to tackle the situation with Nortus yet.

"Lonely… It had not been tended to for some time so it is taking time to make it livable again… I hope it is in good enough condition to be seen by the wedding," said the cleric, swallowing hard as he thought again of all that needed to be done just to make the place hospitable, let alone livable.

"Would you like some help?" asked Eonard eagerly.

Aramis smiled from ear to ear and nodded. He looked around then and said, "Speaking of, where is Nortus... my grandfather?"

The faces of all of his friends lost a shade.

Darlyn started to speak but Eonard held up his hand. The elf appreciated the wizard being willing to tell Aramis what had happened, to help take some of the pain off him, but it was not his place. He hoped his friend would understand and would be able to accept that Nortus had died a hero. He said slowly, "Nortus asked that I tell you that he and your father could not be prouder of you..." then he told him, and the others in the room, all that had happened while he was on the Plains of Vethe.

42

LIFTING
THE VEIL

Haylea was still trying to figure out how she had gone from being treated like a leper to suddenly her parents doting over her like she was their pride and joy again. She also couldn't understand why they suddenly had the money to get all the things around the house that had been falling into disrepair fixed.

She had thought at first maybe a well-to-do lord had asked her father for the hand of Sian, it had been made apparent she was no longer to be offered, but it was her they had taken for several visits to the local dressmaker to have new dresses made – including a wedding dress.

Finally, after two weeks of this, she asked her mother to tell her what was happening and the woman had told her. It was her hand that had been asked for, by a lord from the north.

She was being prepared to go to him at the end of the month. Her mother refused to give her any details, only that she would be very pleased with the choice.

The end of the month finally came and found Haylea standing in front of her freshly painted house. Her parents said it was today that she was to be picked up and taken to Komac, where she was to marry the new lord of said land.

She wasn't certain she liked that she had not seen the man she was being married off to, that she was going to be leaving home or that she had never been to the land she was soon to be calling home but anything had to be better than the weirdness her life had been recently. She hoped, at the very least, she would find some normalness there.

She jumped when she saw a team of four beautiful white horses turn down the lane she lived on. She recognized the carriage that pulled up in front of her house. It was the shiny black one with the burgundy curtains she had seen the day she and her sister had been in the market – the day things in her world began to become even weirder.

The door behind her opened quickly and her mother and father, dressed in their best clothing – also newly purchased – stepped out and walked to stand behind her.

"Please, Mother, tell me his name at least," begged the girl.

"He has made us promise not to, My Dear."

"I don't want to marry a stranger, Mother," cried Haylea desperately.

"He is not," was all she said.

Haylea was uncertain how he could not be a stranger.

The man in the driver seat of the carriage stepped down and bowed to the three standing at the end of the walk. He removed a folded piece of parchment from a satchel at his side and passed it to Rall.

The man saw this had the seal he had now come to know as that of the Lord of Komac, his soon to be son-in-law, the mortar and pestle over an open book. He snapped the seal and read the letter from that lord to himself. It explained that they were to load Haylea's items onto the cart and send her ahead then they were to join her in two days, bringing their other daughter, to help get his fiancée prepared for the wedding, which would happen at the end of the week.

Rall called into the attendant, who was waiting just inside the door. "Bring my daughters trunks out and place them in the carriage.

The trunks they were loading we full of the new dresses and the wedding gown her mother had picked out for her over the last month. She had only worn them the one time to make sure they fit then they were packed away.

"Your mother, sister and I will be riding up in a separate carriage and will see you at Komac castle in two days," said Rall. He took his daughter's hand and led her to the carriage door.

Haylea looked to see if the man she was betrothed to was in the carriage – it was empty. "I am riding up alone?"

"That is Lord Komac's wishes," was all he said.

Haylea couldn't believe her parents would be willing to send her so far away from them and alone. She did find some nice books and some fabric, thread and needles to do some needlepoint with at least. She supposed she at least could be thankful it appeared she had a thoughtful soon-to-be spouse.

It took two days to arrive in the city that was to be her new home. Haylea didn't like it – it was dark and small and there was no market to speak of. She also didn't like the castle sitting on the top of a rise in the terrain – it looked like it was ruling over the town. She decided if this was to be her home she would do her best to make it homier.

She hoped the days until her parents and sister arrived went fast.

Haylea tried to stand and wait patiently as her mother and sister fidgeted with the folds of her dress and her veil, saying they wanted her to look perfect when she entered the great hall.

She had to admit she did like the room she was in. It was nicely furnished in all her favorite colors. At least her new husband had thought to ask her tastes. There was a huge four poster bed and a nice vanity table and seat beside it. A decorated wardrobe closet and a comfortable bench were also in the room. That bench was positioned perfectly under a large window that opened to a view of a large lake with a waterfall and a flower filled meadow. She thought she could sit and stare out the window for hours. The twin suns were burning through that window now, giving the room a warm and comfortable feeling.

She jumped as a knock rattled the door and again as the woman, Sarah, introduced to her as soon as she arrived at the caste as her attendant, said it was time.

Haylea Quinlan walked into the great hall, which was decorated with soft pink roses and ribbons. She saw close to fifty people seated before her; some were her family but most she did not know. She guessed they were her soon-to-be husband's family and friends or visiting nobles that were there only for the wedding.

"What do I call him?" she asked her mother over her shoulder.

"Aramis MaComber," said the woman.

Haylea knew that name but she couldn't say why or put a face to it. "Aramis," she whispered.

She saw several of the faces around her turn to her and that they were smiling at her as if they were genuinely happy to see her – not the rushed and forced happy that her parents were. She thought she knew some of them as well but again – couldn't put names to the faces.

She saw a very handsome elf couple standing near the alter at the front of the chapel. The male elf was beaming and smiling at her, the female elf was beaming and smiling at him.

She saw another couple – also standing near the alter. The man had a strange half black and half all but transparent white hairstyle and the woman had long curly amber hair. She was holding a child to her shoulder. The woman was beaming at her, the man appeared uncertain what he was feeling and unsure how to express it.

She saw King Uther Hundertmark – which surprised her greatly – she fought the urge to stop and curtsy to him and the urge to wave at him – she could be hanged for waving at the king.

She saw another couple, both dressed as if warriors, again both beaming at her, and found herself smiling back at them.

And she saw the back of the man she guessed was to be her husband. He was tall and broad shouldered and had wavy blondish brown hair. He seemed to be nervous, constantly shifting his feet. The elf kept whispering to him and he kept nodding his head.

The names of these people were beginning to come to Haylea as she stepped beside the man that had asked for her hand. She turned to him and saw a handsome face with bright deep brown eyes and a smile that would melt the coldest heart.

The man lifted the veil covering the face of the woman standing before him and said, "I love you, Haylea."

All the months Haylea had spent in the woods with the man before her, the tall warrior, the wizard, the amber haired woman, an old man, a former marauder and the elf came flooding back to her then. She began to cry – tears of joy – as she said, "I love you too, Aramis."

43

BROTHER'S KEEPER

Darlyn waited as long as he could to get away from the festivities. He had something he had to see to. He turned to Iligra and said, "I will see you back at the castle. Please give Aramis and Haylea my praises."

"I can go with you," said the woman.

"No. This is something I must do alone."

The wizard kissed his lover then his son and quickly left the hall where the reception was now being held. He opened a portal as soon as he was out the door and in the center of the courtyard then stepped into it without looking back.

The outside of the tower Darlyn now called home appeared to be made of the same white marble as the rest of

Hundertmark Castle but the very top room, which was used only for storage, hid a secret. A veneer of white marble covered the exterior of it so to all it appeared a solid marble tower but the interior of this room was lined with the stone that had been used to build his original tower. They were in essence living stones – imbued with the souls of hundreds of workers whose lives had been given in their forging. Now those stones acted as a shield of sorts, protecting what was inside the room. No one knew of this room but him. The entrance to it was concealed and he had placed a *proportion* spell on the rest of the tower so it would appear the room below was the top of it.

The wizard looked over the items he had stored there. They were things not fit for the eyes of normal mortals – things he could be punished greatly for having if the Wizards Guild knew. He could not bring himself to destroy the items held in the room – even though some of them were quite dangerous. He could not relinquish all of his desires.

He had come here nearly every day of the last month – waiting. He knew as soon as he stepped inside it that this time he wasn't alone.

"I know you are here," said the wizard in the voice he had not used in close to a year. The one that said he expected to be obeyed and would be quite put out if he was not.

The image of the spirit knight in resplendent armor stepped forward then, out of the wall before the wizard.

"Why did you do it?" asked the wizard. "Why did you take a piece of my lifeforce – a piece that weakened me and could have killed me?"

"You no longer needed me but I was not ready to leave this realm... I was not ready to accept my death."

"I could have offered you assistance; and would have willingly given it," said the wizard.

"I could not ask that of you."

"*Yet you could take it without asking?*" growled the wizard.

Junt had no response.

"You know the consequences for doing this, Junt," said the wizard. This wasn't said as a question because he knew the knight did.

"I do. I swore, upon risk of being dispelled, that I would never harm you when I accepted your request to act as a servant. I am ready to take the punishment."

There was a day Darlyn would not have thought twice of dispelled anyone – be it a soul or living flesh – that had betrayed him. He found he could not harm this soul. For all the betrayal stung he could not fault the knight for not being ready to give up its world. He had only recently given up the chance at immortality, who was he to judge this soul when he had once wished never to see death either?

"I had released you from my service when you bonded with Phineas so you were no longer bound by that promise when you took the bit of my lifeforce. That threat is no longer valid."

Junt was shocked.

"I no longer find as much pleasure in harming others as I once did," said the wizard, uncertain exactly why. He had never felt the need to explain his actions before – he truly respected the spirit knight though and wanted him to know it.

"It was an honor and a pleasure to be your attendant, Master Darlyn Algier," said the knight, sounding quite choked up, as he dropped to his right knee, lowered his head and placed his fisted hand over his heart.

Darlyn was surprised at how choked up he was suddenly. The walls of the room should have reinforced his anger but he barely felt their evil pull. He stepped forward, placed his hand on the semi-solid head of his former servant and said, "I forgive you and release you."

"Thank you," said Junt. He brought his tear streaked face up to the wizard and said, "I have another confession to make... I hope you do not mind that I visited your son. I promise I did him no harm; I only wanted to see him before... I know your brother would be pleased that you chose to name him after him."

Darlyn nodded and said, "Had I any clue that my brother had been manipulated into killing my parents, I would have seen him saved. Bannock did not deserve the life he was dealt... had I been a better brother he would never have had to endure the abuse of our father and he would not have been so easily led by Paitell... I was the one that caused the death of my parents... and him. I suppose I am hoping that by naming my son Bannock I am asking him his forgiveness and am honoring his memory..."

"I believe you are, and know that he would give it," said Junt strongly, then a little quieter, and with a lot of emotion, he said, "I believe I am ready to move on now."

Darlyn was about to tell the spirit knight not to go, that he still needed his services but he knew that would be selfish. He was pleased the former knight had found what it needed to be able to let go. He nodded and said, "Safe journey to heaven, kind soul. May you be reborn to another life and get to enjoy the feeling of the suns on your face again."

Darlyn had never really looked at the face of his ethereal servant before. The fact that he usually was all but transparent most of the time had made it hard to get a good look at him. He did now, and was beyond shocked at what he saw.

The spirit knight smiled a smile the wizard knew very well then became thousands of tiny bits of light. They floated around in a bit of a cloud for a split second them just winked out.

The wizard stumbled to the wall and leaned against it, He had to fight the urge to jump away from the crawling rock but he could not have stood then if he wanted to. He was fighting back tears himself then.

The face of the spirit knight had changed just before he dissolved into the bits of energy, changed into a face he knew well... one with black curly hair and blue-gray eyes – it was the face of his brother, Bannock.

"I never knew," said the wizard as he slumped to the floor and began to sob.

EPILOGUE

Darlyn stepped into the courtyard of Hundertmark castle and opened a portal then stepped through it. He wanted to be certain the threat was truly gone, that there was no chance of anyone ever finding the cave the dark cleric had been held in. He exited the opening on the ledge just before the entrance to the cave. He took a quick look around, to be sure there was no one to see him or harm him if they did. He sensed no danger so he walked into the cave.

The golden doors of the dark cleric's chamber were still open. He slowly walked toward the room, listening to be sure there was nothing to surprise him. He stopped about halfway up the hall, he could hear scraping sounds. He had the words to a defensive spell on his lips but he also pulled his silver dagger in case he needed a faster defense. He inched closer to the doors and peered between them.

The sounds he heard had been two rats that were pulling at the bag of herbs that was on the floor of the chamber, likely wanting it for a nest. They jumped when they saw the wizard then screeched at him and scurried around his legs and down the hall.

Darlyn took a quick look around and saw nothing else amiss so he let some of his guard down.

He walked over to the stone coffin and looked inside it. He was pleased to see the black sword was shattered and lay in tiny bits on the padding. That the sword could be found and used was one of his concerns. The pile of ashes in the coffin, that had been the bodies of Paitell and Mahki, appeared to have been scattered, likely by the rats. He didn't see any signs that anything else had been disturbed. He breathed a sigh of relief.

He said the words that would open a link to the Plain of Vethe the dark cleric's soul had gone to and called out to the clerk-of-sorts that policed this level of Vethe.

"Hello, old friend," said the clerk, not looking up from the book he was quickly writing in with the long white feather quill. "It is not time for you to come here yet, is it?"

"Not yet," said Darlyn.

"That is good; I am not prepared for the tribunals and contests that will require as yet. And, I suspect, neither are you," the clerk looked up then, a strange glint in his eyes and a slight curve to his lips.

"I hope it is a long time before either of us will have to face it," said Darlyn.

"I believe it to be so," said the clerk cryptically. "I can guess why you have contacted me then."

"You can."

"It is done."

"Are you certain," asked Darlyn. He did not doubt the man but he needed to hear specifics.

"The elf managed to do great harm to the soul of the one known as Mahki MaComber, as well as to one called

Paitell Tobac and another, Helon Cetto, but he did not finish the job. It would be many years before any of them would be able to re-combine but Mahki's essence was still causing many ripples with his lingering anger and hatred.

"The souls were dissolved. Only small bits of them remain, not enough to ever fully reform as cohesive souls again." The clerk did not look up as he said this, writing in the journal the whole time.

"No part of them can remain. They need to be erased completely," spat the wizard.

"You know well that cannot be done, wizard. Do not worry; they will not threaten Ernel again."

Darlyn wasn't comfortable with this answer; it implied there was still a threat.

"I must ask you not to contact this plain, nor any other, again until it is your time to come before me," said the clerk, obviously dismissing the wizard.

"I may have need…"

"*DO NOT TEST ME!*" spat the clerk. He thrust the quill down, breaking it in half on the top of the desk. "The next time you open a doorway to this realm you *will not* leave it."

Darlyn was never one to like being told what to do but he valued his limited time in the living world more than he wanted to push the envelope. He nodded and let the window to the Plain of Vethe close.

The wizard stepped back into the hall and walked down the length of it. He opened a portal at the end of it but did not immediately step through. He whispered an apology to the Wizards Guild, he had sworn never to speak the words to the spell, *Bafefire* but it was the only spell he knew that would do what was needed. He had done it once previously, the last time he was in this chamber, wanting to destroy Paitell and stop him from raising the dark cleric. Now he was doing it to end the evil that had been held in this mountain for so long.

He sent the powerful waves of magical fire down the hall and watched the ball of flame erupt in the chamber then he stepped through the portal. He exited the void on the other side far enough into the valley to be able to see the cave entrance but not be hurt by any after-effects. The ground beneath his feet began to shake as the magically induced quake went through the fault under the cave.

He realized the shafts of the extinct volcano that had formed the mountain must be collapsing from the force of the spell. He watched trees around him starting to fall. He threw a shield spell over himself just as one beside him started to topple over. He held the spell in place until the ground had stopped shaking. He lifted the bubble of the shield and pushed it outward which made the tree that would have crushed him roll off and come crashing to the ground behind him then he walked back toward the cave opening.

It was gone. A small crack, only big enough for the rats he had disturbed remained but nothing that would ever indicate a cave large enough to walk through had ever been there. He turned around then and looked over the expanse of trees around the mountain.

Danbar Forest looked beautiful from up here. He had no way to know if the pockets of evil that had formed throughout it would go away naturally now that the anachronism that had caused them had been destroyed but he would see to it the entire forest was checked and any residual pockets dispersed so the once peaceful forest could reclaim its glory and no longer be called the *forest of shadows*.

The wizard drew in a deep breath then slowly blew it out. He wanted only to go home and see his lover and son but he had one last thing to do before he could truly be with them.

He opened another portal and stepped through.

Darlyn Algier stood before the garish home of the Lord of Sheffield trying to convince himself that he needed to do this – how shaky his legs felt right then gave him his answer. He hoped the lord's steward, Antrim, had been honest when he said he would finish the cleansing of his soul when he had last seen the man. He hoped he was ready himself for how much the cleansing would take out of him. There was only one way to find out.

He walked up to the door and knocked on it.

THE END